ELIZABETH SINCLAIR

❖

Eye of the Dream

Jewel Imprint: Amethyst
Medallion Press, Inc.
Printed in USA

S0-BVO-051

DEDICATION:

With much love to my three children: Linda, Toni and Bobby, and my four grandchildren: Rian, Sean, Meghan and Emily, and to Bob, my hero and my love.

Published 2006 by Medallion Press, Inc.

The MEDALLION PRESS LOGO
is a registered tradmark of Medallion Press, Inc.

Typeset in Simoncini Garamond

Printed in the United States of America

10 9 8 7 6 5 4 3 2
First Edition

ACKNOWLEDGEMENTS:

Many, many thanks to my critique group, the inimitable Plot Queens: Dolores Wilson, Heather Waters, Vickie King, Laura Barone and Kat McMahon, and the Ladies of the Suwannee: Kat McMahon, Cheri Clark, Judy Peters, Nancy Quatrano, and Vickie King for their guidance and encouragement in helping me to bring Kaine and Laura's story to life.

Prologue

A gauzy mist swirls around her. It cloaks her in a smothering, ethereal blanket. She gasps for air. It smells earthy, like the thirsty desert sands after a torrential rain. She spins away into another wall of white nothingness. The mist thickens, robs her of all sense of direction, pulls her ever deeper into the milky haze. Panic paralyzes her. She opens her mouth to call out. No sound emerges. The mist thickens. Her panic becomes palatable, breathing more difficult.

Suddenly, as if an unseen force has taken charge, the mist parts. Fearing it will close and trap her again, she runs through the opening, unseeing, uncaring about what waits on the other side. She knows only that she must escape the suffocating, white fog.

As she adjusts her eyes to the glaring brightness, a strange scene takes form. A withered old Navajo sits cross-legged before a boarded-up hogan; a twisted mesquite stump to his right resembles a snake coiled to strike. His ancient, leathery face bears the evidence of many summers spent beneath the hot, desert sun. Observing her closely through large, owl-like eyes, he measures her approach. That sharp, brown-eyed gaze, brimming with the wisdom of his years, never wavers from her.

With a sharp wave of his gnarled hand, he motions for her to join him on the ground. Welcome serenity replaces her panic. She obeys.

From beside him, the old Navajo picks up a small, leather pouch, then taking her hand, dumps the contents into her palm. She stares down at a silver chain coiled around a rainbow pendant. With her fingertip, she nudges the chain aside to better see the pendant. Inlayed with bands of turquoise, abalone, jet, and white shell, the rainbow's arches catch the sunlight and glitter, as though alive.

His guttural voice, crusty and angry, comes from inside her head. "Sa?ah naghai bikeh."

The pendant suddenly takes on an eerie luminescence, and with it, comes heat that intensifies steadily until it burns her palm. She cries out, but the sound is only in her mind. Dropping the necklace, she looks to the old man for an explanation. He's vanished and so has the necklace.

In his place stands another man, younger, his muscular body untouched by time. His features, concealed in shadow behind a swath of dark hair, need not be illuminated for her to know his identity. As familiar to her as her own mirrored reflection, they live in her dreams nightly and reflect from *her son's face daily.*

Hair, dark as a desert night. High cheekbones carved out by shadows. Eyes, dark and mysterious, haloed in amber, luminous, haunting, judging, accusing. And his mouth . . . Lord, his mouth. The mouth that loved her to the heights of passion and took her to worlds far beyond earthly reaches. His lips turn up slightly, as if reading her thoughts and finding amusement in her reaction.

A phantom breeze picks up his long, black hair from his broad shoulders and whips it away from his face. Light bounces off the contours of his coppery skin. He towers like a giant oak, strong, immovable, silent—always silent.

Radiating ferocity as strong as the foreboding prediction of a storm's onslaught, he beckons, drawing her with his powerful magnetism. She reaches for him, the need to touch overriding all else, compelling her as surely as her need for her next breath.

Then he vanishes. The fog closes in again, swirling, suffocating, threatening. The panic returns.

✤ ✤ ✤

Laura Kincaid bolted upright in her bed, choking and clutching at her throat. A soft, early, summer breeze laden with the fragrance of the rain-soaked Arizona desert blew through the open bedroom window. The air currents played with the white, organdy curtains, encouraging them to writhe in a mocking, ghostly dance, a twin to the mist of her nightmare.

She tore her gaze away and dragged deep breaths into her starving lungs. Finally able to breathe easily again, she fell back against the pillows, exhausted.

Rolling to her side, she checked the glowing face of her bedside clock. Four AM. Trying to shrug off the nightmare as the byproduct of her late-night, fast-food supper the evening before, she snuggled deep into the warm folds of her blankets.

But the panic she'd experienced in the dream remained with her. Even though she didn't understand them, the harsh, angry words of the old Navajo settled heavily on her soul, chilling her to the bone. As hard as she tried to dismiss their dire tones and make the excuse that some gastro-connected upset had caused her to dream about the old Indian, it still sent chills down her spine.

Not surprisingly, she found the appearance of the younger man, the man she'd walked out on eight years ago, the man who had haunted her dreams many times before last night, even more upsetting.

From her vantage point atop the slope of green lawn, Laura Kincaid scanned the rows of booths marching across the fairgrounds like soldiers in a dress parade. Red, white, and blue bunting fluttered in a warm desert breeze. The mixed aromas of pizza, tacos, hot dogs, re-fried beans, and cotton candy wafted out over the crowds milling about, tantalizing their palates, enticing them to sample the vendors' wares.

Laura couldn't hold back a satisfied smile. It looked as though the Tucson Children's Clinic would have more than enough reserve-fund cash to underwrite the Organ Transplant Program. The hard work she and her aides had done had paid off. Justifiably proud of her efforts to gather funds for the medical facility, she sighed; glad that today marked the last in a weeklong task that had sapped her energy.

A young boy in a Dallas Cowboys T-shirt whizzed past her, obviously targeting the money clutched in his hand for the cotton candy booth. Thank goodness her best friend and neighbor Anne Yatzee had volunteered to take Peter to her clan's powwow or Laura's son would be darting about the crowd as well. Keeping track of him in this confusion, while still monitoring the booths, would have been impossible. Not to mention, he would have wanted one of everything.

She chuckled. Typical eight-year-old.

For some unknown reason, the thought of Peter triggered the memory of her dream from the night before. If she wanted to be honest, figuring out why one prompted the other didn't really take much effort. It was an inevitable connection. Seeing Peter's father, even in a dream-state, had a way of disrupting her thoughts for days afterward, making her wonder if, when she'd elected to keep Peter's birth from him, she'd made the right decision. But eight years of silence made that a moot point. Even if she wanted to, she could hardly walk into the man's life now and announce he had a son that only she, Ada and her friend Anne knew he'd fathered.

Kicking both problems to the back of her mind, she concentrated on aiming what energy she had left toward the successful concluding day of the fair.

Picking up her purse and the clipboard she'd used for making notes over the last three days, she got ready to make her way along the wooden booths where vendors hawked everything from abstract art to stuffed, toy zebras.

She glanced at her watch. Two more hours, then this year's fair would be a memory, and she could relax. If she took the time to close her eyes, she could already smell the fragrant aroma of a soothing bubble bath. Visions of a decadent supper of pizza and Rocky Road ice cream began to fill her mind, but when she recalled the aftermath of her last fast-food binge, a nightmare to end all nightmares, she decided instead on a healthy salad.

A movement at the end of the row of booths drew her attention, effectively erasing all thought of food. "Mary Jane, who's that?" she asked an aide who had dashed past her to the cashbox for change.

"Where?" The aide strained to see where Laura pointed and then laughed. "There are too many people. You'll have to be more specific."

"Down at the end of the sixth row. It looks like someone's just setting up booth 6F."

"Are you sure? Maybe they're breaking down their booth early." The aide's wide-eyed gaze zeroed in on the spot Laura indicated. "Gee, Laura, I don't know, but you're right. It sure looks as if they're just setting up." She grinned. "They're gonna be real surprised when we close up in a few hours." She grabbed a pack of singles out of the box, closed it, and then snapped the padlock shut. "After I take these singles to Mrs. Rodriguez, do you want me to check it out for you?"

"No. I'll take care of it. I was just about to take my

hourly stroll through the multitude." She smiled at the young redhead. "You better get that change over to Mrs. Rodriguez. You know how easily she panics."

The aide tucked the bills in her pocket and then started down the hill. Halfway down, she stopped. "Great fair, Laura!"

"Thanks. I couldn't have done it without my able-bodied staff of aides."

Even as she mouthed the words, in her heart she knew that while she felt satisfaction in the fair's success, it was a long way from filling the niche inside her that had been carved out for her and her alone. As a fair organizer and nurse, she excelled. Beyond that, beyond her job, there was only Peter—and, as much as she doted on her active, young son, she needed more.

The girl grinned. "Think we're over the top from last year?"

"I'm about certain. Now, get those singles over to booth twelve."

"Gotcha." The young girl gave Laura a thumbs-up, and then trotted off at a run down the slope.

Laura checked her clipboard for the name of the vendor who'd rented that booth. The line beside 6F was empty. She frowned and recalled that, oddly enough, 6F had been the one booth she hadn't been able to rent. Shaking her head in confusion, she followed Mary Jane down the slope at a slower pace.

Ah, the vitality of the young. She could use just a

small portion of Mary Jane's energy today. She'd always been an early riser, but four o'clock pushed the envelope too far, even for her. With that disturbing dream still fresh in her mind, relaxing enough to go back to sleep last night had not been an option or a possibility.

The dream. Peter's face popped into her mind. Was he all right? *Oh, for Heaven's sake, Laura, get a grip. One dream and right away you begin imagining the worst.*

Dismissing her uneasiness as lack of sleep playing games with her head, she zeroed in on the renegade vendor and made her way through the milling throng of people. Oblivious to the fair and the bright Arizona sun, her thoughts and direction centered on booth 6F.

Nearing the booth, she caught sight of a woman in traditional Navajo dress, a long-sleeved, white velvet blouse and a flowing skirt of the same color, balanced precariously on a stool while hanging a colorful rug to the booth's crossbeams. Her black hair, caught back in a figure-eight, bulged on both ends of a bun bound in the middle by a strip of snowy cloth.

While waiting for her to come down from the shaky perch, Laura surveyed the items the Navajo woman had lain out for sale. Arranged on what appeared to be a beautifully woven rug, pieces of silver jewelry glittered in the sun, one more exquisite than the next. Squash-blossoms made from finely cut and polished needlepoint turquoise shared space with chunky, coral-encrusted bracelets and *concho* belts buffed to a bright, silvery sheen.

The woman finished her task, made her way down off the stool and then turned to face Laura. For a long moment, her chocolate-brown gaze held Laura's; then, almost imperceptibly, she nodded.

All thought of Laura's original reason for approaching the booth evaporated from her mind. She studied the heavy necklace the woman wore. With perfectly round gemstones, it was surrounded by featherlike rays made of turquoise and abalone. At its center black, slitted eyes peered at her from a face made up of geometric shapes fashioned of turquoise, coral, abalone, and jet. She recognized it immediately as a *tewa*, the face of the Navajo Sun God. Without a doubt, a very rare piece and one of the most intricate bits of silversmithing Laura had ever seen.

Realizing she was being rude, she dragged her gaze from the mocking sun to the woman's face. Lovely; and, in a strange way, familiar. Time had not yet sketched the woman's skin with wrinkles and the hot sun had not baked lines of weathering into her smooth copper flesh. While not really attractive, she seemed to possess an inner beauty that lay hidden in her course features like a cactus flower awaiting the kiss of a refreshing rain to burst forth into breathtaking loveliness.

"Your necklace is very beautiful," Laura offered, hoping to divert the woman's piercing stare. Laura gestured to the jewelry display. "It's too bad you got here so late. These pieces would have sold like hotcakes."

The woman shrugged, as though selling the jewelry

mattered little, reached into the pocket of her skirt and then extracted a small leather pouch much like the one the old Navajo had had in Laura's dream. Removing something from the pouch, she cupped it in her palm and then returned the pouch to her skirt pocket. As the old man of the dream had done, she reached for Laura's hand.

Laura felt the chill of the cold metal against her skin. She looked down and gasped. A wave of déjà vu passed over her. Nestled in the center of her palm lay a silver chain coiled around a rainbow-shaped pendant—an exact duplicate of the pendant from her dream. Unlike in her dream, however, the metal chilled Laura's palm, sending an inexplicable sense of urgency surging through her.

I must have this necklace.

When she reached for her purse to pay the woman, a graceful hand closed over hers. The woman shook her head; then slipped the chain around Laura's neck. Laura blinked and looked down at the pendant lying against her blouse. When she looked back, the woman was gone. Laura looked around her to see where she'd disappeared to, but she saw no one that even resembled the Navajo woman. If it hadn't been for the weight of the necklace around her neck, Laura would have sworn she'd been dreaming again.

By the time Laura returned home, the mystery that

surrounded the connection to her dream and the sudden appearance, then sudden disappearance, of the Navajo woman still gnawed at her mind. As crazy as it seemed, the more she thought about the extraordinary circumstances, the more she believed the woman had come to the fair, not to hawk her wares to the fairgoers, but specifically to give Laura the necklace. But why? Why would a Navajo seek her out and then give her such a valuable gift with no explanation? And why the same pendant from her dream? And how had she disappeared within the space of a few seconds?

This series of sudden and inexplicable happenings and their connections to the Navajo made Laura very uneasy. Aside from Anne Yatzee, who had befriended her from the day she'd arrived in Tucson and had become Laura's closest confidant, she'd studiously avoided any close contact with Arizona's Native Americans ever since she'd walked out of her Navajo husband's house eight years earlier. Now, they appeared to be pushing back into her life. Why? Whatever the reason, she couldn't allow it. She had too much to lose.

Standing just inside her living room, she glanced down to where the pendant's bright silver setting glowed starkly against her black silk blouse. Her hand went to where it nestled between her breasts. At the precise moment before her fingers closed around the metal, her gaze locked onto Peter's school picture sitting on the mantel. The urgency she'd felt at the fair returned. This time sheer terror accompanied it.

"Peter!"

From deep in her gut came the certainty that something was wrong with Peter.

Quickly dumping the contents of her purse on the coffee table, she rummaged through it for the slip of paper Anne had given her containing her cell phone number. When it wasn't immediately forthcoming, she began to tear frantically at the purse's contents. Still nothing.

"Where is it?" she cried, her gaze darting around the living room.

She cursed herself. Why hadn't she tacked it to the kitchen bulletin board? Over and over she searched through the pile of items she'd emptied from her purse. It wasn't there. Again, her gaze shot around the small, Southwest-style room.

"Think! Where did you put it, Laura?"

Clawing through the purse's contents once more, she cursed herself anew, this time for letting Peter go with Anne. Why? He was only eight years old, for God's sake. Close to tears, she threw herself on the sofa and covered her face with her hands, trying to think.

The pendant hit her wrist.

Unconsciously, she clutched at it like a lifeline. Slowly, very slowly, her nerves began to loosen from the tangled ball they'd formed, and she began to calm down. Her taut body began to relax. The urgency ebbed. Rational thought replaced the panic.

She had to get a hold on herself. Between that weird nightmare last night and the old Navajo woman today, she had built a case out of thin air brought on solely by exhaustion. Despite her weird dream and even weirder experience with the Navajo woman at the fair, Laura was convinced that nothing except her sleep-deprived mind indicated Peter was in any trouble. Anne would have called if anything had happened. Her gaze flew to her answering machine. The dark message light indicated no one had tried to reach her during her absence.

She had to calm down. Her decision to allow Peter to go with Anne had been sound. Peter had begun asking questions about his Navajo heritage. No matter how she felt about her husband, Peter had the right to know who he was and understand what that meant. She owed that much to him and Peter's Navajo father.

One badly digested Super Buddy Burger had turned her into a paranoid mother experiencing the throes of a first-time separation anxiety from her child. The rest, the dream and the woman in white and the pendant, were all just weird coincidences that, after a good night's sleep, she'd find easy enough to explain. She scoffed at her own foolishness.

Feeling more at ease, she kicked off her shoes and then padded to the kitchen. A good, strong cup of coffee would help clear the cobwebs of exhaustion from her brain and get her thinking straight. The cold, ceramic tiles felt good on her aching feet. As she prepared the small coffeemaker, she inhaled the aroma of the ground coffee.

A smile crossed her lips. Peter always said he was going to find her perfume that smelled like coffee beans because she liked it so much, and then he'd produce that grin that tore at her heart. Looking into Peter's smiling eyes reminded Laura of looking into his father's, seeing herself reflected in their luminous depths. Many times she'd gazed at her beautiful son and had to hide the tears that sprang to the surface so easily. And contrary to what everyone said, time did not make it easier. Only to herself could she admit that she'd never completely gotten over Peter's father.

A shrill ringing roused Laura from her thoughts. She quickly grabbed the beige receiver from the wall phone next to the refrigerator.

"Hello. Yes, this is Laura Kincaid."

Apprehension filled the room while Laura listened to the deep voice of a Navajo Tribal Police officer tearing apart her world, her life, her heart. Peter had wandered away from the powwow and was lost somewhere in the Arizona wilderness.

"What do you mean you're calling off the search?" Laura's voice rose in panic. She strained toward the uniformed Navajo Tribal Police Lieutenant sitting behind the desk in the cramped office. "It's only been three days. That's not nearly long enough to search. You've barely gotten started." She swallowed hard, frantically trying to hold back the terror that had been threatening to choke her since she'd arrived in town three days ago. She might never see Peter again. Reddened and stinging from too little sleep and too many tears, her eyes burned in their sockets, like hot coals.

"In Canyon Country, three days *can* be too long, Mrs. Kincaid." The coarsely featured, young officer shifted uncomfortably in the cracked vinyl desk chair. He placed his elbows on the desktop, steepling his hands in front of him. After peering at her over his fingers for several seconds, he closed his eyes, as if the sight of her pain-ravaged face was more than he could stand. Finally, he opened them and looked at a spot somewhere over her right shoulder. "We've exhausted every avenue. Other than your friend's account, we haven't a clue as to where to look for the boy."

She flinched. "Peter. His name is Peter." Somehow, making the Navajo officer use Peter's name made the situation less impersonal, less hopeless. "He's my son, Lieutenant Klah, not a nameless statistic."

The lieutenant dipped his head, thin raised his gaze to hers. Genuine compassion shown from his deep brown eyes. "I'm sorry. Peter."

His softly spoken apology made her regret her sharpness. Laura shook her head. "No. I'm sorry. I shouldn't be taking my impatience out on you. I know you're doing everything possible to find him. It's just . . . so frustrating."

He smiled. "No problem. I don't bruise easy. Fear and grief make people do and say things that, under normal circumstances, they would never consider."

Grief? Did that mean . . . ? She swallowed again, afraid to ask the next question, afraid of what his answer would be. But she had to know. For her own sanity. "Are you saying Peter is. . . ?" Try as she might, the word wouldn't come. She licked her dry lips and shifted her gaze from her cold hands to the officer's face, hoping he wouldn't make her say the word she dreaded hearing.

"No, ma'am. I'm saying a lot can happen out there. I'm saying there are no clues, no footprints, nothing to tell us where to start looking for Peter. It's as if he vanished like a puff of smoke."

Laura bit down on her bottom lip to keep from screaming. Not Peter. He was all she had, all she'd had for a very long time. When Ada Dooley had found her eight-and-a-half years ago, pregnant and hungry, wandering the streets of Los Angeles, she'd taken her in. For the last eight years, she'd had Ada and Peter, but then ten months ago her friend and mentor had died suddenly, leaving her only Peter. She couldn't lose him, too.

The world closed in on her, suffocating her. She had to clear her mind. She had to think about how she could convince the lieutenant to continue the search.

While searching her mind for answers, Laura scanned the dusty room and its meager furnishings. A coat tree, holding a khaki jacket that bore the green and yellow

Navajo Tribal Police emblem, stood near a windowless door. A fan, churning noiselessly in front of an open window, sucked in dust and warm air from the street and did nothing to dispel the stuffiness from the room. On the scarred, wooden desk, backed up by an old, brown vinyl chair that squeaked every time the lieutenant moved, a coffee mug with a laminated picture of three children, their copper-skinned faces grinning at her from beneath black type reading #1 Dad, taunted her.

Would she ever see Peter's toothy grin again? Would she ever groan at his humorous antics again, or smile tearfully when he said or did something that reminded her of his father? Pain seared a path through her heart, nearly making her double over with agony.

She tore her gaze away from the lieutenant's little family and concentrated on the map of what the Navajo referred to as the Big Rez hanging behind the desk—the twenty-six thousand square miles of land making up the Northern Arizona Navajo Reservation. Round-headed pins in various colors protruded randomly from the map, marking, she supposed, the crime scenes the NTP was investigating.

On the north rim of the canyons, a single red pin glared at her. The place where Peter had last been seen. Her hand went automatically to the rainbow pendant still hanging around her neck. Calmness stole over her like a wash of warm water.

"Mrs. Kincaid?"

Laura swung her attention back to the lieutenant.

"You can't give up," she said, her voice controlled and reasonable. "He's out there somewhere, alive." He raised a dark eyebrow at her words. How did she explain to a man about that built-in instinct mothers have concerning their children? A great sense of frustration settled over her.

"Mrs. Kincaid, we—"

"Lieutenant, I'd feel it if Peter were . . . dead. He's alive. I know it." She placed her hand over her heart, telling him without words where this intuition came from. "Somewhere, out there, he's alive."

Lieutenant Klah rounded his desk. He perched one hip on the rough, wooden surface, then leaned his forearms on his knees, putting his face on the same level as hers. He gently took her hand from the pendant and enfolded it in his. His eyes held understanding, sympathy, compassion, but no sign of relenting.

"I've been at this job for over six years. Sometimes, I think six years too long. I've put those red pins in that map, and I've removed them. Sometimes, we never find the missing person—alive or dead. There's a great many things out there in those canyons that we can't explain. There are even more that we can explain, and they all spell danger."

"But—"

"Ma'am, please try to understand. This country is wild and inhospitable to adults. For kids . . . well, for kids it's worse." Pain glittered in his velvet eyes. A deep frown creased his wide forehead.

Nothing he could say could convince her. Stark fear returned. "He's alive. I know he is." Laura pulled her hand from his before again clutching the pendant. Calm ebbed through her. "If you can't find him, I'll look for him myself."

"That's foolishness." The officer sat up straight. "You know nothing of this country. What can you do that we haven't already done?" His strained patience began to make itself evident in the tone of his voice.

"I don't know yet, but one thing I won't do, Lieutenant, is give up." She stood and gathered her purse from the desk. Releasing her death grip on the pendant, she shook his hand. "Thank you for all you've done. I know you did your best. It just wasn't enough."

Turning, she made her way to the door.

"Mrs. Kincaid?"

Laura stopped. She glanced over her shoulder at him. He scribbled something on a small notepad, ripped the sheet off, folded it, then held it out to her.

"If you do decide to go into the Canyon Country, and I sincerely hope you'll change your mind, call this guy. A good part of the canyon is sacred to the Navajo and restricted to *bilagáanaas*, Anglos. You'll need a permit and a Navajo guide to get in there. This man was raised there. He knows the canyons as well as he knows his reflection." Lieutenant Klah paused, and then flashed an encouraging smile. "If Peter can be found, he'll find him."

She accepted the note. She liked this man. He knew

what she was up against. And, even though he couldn't do any more to help her, she had a feeling, if his child were lost out there, he'd do exactly what she planned to do. But with his hands tied by rules, he could offer only this name and his heartfelt concern, and right now, she needed them both.

"Thanks."

"Good luck."

She nodded and left the office.

Clutching the paper, she exited the Window Rock substation. As she stepped into the dusty street, the sun beat down on her, warding off the chill that threatened to overcome her again. Dust devils chased each other across the asphalt parking lot. A hot breeze ruffled her shoulder-length hair, its careless fingers flinging the loosened black strands across her eyes. Impatiently, she swept them behind her ear.

Unidentifiable cooking odors mixed with the dry air. When had she last eaten? No answer came readily to mind, and she didn't search farther. Locating the Navajo guide who could help her find Peter filled her mind to the exclusion of all else.

Slipping behind the wheel of her rented, blue Ford Taurus, she carefully unfolded the paper the lieutenant had given her and read the name he'd scrawled across it. Her blood ran cold. The name rose off the paper like the heat waves wafting up from the baking earth, branding the identity of her only hope across her heart.

The one person she loved most in the world had wandered into the Arizona wilderness, and the man who could locate him was the man she'd been avoiding for eight years, the man who could take her son from her, the man from her dream—Kaine Cloudwalker, Peter's father.

Chapter 2

Kaine Cloudwalker dragged several French fries through a smeared puddle of ketchup, popped them in his mouth, and chewed thoughtfully. He hadn't done it because he was particularly hungry. The hamburger, salad, and apple pie he'd just finished had served to appease the hunger that had been gnawing at his gut since noontime. The French fries simply filled his mouth and gave him thinking time to answer the two men sitting across the booth from him.

While he chewed, he silently studied each man.

Agent Henry Oates was relatively new to the area, assigned six months ago to the Sedona FBI offices. Having spent most of his time in a comfortable office in Washington, the desert sun had turned his virgin facial skin bright red with sunburn. Kaine wondered absently what infraction the agent had committed to be sentenced to duty out here in the wilderness. Whatever it had been, he also decided the agent wouldn't last long in Arizona. He didn't understand the People or the land and from the looks of his sunburn, the climate. And out here that could kill you in many ways.

Oates frowned at Kaine's silence and draped one arm over the back of the red vinyl booth. His wrinkled blue suit fit his overweight body badly and where his jacket gaped open, dark perspiration stains radiated from his armpits. In the twenty minutes he'd been here, he'd guzzled two glasses of iced tea, but sweat still beaded his wide forehead, despite the iced drinks and the AC that cooled the diner's interior.

As he waited for Kaine to speak, Oates' beady blue eyes studied him. The fingers of his right hand drummed impatiently on the tabletop. Everything about the agent fairly screamed *tension*.

Jim Longtree, from the Bureau of Indian Affairs, had grown up here. He knew this land, the climate and its people well, and he revealed his impatience as any Navajo would, only through his eyes. His gaze centered on Kaine, hard and unswerving. Longtree's well-built, athletic body, tanned by the desert sun, appeared relaxed. Kaine knew that it was just a front. Like other Navajos, Jim held his emotions carefully within him, so as not to disturb the *hozho* of those around him. Harmony was a very important part of the Navajo life. Everything had a black and white, a good and bad, a positive and a negative, and they worked hard at making sure that balance was never disturbed.

"Let me get this straight. You think skinwalkers are pillaging the burial sites out there?" Kaine was sure his skepticism showed on his face, and he did nothing to cover it up.

"That's what we're told," Oates said, but his tone told Kaine he didn't think the mythical man/animal legend any more credible than any other Anglo. "The guy who saw it described it as an animal moving on all fours with glowing, red eyes. Jim tells me that's a skinwalker."

Kaine chuckled. He'd heard tales of skinwalkers since he was a child, but had never encountered one himself. A few years back Kaine might have believed it to be skinwalkers, too, but not anymore. Now, Kaine believed that it was no more than the vivid imagination of a frightened man who saw what he wanted to see, an explanation for the inexplicable. "And I take it that this skinwalker was carrying pottery in his teeth; or maybe he had a backpack?"

Jim glared at him. "This is not a joke. How do you explain the prints that were found that turned from a man's to an animal's?"

Kaine scoffed and shook his head. "You've worked on enough of these grave robber cases to know that the robbers will invent any means they can to use the Native Americans' beliefs to spook them and to throw the authorities off their trail. My bet is that, when you find these guys, they will be no different than you and me. They'll walk upright and their eyes will be blue, green, or whatever."

Jim looked out the window at a car pulling into the diner lot.

"Well, Cloudwalker?" Oates pulled an off-white handkerchief from his pocket and swiped at the latest crop of moisture gathering on his forehead. "Are you going to help us?"

Kaine took a deep breath, pushed his dinner plate to the side and then leaned on the table. "No, I'm not." He had no desire to go roaming around the canyons with these two looking for bad guys wearing animal skins to scare the hell out of the locals.

Oates cursed softly under his breath while cramming the handkerchief back into the pocket of his jacket.

For the first time, Jim displayed emotion. His fingers tightened into a balled fist on the table. "I remember a time when you would have jumped at the chance to get to the bottom of this, to protect what belongs to your ancestors."

"Yeah. Well, no more. I gave that up a long time ago." He offered no more explanation, explanations that could drift into memories of his mother and of Laura that were too painful to think about. "Besides, as of three hours ago, I'm on vacation." He smiled. "First one I've taken in years, and I have plans for how I'm spending it, and it's not with the two of you."

Once more, the memories tugged at him. Once more he fought them off.

"Have you forgotten you're Navajo? Those relics

are as much a part of you as your heritage is." Jim's jaw worked spasmodically.

Kaine sat back. No, he hadn't forgotten. How could he when his so-called heritage had stolen his mother and his wife from him? He may be full-blooded Navajo, but that's as far as it went. The only reason he'd remained here was because he loved the canyons, the risks they represented and the danger. He loved the freedom his job afforded him.

"You owe your people."

Unaccustomed anger exploded inside Kaine. "I don't owe them shit!" he said, slapping the palm of his hand on the table and making Oates jump nervously. "I paid my debt a long time ago. I spent years of my life in Washington preaching to a bunch of deaf, white-collared Congressmen about Indian rights. What good did it do me? What good did it do the People? Washington ignores them and they go right on shunning the Anglos' medical help, singing their Ways, making their sandpaintings, immersing themselves in a past made up of legends and myths, and then they die anyway."

He stopped talking abruptly, realizing he'd strayed from the subject of the stolen Indian relics that concerned Oates and Longtree and had begun venting about things he'd never spoken of to anyone. He leaned back and crossed his arms, as if holding the rest of his thoughts at bay.

"Find someone else to take you into the canyon to find your ground-pickers."

"They aren't ground-pickers." Oates wiped his pudgy hands on the handkerchief. His dark eyebrows drew together to form a straight line across his eyes. "Whatever these guys are, they dig. They're grave robbers, and whether or not I believe the Navajo mumbo-jumbo about skinwalkers, that's against the law. They're finding caches of Mimbres pottery that are making them damned rich. Someone is feeding them information, and we can't figure out who it is. We think, if we go into the canyons, we can follow them and see where they go, then track them back to the brains behind this." He wagged a finger at Kaine. "That's where you come in."

"No, that's where I go out. Besides, Jim knows the canyons as well as I do. He can guide you through them."

Jim shook his head. "I've been away from the land for too long, forgotten too much. There's no one around here who knows the canyons like you do, Kaine. Reconsider."

Kaine stood, took a few bills from his jeans pocket and dropped them on the table. He paused and looked from one man to the other. "Good luck."

He stopped long enough to pay his tab at the cash register and then strode from the diner to his Land Rover. Halfway down the street, he noted a blue sedan in the parking lot beside the NTP substation. Inside the car, a woman stared down at a piece of paper she held against the steering wheel. It was her long, dark hair that caught Kaine's attention. He did a double take and then looked away, cursing himself for every kind of fool.

For one split second, he'd thought the woman was Laura. Then his sane mind cut in, and he knew it was nothing more than the power of suggestion brought on by the long-suppressed thoughts of her that had surfaced in the diner.

Use you head, Kaine. What would Laura be doing here?

Eight years ago, she'd gotten away from him and this country as quickly as she could. He'd be willing to bet that it would take a team of wild horses to drag her back.

With a huff of impatience with himself, he steered the Rover toward Jesse Begay's hardware store. With any luck, Jesse had been able to get the building supplies Kaine had ordered and tomorrow, he could start the long-awaited renovations on the house where he and Laura had lived, sell it and finally close that chapter of his life. But even as he tried to picture the new porch he had planned, visions of a dark-haired woman intruded.

Moments later, memories of the night he'd come home to find Laura's terse little note began to bombard him. He'd been away for three weeks and had missed her with an intensity that had astonished him. All the way back on the plane from Washington he'd been entertaining the idea of slipping into their warm bed, pulling her into his arms and making passionate love to her for hours.

Many other times, since they'd gotten married, he'd had to go to Washington on behalf of his people, but for some reason, this time, leaving Laura had been like tearing off his arm. He'd felt less than whole for the entire three weeks and had made up his mind that this trip would be his last. He'd leave the lobbying for Indian Affairs to the younger men, and he'd stay home, and spend more time with his wife, maybe even start a family.

Their house had been quiet, which he'd expected at two in the morning. What he hadn't expected was to walk into the bedroom and find the bed empty and undisturbed and an envelope propped against his pillow. Even now, the pain of her abandonment had hit him like a gunshot to his gut.

Less than a year later, his mother succumbed to cancer while a so-called *hataałii* sang over her and drew pictures on the ground with colored sand. Kaine had begged her to go to the Anglo hospital in Phoenix, but true to the Ways of the People, she'd refused. Her death had marked the beginning of Kaine's disillusionment with his heritage.

That was saying a lot considering that at one time he'd trained to be a singer at his grandfather's knee. His grandfather, Brother To The Owl, had been one of the most powerful singers his people had ever known and word had it that Kaine possessed even greater powers than his grandfather. But even by invoking the help of the Holy People, there had been no way to save Kaine's mother.

Over time, Kaine had come to terms with his mother's death and his loss of faith in the teachings of his people, but the bitterness he felt for Laura remained as strong today as it had been the night he'd read her note.

✜   ✜   ✜

Laura guided her car carefully though the growing desert twilight. Beside her on the seat were the directions the woman at the diner had given her to Kaine's house. As she'd suspected it would be, it was isolated, far from any friends and neighbors he might have enjoyed in town had he one social bone in his body.

Her nerves were strung as tight as the strings on a guitar. The steering wheel was slick with sweat from her palms, and the uneven ground upon which she drove made it hard for her to maintain control. Motivated by her jangled nerves, haunting questions skittered through her mind.

What if Kaine found out Peter was his son? What if he wanted Peter to come live with him?

From what she could recall, these men were very possessive of their children, especially the boys. She remembered an incident when a woman had run off with her child and her husband had gone after her, left her behind, and brought the boy home with him. They'd heard months later that she'd committed suicide over the loss of her son.

When she'd mentioned it to Kaine, he'd agreed with the father's actions.

"A boy belongs with his father," Kaine had said firmly, "with his people, not in a strange society where he'll lose his heritage and his identity. If it had been me, I would have done exactly the same thing."

Now, here she was, driving through the Arizona wilderness to ask for Kaine's help in finding his son. Could she do this and not tell him? Could she risk losing Peter?

She gripped the steering wheel tighter. A humorless laugh burst unbidden from her pursed lips.

Fate had a warped sense of humor, she decided, navigating around a large saguaro cactus that had sprung up in front of her car out of nowhere. Eight years ago she'd have staked her life on it that she and Kaine would never cross paths again and here she was meeting him to ask him to do one of the most important favors she would ever ask of anyone. What chance did she have that he'd agree?

Despite her trepidations at coming face to face with her estranged husband, the closer she got to Kaine's home, the more a strange anticipation grew within her and the more Laura's heartbeat increased in equal proportions to the decrease in miles she covered.

What would she say to him after all this time? Would he slam the door in her face?

Before she was ready for the confrontation, a house appeared around a curve in the road. Her headlights washed over the plain adobe structure. A Land Rover was parked haphazardly parallel to the porch that spanned the front of the house.

For awhile, she sat in her car and stared at it. Then making up her mind that her nervousness at seeing Kaine was far outweighed by Peter's disappearance, she slipped from the car, closed the door softly, and then climbed the steps to the front door. Taking a deep breath, she knocked.

Chapter 3

Kaine unfolded his tired body from the rickety kitchen chair, stretched his cramped, tired muscles, and then strode to the sink. He deposited his dirty coffee mug atop an ever-growing pile. If he didn't wash dishes soon, he'd be eating off the bare table. Unconcerned with the possibility, he moved into the small living room. Throwing himself into his easy chair, he stared moodily out the window at the purple and orange streaks crisscrossing the evening sky.

Tomorrow would begin the first vacation he'd had in years. Having a few days to himself would be a real novelty. He'd done little lately except scour the Arizona wilderness for some damned-fool tourist who couldn't read a map and didn't have enough sense to stay out of a land that offered no forgiveness for ineptitude.

The change of pace would be a pleasure. He knew better than to plan on sitting around doing nothing. He'd go nuts. Besides, inactivity gave him too much thinking time. It had been too long since he'd had his life to himself, and he planned on taking advantage of it by starting repairs on that porch and roof of the house he'd shared with Laura, thus closing that part of his life for good. Maybe then he could get through a day without thoughts of her invading his peace of mind.

Tomorrow, Jesse Begay's man would deliver the supplies Kaine needed to the old house. He'd get up early and go out there and take the first step toward purging the past. Now that he had no scheduled guide trips into the Canyon Country, he couldn't make excuses any longer.

He ran a hand over his face from forehead to chin. Who in hell was he kidding? He hadn't wanted to go back there, to face the memories that still haunted the place. If he wanted to be truly honest about it, it wasn't just the memories. He'd lost the fire for everything but his job after Laura left.

Ever since the night he'd read the words in her note, *I just can't live this way anymore*, he'd been content to spend more and more time in the canyon wilderness, playing with danger. At least then, he felt alive.

Once more, memories of that night began to trickle into his conscious mind. He firmly slammed the door. He didn't want to resurrect that part of his life—couldn't resurrect it. Thoughts of Laura still hurt far too much, something, in the true Navajo tradition, he admitted to no one but himself.

Would the pain of losing her ever go away? He hoped getting rid of their house would be a start. But he had to wonder if, even after someone else lived in it, the memories of his life with Laura would remain behind to taunt him every day like the pain of his mother's senseless death, a death that could have been prevented had she believed more in the Anglos' medicine and less in the mumbo-jumbo sung over a sandpainting?

However, while his mother's memory brought an aching sense of loss, Laura's memory brought the kind of pain a man never forgets or forgives.

He shook himself, finding it strangely disturbing that Laura suddenly occupied so much of his thoughts. It had to be his decision to fix the house that had brought her ghost to life with a vengeance.

Kaine decided to get a beer from the kitchen. Just as he opened the refrigerator, a rapid tattoo sounded on the front door. He glanced at the clock above the stove. Eleven-fifteen. Late for visitors.

Pulling a frosty can from the shelf, he closed the door, popped the top, drained most of its contents, and sauntered toward the front entry. Another round of knocks came. More insistent this time.

"This better be important," he growled under his breath. *And it better not be Oates and Longtree making one more plea for my help.*

Grasping the latch and with words that would reinforce his decision not to help them find their skinwalker hovering on his lips, he swung the heavy door toward him. With the beer halfway to his mouth, he froze, his mind a sudden blank.

His hand dropped to his side, the beer forgotten. The woman in the car outside the NTP substation flashed through his mind. His instincts had been right after all. He knew without a doubt it had been Laura and now, she was standing on his doorstep looking at him like he held the answer to world peace.

Having been hit head-on by a charging bull would have left more air in his lungs than seeing Laura again after all this time.

Careful not to give any hint of his loss of composure, he leaned negligently against the doorjamb; but his stance appeared supportive, and was not the casual pose he had hoped to project.

"Forget something eight years ago?" he drawled.

She stared up at him with red-rimmed, green eyes. Dark circles shadowed them. She looked like a deer caught in the headlights of a car. She'd been crying— a lot. Another smart remark hovered on the tip of his tongue, but he stifled it and fought the need to comfort her. He battled against the lurch of his heart and the overpowering urge to haul her into his arms and make everything all right. Instead, he deliberately summoned the pain. With the pain came the anger, and he could deal with that far better than the wanting, the needing. He tightened his grip until the soft sound of crumpling metal reminded him he still held the beer can.

"Kaine, I need your help." Her voice quivered, as if on the edge of more tears.

"And hello to you, too."

She blinked. "I'm sorry. Hello, Kaine. How are you?" The words rushed past her lips as if she begrudged the time the simple greeting took.

He did a quick inventory of the face of the woman who'd claimed every ounce of love he'd had to give, then threw it away, leaving none for anyone else, not even himself. She looked like hell. Her long, black hair appeared as though it hadn't seen a comb since early that morning, and her wrinkled pink T-shirt and soiled white jeans looked as if she'd slept in them. She—

He stopped himself. What the hell did he care if she looked like any minute she'd shatter into a million pieces at his feet?

"Please. May I come in and talk to you?"

Without a word, he stepped back and waved her into the living room with the hand that still clutched the smashed beer can. For a minute, he stood still, studying her liquid gait. How many times had he imagined her here? How many nights had he lain in that bed down the hall, dreaming of her curled against him, only to wake and find the bed cold and empty?

A chilly gust of desert night air swept through the door, cooling his dangerous thoughts.

He laughed harshly. "This is sure a turnaround,

considering that eight years ago you made it clear that I didn't have anything you were interested in, including my help." He lowered himself into the chair he'd abandoned moments before, then propped his dusty boots on the edge of the footstool in front of him.

Laura stood before him like a little girl about to be reprimanded by her elders. He hadn't missed the way she'd flinched at his harsh words. Instead of the satisfaction he'd expected, guilt prickled his conscience. *Guilt?* Why in hell should he feel guilty? *He* hadn't walked out on *her*.

"I don't want to rehash the past, if that's what you mean. Believe me, if there had been anywhere else I could have turned, I would have."

Kaine laughed harshly. "I don't have a doubt about that. Must be playing pure hell with your pride to have to come here and ask me for anything." He placed the can on the side table. "So. . . ."

"My son is lost in the Canyon Country. I need your help to find him." The hurried words caught on a sob. She swallowed hard and then gripped her hands tightly around a manila folder she held in front of her like a shield.

Laura had a child.

Kaine struggled for composure. A son. A son who should have been his, but who had been fathered by another man. The sight of her suddenly sent his anger spiraling to new heights. He stood and walked to the window. Pushing aside the curtain, he stared blindly into the black desert night. The hand at his side formed a fist. God, he wanted to hit something, anything that would stop the pain.

But he didn't. He did as he always had. He swallowed his feelings and consigned them to the place deep inside him where they wouldn't hurt him or anyone else. That was one Navajo tradition he had no trouble understanding. Since his mother's death and Laura's desertion, it had served him well. He turned toward her. She'd taken a seat on the couch, poised on the edge, as if ready to flee at any given moment.

"Why me?"

"The NTP told me you know the canyons better than anyone."

He should. He'd spent enough time there and probably knew every rock and crevice in the one hundred thirty square miles it covered. He'd grown to manhood spending summers with his family's sheep in the shade of Spider Rock. He'd pulled tourists out of places in the canyons that no other man would go. Some of his friends claimed he had a death wish. Maybe he did.

"How old is he?"

She hesitated for a fraction of a second before answering. "Eight."

Eight. She hadn't wasted any time replacing him. Anger bubbled up from that hidden place. He tamped it down. "Where'd he disappear from?"

"A powwow on the north rim." While she filled him in on all the facts, as she knew them, he listened quietly. "He's been gone for three days, and the NTP gave up looking. They said it's as if he just vanished from the face of the Earth."

Enclosed in contemplative silence, Kaine mulled over what she'd said. Chances were the kid wasn't alive, but after taking one look at her, he couldn't tell her that. She looked too damned fragile, like one word from him and she'd blow apart like a dandelion's seed head. He wanted her to suffer, but not even he was heartless enough to do it that way. He wanted to tell her to find someone else to look for her kid, but he couldn't do that either. As much as he wanted to see her hurting, Kaine couldn't take his anger at her out on a child. If the kid was still alive, every day counted. By the time she did find someone else to search for him, it might be too late—if it wasn't already.

"I'll start tomorrow, but I'll need all the information you can give me, and it's not gonna be a freebie just because we have a history." He named his fee.

To his amazement, Laura nodded eagerly before bolting off the couch. For a minute, he thought she'd throw herself in his arms, but she quickly regained her composure and took a step backward. She gripped the folder tighter against her body. Regret lapped rebelliously at his insides.

"Here are the copies of the case folder the NTP gave me." She moved closer, handed him the folder, and laid her hand on his arm. "Kaine, I don't know how to thank you for this."

Grabbing the folder, he shook her hand from his sleeve. "Thank me by staying out of my way and letting me do my job."

She smiled, and his heart turned over in his chest and his skin warmed as though the sun had invaded the house, stealing the chill of loneliness from all the corners. Some things never change.

"I promise I won't be a bit of trouble. You won't even know I'm around. I'll—"

He swung on her. "Hold it. What do you mean I won't know you're around? You don't have some crazy idea that I'm going to let you come with me, do you?"

She stiffened. Her hand went to the front of her T-shirt and clutched something beneath the material. Perhaps whatever hung suspended from the silver chain around her neck? She pursed her lips and knitted her brows.

He knew that look all too well. Stubbornness mixed with a large helping of pure hard-ass determination.

She raised her chin. "I most certainly do. He's my son, and I expect to be there when you find him."

If I find him. "Go, and you go alone." He threw the folder on the footstool and skirting her, moved to the fireplace. Grabbing the solid iron poker, he speared it into the burning logs. A shower of sparks rose up the chimney with the smoke.

Laura stood closer to the low hearth. "Kaine, be

reasonable. I'm his mother. I know my child. I could be of help."

He avoided her face and continued to rearrange the logs, nearly extinguishing what had been a strong, blazing fire. "You'd be a liability."

She made an impatient sound which drew his gaze against his will. Moisture lay imprisoned behind her long, dark lashes. He quickly averted his attention back to the heart of the flame.

"How can you say that? If I promise to do exactly as you say, how can I be a liability?"

"You'll do exactly as I say? Is that a promise?"

"Yes."

He ignored the light of hope that had blossomed in her eyes. "Then go back to your motel room, and stay out of my way."

From the corner of his eye, he saw her stiffen. "I will *not* wait in a motel room and go slowly crazy wondering."

"You will if you want me to find your kid." This had gone beyond her holding him back in his search. Now, it included self-preservation—his. After being in the same room with her for the past few minutes and waging this battle of emotional survival, even sharing the vast isolation of the Canyon Country with her would be courting trouble. "Laura, I can't put it any plainer than this—I don't *want* you with me."

"Kaine, this isn't about us. This is about *my* son, and I will do anything I have to for his welfare, including following you, if you refuse to be reasonable."

He covered the angry eruption inside him at her possessive tone with sarcastic laughter. "Is that supposed to scare me into letting you go?" When she didn't reply, he turned to look at her.

She stared back at him with those wide, green eyes, the eyes that had first captured his heart at the Indian Rally in Los Angeles over eight years ago. A tear had escaped and left a silvery trail down one of her tanned cheeks. "I'm not foolish enough to try to scare you. I'm just stating facts."

Forced to look away before he blurted out the truth of what he was feeling, he poked viciously at the fire. Sparks flared. Didn't she know that just by being here, just getting within touching range of him, just inhaling her special fragrance, scared the living hell out of him? He'd spent every minute since he'd found her on his doorstep looking so damned vulnerable, so damned beautiful, being scared. No other woman on the face of the Earth could do that to him. No one but Laura. And he hated her for it.

He took refuge in his anger again. "Then you take your facts and tuck them into your bedroll and get on your best hiking boots. You'll need them."

She brightened and flashed that damn gut-wrenching smile of hers. "Then you'll take me with you?"

"No."

"But—"

"Wake up, Laura." He threw the poker onto the hearth. The metal clanged loudly against the adobe. He shifted his body, positioning his face inches from hers. "This isn't a *bilagáanaas* church social you're planning to attend. That's damned rugged country. The kind that drains all your energy and then asks for more. The kind with dangers that make good nightmares." A soft gasp escaped her. The sweet smell of her breath wafted to him. His gut knotted. "Go back to your safe motel."

He retreated to the window. Laura watched him. His body moved with the combined grace of a mountain cat and Mikhail Baryshnikov. Every move noiseless, every move counting for something more than just propelling his body from one place to another, every move accentuated by the flowing grace of his ancestors.

His long, muscular legs ate up the space between her and the window, moving him as far from her as the small room would allow. That pricked her sensibilities.

She'd always loved to watch him walk. And from the way her heart fluttered in her chest, that hadn't changed.

Coming here had been one of the hardest things she'd ever had to do, but for Peter, she'd walk through hot coals. Now she was discovering to her chagrin that the attraction she'd always felt for her estranged husband hadn't diminished one ounce in eight years. Not a healthy concession for a woman planning on spending indefinite hours with that same man combing the wilderness. Still, she couldn't take her gaze off him.

At the window, he moved the curtain aside and stared out into the black night. His face in profile accentuated the deep grooves and valleys of his Native American features. A muscle twitched spasmodically in his jaw.

So, Mr. Cloudwalker, you aren't as composed as you'd like me to believe.

The idea that she still had an effect on Kaine pleased her. Maybe too much. But maybe she could use it to her advantage. Before she could act on her notion, his face hardened to that impenetrable profile she knew so well.

What had happened to the gentle, sensitive man she'd met and married in Los Angeles? When had he turned as stony and unfeeling as the canyon walls that flanked his little house?

Quickly, she reminded herself that, back then, she hadn't known Kaine as well as she thought she had. If that had been the case, she'd have realized he didn't love her long before she'd married him and moved to the Big Rez. But even taking that into consideration, she knew even less about this stranger who lived in Kaine's body now. And she wasn't sure she wanted to know him.

When she'd come here tonight, she'd been prepared for his anger, his hatred, but not his unfeeling, bullheaded stubbornness. How did she breach it? And breach it she must. She could *not* wait quietly in a motel room while her son wandered around the canyons alone and hungry. The sooner Kaine understood that, the easier this would be on both of them.

"I'm *not* going meekly back to that motel room. I've spent too much of my life waiting for . . . well, waiting. This time, I'm doing what *I* want."

He continued to stare stoically into the dark night. Anger rose up to choke her. How she'd learned to hate that closed part of him, the Navajo part that shared nothing of himself with anyone. She hated it as much now as she had the night she'd walked out on him—pregnant, with nowhere to go.

"What will you do if he cries, if he's hurt, if he's sick?"

Kaine drew his gaze from the contemplation of the night and glanced at her. "Dry his tears, bandage his wounds, bring him home to Mommy." The words sounded as emotionless and unfeeling as if he'd been talking about an injured horse.

Her anger flared red hot. "Dammit, Kaine! He's—" She bit down on the rest of her sentence. For one brief flash of time, she'd thought to sway him by telling him Peter was his son, and then she'd stopped herself. She had more than her share of battles to fight right now. She didn't need to spar with Kaine over why she'd never told him about Peter. Nor did she want to think about him taking her son from her when the truth was out. Finding Peter as quickly as possible took precedence now.

"He's what?"

"—just a little boy, who needs his mother." The words fell from her in a rush to cover her blunder.

"Where's his old man? Why isn't he here spearheading

this operation to find his son?"

She could tell by his disapproving tone that he didn't think much of a man who would let a woman take on this task alone. Guilt walked over her with cold feet. She shivered.

Laura chose her words carefully. *Stay as close to the truth as you can. Lies have a way of getting tangled and strangling the liar.* "His father doesn't know about Peter."

When Kaine threw her an accusing glare, she winced inwardly, but met his gaze head-on. Better he think Peter the product of a one-night stand than find out the truth. She surprised herself by adding *at least for now.* It was the first time since her son's birth that she'd ever seriously considered telling Kaine he had a son.

Finally, he stepped away from the window and faced her. His expression startled her. Despite his mask of stoicism slipping firmly into place, his eyes shimmered with an emotion she read as pain. Why?

Before she could analyze it, he shuttered them and walked to the front door. Throwing it wide, he looked pointedly at her. "I need to get some sleep so I can get an early start tomorrow."

Feigning nonchalance, she crossed the floor to stand in front of him. His earthy fragrance nearly undid her. "And what time would that be?"

His answer took the form of a smile. A genuine, heartbreaking, bring-a-woman-to-her-knees smile. Laura's hard-won composure rocked on its heels. She struggled to right it.

"Okay. It was worth a try. You might have been so bowled over by my charm that you'd have inadvertently answered my question." She could have bitten off her tongue. Too late she realized how much her words sounded like the flirting they used to engage in. She'd just given him an opening for another barb.

He didn't miss his chance. His grin broadened. "A smart man never makes the same mistake twice. No matter how tempting it might be."

She'd asked for that, but she wasn't beaten yet. "Kaine." She laid her hand on his bare forearm and felt him flinch. Did he detest her touch that much? She could recall when an innocent gesture like that had sent them scurrying for the nearest bed. But that was back when he'd loved her—or when she thought he had. "How can I thank you for this? Somehow money doesn't seem to be enough."

He removed his arm from her grasp and swept his thick, straight hair from his forehead. It fell softly back to almost where it had lain before, framing his rugged features and making him appear savagely enticing—the grown counterpart to her son.

"Money'll do," he drawled.

Quickly, she dragged her gaze from his and slid past his towering body. Nearly through the door, she thought she heard him add softly, "For now."

✣   ✣   ✣

After Laura left, Kaine got another beer and went back to the easy chair. This time, he'd turned off the lights. Surrounded by darkness illuminated only by the blazing fire, after her physical presence had gone, he wouldn't have to fight off the images of Laura in the room, the images that had remained behind to taunt him. He threw a glance at the folder he'd tossed on the footstool and then toed it aside.

"For now?" he asked the darkness. What the hell had he meant by that? Unable and unwilling to answer his own question, he blocked it out of his mind and thought about what lay ahead of him tomorrow.

The section of the canyons that she'd indicated Peter had disappeared in was largely impassable except on foot. He'd only been there once when he was a young man and when he believed that the ghosts that lived there were something he had no desire to encounter. They were filled with lethal slot canyons that flooded unexpectedly and legend had it, they were the home of the skinwalkers. It was not going to be an easy trek.

At least he wouldn't have her tagging along, getting in the way and whining about the heat, the lack of amenities and the blisters on her feet. As he recalled, the Laura he knew from eight years ago was not by any stretch of the imagination an outdoorsman. Hopefully, before he saw her face-to-face again, he'd have his emotions pigeonholed and under control. He'd give her son back and then be on his way, and once the house was gone, too, he'd be free of her forever.

Laura's son. Peter she'd called him. Kaine wondered if he'd inherited his mother's black hair and haunting green eyes. Or did he look like the guy who'd jumped Laura's bones, got her pregnant, and then disappeared from her life? The mere thought brought his blood to a rolling boil. He bit down hard on his emotions.

What the hell was he doing? Laura and her personal life had ceased to be his problem a long time ago, but still . . . Kaine rerouted his thoughts.

What if the kid was dead? The possibilities were very good. Three days was a long time for a grown man to be lost in the canyons without food, water, warm clothing, bedding and that didn't even take into account the wild animals. For a kid . . . it didn't look good.

If the kid was dead, how would he break the news to Laura? How could he stand by and watch her fall apart without it affecting him?

Questions piled on questions, and nowhere did he see any answers. He sighed. Suddenly exhausted, he laid his head against the back of the chair and closed his eyes.

✛　　✛　　✛

From nowhere a bright light fills the room. Kaine bolts upright in the chair, exhaustion forgotten. The light changes and moves, suddenly taking on all the vivid colors of the rainbow. Mesmerized by the shifting and turning, he stares into the bright white spot in the center.

A shadow appears, first indistinct, then gaining definition. Another shadow joins the first. They move in unison toward Kaine, shifting and slowly taking form. Still, he stares, unable to move, nor, strangely, does he have any desire to.

The light grows stronger, blinding him with its brilliance—then suddenly goes out, as if someone has thrown a switch. The flashbulb effect brings with it dancing specks of colored light. He blinks several times to clear them from his vision.

When they disappear, he stares, certain the lights are still playing tricks on him. But the two figures standing silently in his living room remain. Oddly, he feels unaffected by this phenomenon.

He recognizes the man as his grandfather, Brother To The Owl, but not the woman with him. That he accepts the appearance of his grandfather so casually surprises him. The old man died five years ago.

The woman, garbed from head to toe in the traditional female Navajo dress, is lovely. Her skirt and blouse, the same shade as the white shell in the squash-blossom necklace suspended from her neck, sways as she steps forward. Firelight reflects from the hammered silver face of the sun, the centerpiece of the necklace, giving strange life to the pendant's frozen features.

"Who are you?" Kaine hears himself ask.

"Have you forgotten the Ways of your people so com-

pletely? The Diné *call me Changing Woman, Daughter Of Long Life Boy and Happiness Girl, Wife Of The Sun, Mother Of The Monster Twins, Mother Of Creation." Her voice emerges as a musical chant.*

Blinking several times in hope of rousing himself from this dream, Kaine shakes his head. "I don't believe this."

"Do you need proof that the sun will shine tomorrow or that the flowers will bloom after the rain?" He shakes his head again. "Why then do you need proof of who I am?" He doesn't reply. "Ask your wife of a woman known to her as Ada Dooley."

"Laura? You know Laura?"

The woman answers with a smile. "I know many."

"Why are you here?" Kaine can't shake the feeling of being a spectator. His voice seems to come from within his head.

His grandfather—taller, younger, straighter than Kaine remembers him—steps forward.

"We have come to tell you time is running out." He gestures to Changing Woman. "She is in her first phase as Whiteshell Woman. She has only three more phases to pass through before her lifecycle will be done. For her a new lifecycle will begin, but for you, time will be over. There will be no going back. What is not done in this lifecycle will forever remain undone."

"Time for what?" Confusion crowds Kaine's mind.

"For you, Ligai Atsá," the woman whispers. "For your happiness."

Kaine starts. White Eagle. *His war name. No one knows his war name except his mother and him. Not even his grandfather. War names are guarded fiercely, never spoken. To do so will cause them to lose their powers in the Underground Hereafter.*

"*I don't understand.*"

"*You have lost your courage and your faith in the Ways, my son.*" *His grandfather steps back. The circle of light returns, growing in brightness by minute degrees.* "*You have disturbed the* hozho."

A mixture of indignation and frustration propels Kaine from the chair, but while his mind follows the retreating figures, his body remains seated, unmoving.

Stung by the old man's insinuation that he has become a coward, Kaine strains toward his grandfather. "*I am not a coward.*" *Then, because he can't resist, he asks,* "*Courage for what?*"

"*The courage to dream.*" *The disembodied voice comes to him as a singsong chant.*

"*Dreams are for fools,*" *he hears himself retort.*

The images fade into the glowing center of a brilliantly colored ball.

"*The fool stays awake, afraid to dream and risks nothing. In the end, he has nothing. The wise man welcomes sleep and risks all by stepping into the eye of the dream. When he emerges, he brings with him wisdom, strength, and a full heart. Step into the eye of your dream, Kaine Cloudwalker, before it is too late.*"

✤   ✤   ✤

Kaine jumped, roused instantly from sleep. Absently, he watched the slow progress of the beer can he'd been holding as it rolled across the wooden floor and came to rest against the adobe hearth, leaving a thin trail of liquid behind it. The dream replayed itself through his mind again and again. Finally, he stood and shook his head.

"Dreams are for fools."

But, as he walked toward his bedroom, he could still hear the echo of his grandfather's words reverberating though his mind.

"Step into the eye of your dream, Kaine Cloudwalker, before it is too late."

Chapter 4

Kaine stared at the ceiling waiting for sleep to come, but in vain. His mind worked tirelessly, but not at finding sleep. Visions of Laura danced through his head: her smile, her sad eyes, her tears, her lips so full and moist and begging for his kiss. Much like the first time he'd met her.

He'd been at a Los Angeles rally with his Pechanga Indian friend, Tommy Twotoes. Kaine had felt her before he'd seen her. He experienced a feeling of being watched intently by a single pair of eyes. Since a crowd of over seventy-five people were centered on him, there was no reason for this strange sensation.

Then he'd seen her standing alone on the edge of the crowd gathered in the small park. The wind had picked up her long black hair and scattered it over her shoulders. A strand had blown across her face, and she'd shoved it back impatiently, as if annoyed that anything had come between her and the object of her concentration. A soft smile curved her lips when she saw she'd garnered his attention.

Kaine's mind had gone instantly blank and all his sense had jumped to alert mode. He'd stepped down from the platform, leaving his friend to go on with his speech without him. Never taking his eyes off her, he'd walked slowly toward where she stood. A couple of feet from her, he stopped.

"Hello." Her voice was as sexy as her sea-green eyes.

"Hi."

The crowd reacted noisily to something Tommy had said, but neither of them paid any attention. For them, the world outside had ceased to exist. Kaine had not been able to talk or breathe. Her beauty just overwhelmed him. And that smile reached down inside him and brought emotions to life that he had no idea he even possessed. He'd felt alive, more alive than when he rode his horse at top speed through the Arizona wilderness. More alive than when the wind wiped through is hair and the sun kissed his face.

"Wanna get some coffee?" he'd said.

Without hesitation, she'd nodded and held her hand out to him. He'd taken it in his and at that precise moment, Kaine's heart had ceased to belong to him.

He'd never forget the electricity of their first touch. In his soul he'd known she was the one woman who could complete him. He never wanted to let her go.

They went to a small café not far from the park and talked as if they'd known each other all their lives. She told him how she'd come down from her Nob Hill home in San Francisco at her friend's urging to attend the rally.

At the mention of where she'd come from, he should have know this relationship was headed for disaster, but all he'd been able to think about was how lovely Laura was, how he wanted to never let her out of his sight, how he wanted her at his side for the rest of his life.

Two weeks later, they were married, and he was carrying her over the threshold of his tiny adobe house. For the first few weeks, life had been idyllic, perfect. Then he'd gotten word that the Rainbow Arch bill was going before Congress for a vote and he was needed to lobby in Washington.

Leaving Laura had torn his heart to shreds, but he didn't let her see it. Her tears were enough to tell him how she felt. That had been the beginning of his trips to D.C. Each time, the parting became harder and each time, the reunions more stilted. Each time Laura had been more withdrawn until finally, he came home and she'd been gone.

Kaine's ringing alarm clock roused him from his reminiscence. He hadn't gotten a wink of sleep and he had to start his search for Laura's son. He dragged himself from the bed, knowing this was gonna be on hell of a long day.

Twenty minutes later, he slipped from his front door and stopped dead on the porch. Parked under a mesquite tree was Laura's blue sedan. She'd stayed out there all night. Probably so she could follow him. He shook his head. She hadn't lost one ounce of her determination in eight years.

Carefully, he got into his car, pulled the door shut as noiselessly as possible, held his breath, and started the engine. He glanced toward her car and saw no movement. Slowly, he drove out of the yard and onto the road.

✣   ✣   ✣

"How stupid can one person be?"

Laura glared at the spot where Kaine's Land Rover had been parked the night before. She picked up the book she'd brought with her and planned on reading to keep her awake, just in case Kaine tried to get away without her. She threw it onto the car seat in disgust. She hadn't counted on the many nights of lost sleep since Peter's disappearance catching up to her with such a vengeance. Now, by the time she'd awakened, Kaine had sneaked out and her car's battery had long been dead from keeping the dome light on all night.

"Damn! Damn! Damn!"

She'd never find Kaine now. Once he'd left his driveway, she could wander forever trying to locate him. She glanced around the unfamiliar, rocky landscape. She'd never had any sense of direction, even in familiar territory. Out here, she could get hopelessly lost in less time than it would take to start her car and head it out the driveway.

Opening the car door for air, she draped her arms over the steering wheel and then rested her head against it. Frustration ate at her. If she was stuck here, what good could she do Peter?

Damn you, Kaine Cloudwalker. Damn you to hell.

The sound of an approaching vehicle silenced her raging thoughts. Kaine pulled his Land Rover up beside her car. Slowly, she raised her head and fought back the grin tugging at her lips. Not knowing what else to do, she let the smile break through. He frowned.

"I don't suppose you brought any hiking gear with you." A distinct hint of hopefulness colored his question.

"Yes. Yes I did." She scrambled out of the car, hurriedly unlocked the trunk, and turned to him.

"Well, don't just stand there. Get your gear in the car. By the time we reach Willoughby's Trading Post for supplies, it'll be noon."

Before he could change his mind, Laura had her knapsack and bedroll in the back of his car and then deposited herself next to him in the front seat. She wanted to ask what had made him change his mind, but decided that subject might be better left alone—for now.

Never question good fortune, Ada, Laura's friend and mentor, had always said. *The gods might decide to take it back.*

"Thanks, Kaine." What more could she say without groveling? That she'd have rather suffered the tortures of the damned than be left behind to worry and wonder while he searched for her son—their son? Or that his company didn't make her one bit happier than hers made him?

He grunted his reply, but kept his gaze centered on the road, twisting and turning the wheel to avoid the chugholes dotting their path. If his white-knuckled grip on the steering wheel was any indication of his mood, she'd forego any explanation and settle for the grunt.

✦ ✦ ✦

Almost an hour later, Kaine finally spoke.

"You know anybody named Ada?"

Having been totally immersed in thoughts of Peter, Laura jumped. How did he know about Ada? She cast a glance in his direction and then looked out the windshield; she was sure that her features revealed her surprised reaction to his out-of-the-blue question. For a while before answering, she studied the dirt road they'd been traveling for some time, swallowing the lump of sadness thoughts of Ada brought with them.

"Yes. I lived with her. She took me in before Peter's birth. She died about ten months ago. Why?"

"Oh, no reason. Just asking." He looked away, seemingly preoccupied with his thoughts.

No reason! Who did he think he was kidding? Kaine didn't do idle chit chat. And how in blazes had he found out about Ada? She opened her mouth to ask; then thought better of it. In the mood he'd been in since they left his house, she wasn't about to push for a more satisfactory answer and end up on the sharp end of another of his double-edged, sarcastic remarks.

"Took you in? What about your parents?"

Uncomfortable with this whole conversation, Laura opted for evasiveness. "What about them?"

"Why didn't you just move in with them?"

"They didn't want me."

A derisive laugh broke from Kaine's stiff lips. "Still haven't forgiven you for marrying an Indian, huh?"

Laura wanted to tell him that wasn't the reason, but it would have been a lie. Instead, she ignored him and allowed thoughts of her friend to push away her worries about Peter and her impatience with the detached man glaring out the windshield like he harbored a grudge against fate for putting them on the same planet.

Laura had met Ada within two weeks of leaving Kaine and returning to Los Angeles, only to find her wealthy parents would have nothing to do with either her or her "savage's brat," as they referred to her unborn child. She should have been surprised at their attitude in this day and age, but she wasn't. They'd warned her, when she'd decided to marry that *heathen*, that they'd have nothing more to do with her, that for them, their daughter was dead. But she'd loved Kaine, and went against their wishes to marry him anyway, assuming time would change her parents' prejudicial thinking, but it hadn't. If anything, it had grown more narrow-minded.

Left with nowhere to go, Laura had wandered the

streets. When Ada stumbled on her in a rat-infested alley, Laura had been experiencing premature labor pains and had started spotting blood. With Ada's love and care, she'd kept her baby and carried him full-term. In the interim, Ada had seen to it that Laura went to college to earn her nursing degree, so she'd have a profession with which to support her child and herself.

Unfortunately, her guardian angel, which is how Laura always though of her because Ada had been wearing white the first time she saw her standing over her, had died ten months ago. Laura smiled. As long as she'd known Ada, she'd never worn anything but white, turquoise, an iridescent shade of coral and black. She'd been wearing black the day she died, as if somehow she'd known the end was near.

Even beyond the grave, Ada had continued to watch over her little adopted family. She'd left her house to Laura and a small insurance policy. When the job opened up as head nurse in the Tucson Memorial Children's Hospital, Laura had applied and been accepted, then she'd sold the house and moved herself and Peter to Tucson. With her inheritance from Ada, Laura had bought a small house in a nice neighborhood, not far from Peter's school and her work.

The day she had moved into her new house, Anne Yatzee had appeared on her front doorstep with a complete meal for her and Peter. Anne and her son David had joined them, and that day had been the start of a wonderful friendship for both Laura and Peter.

It had all happened neatly, as if following some master plan.

Not a day went by that she didn't think of Ada. Sometimes, Laura could almost hear Ada's voice saying the phrase she always called after Laura when she left the house. "Walk in beauty, Little One."

"What's the smile for?"

Kaine's voice snatched Laura back to the front seat of his truck and eye-to-eye with Peter's disappearance. She stole a glance at his stern profile.

"Just thinking about some happy memories."

"Guess that leaves me out."

He turned and met her gaze with those amazing eyes. Her face reflected back at her from their deep, velvety depths. No man on Earth had eyes like Kaine's. She recalled the very first time she'd looked into them. She'd felt like she was being sucked into a swirling stream, then forced to try to keep her head above water to breathe. Truth be known, they still had that effect on her. Quickly, she averted her gaze.

She could feel him dividing his attention between her and his driving. Gooseflesh prickled across her skin. Despite wanting to squirm away, she sat stone still.

"So, tell me about your kid," he finally said.

Exhaling a sigh of relief that he'd again centered his attention on the road exclusively, she relaxed.

"He's a great kid, wonderful sense of humor and loving nature. He loves sports and is really good at track.

You should see him run. I guess it's his"—she stopped abruptly before adding *Native American bloodlines*, the words that would tell him more than she wanted Kaine to know—"his size. He's not terribly big for his age. I think he takes after my side of the family for that."

As if he'd actually touched her, she could feel Kaine's gaze rake over her body, gauging her statement for accuracy. The gooseflesh rose anew.

"So, he's little. Does he have your hair and eyes, too?"

"No. He's a mirror image of . . . his father." As grateful as she'd been for the distraction moments before, now she wished he'd drop the subject. This topic suddenly held too many pitfalls for her peace of mind.

When he said no more, she glanced in his direction. His jaw muscle worked spasmodically, and his wide forehead had creased into a deep, angry frown. What had she said to set him off this time?

"Kaine?"

"We're about at the trading post. Just the other side of that rise up ahead." He pointed with one long, tanned finger, but kept the rest of his fingers curled around the steering wheel to maneuver through another cluster of chugholes.

Gratefully, she dropped the subject.

✤   ✤   ✤

Kaine pulled the car up to the front of Willoughby's, still fighting off the visions of Laura and another man,

Laura and the son that should have been his. Whatever had possessed him to go back for her? When had he become masochistic and started listening to little voices in his head? Laura interrupted his thoughts.

"Is there a ladies room here?"

A chuckle escaped him. "There's a two-seater just around the edge of the building," he told her, waiting for her to turn up her nose.

"Great!" She jumped from the car and disappeared around the side of the trading post.

Was this the same woman who'd gotten all bent out of shape because the house they'd lived in eight years ago didn't have indoor plumbing? He followed her with his gaze until she disappeared around the corner. Shaking his head, he turned off the ignition and slid from the driver's seat.

For a moment, Kaine stood beside the car and looked at the building before him. It had been here as long as he could remember, unchanged. The roof still tilted at a strange angle, as if any minute it would slide off into the sand. The building sprawled across the land like a chameleon, changing color and texture as it went: adobe brick, clapboard, the plywood painted white. On the front porch lay a sleeping, large, white dog of indefinable breed that Kaine had never seen before. A loud squeak announced the opening of the front door. The dog's ear twitched, and its clear blue eyes opened and followed Kaine.

Willoughby, a slender man in his late sixties, emerged;

the sun glinted off his tanned, bald head, making it shine like a new penny. Kaine had been stopping here for supplies ever since he'd begun guiding tourists into the canyons. Other trading posts were more accessible, but Willoughby had an ear to the ground for gossip; knew more about these canyons and the surrounding country-side than anyone; and sometimes, when Kaine searched for a lost tourist, the old man's gossip helped Kaine choose the path he'd follow. Hopefully, today would not be the exception to the rule.

"Well, if it ain't the warrior," Willoughby called by way of a greeting. "Your call last night to order supplies surprised me. Thought you were taking a few days off."

Kaine climbed the rickety steps and shook the of-fered hand. "Something came up that changed my mind. Last I heard you were sitting on death's doorstep. What happened?"

Willoughby laughed nervously and looked away. "I made a deal with the devil to let me have a few more years."

Kaine smiled and then glanced toward the Navajo woman, Willoughby's wife, weaving a rug on a loom situated under a ramada in the front yard.

"So what's important enough to drag you away from your vacation time?"

"There's a kid lost in the canyon."

Willoughby's smile faded. "I haven't heard anything about a kid being lost." He followed Kaine inside. "When this happen?"

"Three days ago. Disappeared from the north rim. Clan powwow."

Shaking his head, Willoughby moved behind the wooden counter. He fussed for a moment with an addition to his collection of pawn jewelry, and then turned back to Kaine. In a far corner two young Navajo men watched Kaine silently while they sipped soda and spoke softly between themselves.

"You might want to talk to my wife. Her sister just came back from getting her sheep outta the canyon." Drawing his bushy eyebrows together, he rubbed his stubble-covered chin in thought. "Maybe yesterday or the day before. Can't say for sure. Seems like time just whizzes by. Guess it's age." He took out the slip of paper he'd written Kaine's order on as he'd dictated it over the phone the previous night. He began assembling the final few items on the counter while he talked. "The older I git, the faster the dern time seems to fly. Ain't right. When a fella reaches his golden years, time shouldn't move so quickly. He should have more than a measly Social Security check and old age to look forward to." He sighed and leaned on the counter. "I'm tired. I want to retire somewhere where I can sit back and relax."

The men in the corner moved about noisily. Willoughby glanced in their direction, frowned at them and then quickly busied himself with finishing up Kaine's order.

Willoughby's assessment of time brought back the dream from last night and Kaine's grandfather's warning about time running out for Kaine. What in hell did that mean? Was he going to die? He didn't think so. For some reason, he thought the old man had been referring to some other kind of time. And why in hell did it bother him at all? Dreams held no prophecies of the future or wisdom from the past. Dreams were dreams. Something for a man's mind to do at night. Nothing more. Then why *was* he letting the stupid dream bother him? He'd stopped believing in all that hocus-pocus the night his mother had died. Let the rest of the Navajo Nation live on their dreams. He had better places to channel his energies.

He'd long ago lost any fear of dying. Death for Kaine meant only regret. Regret that he'd never hold Laura again. That thought stopped him in his tracks.

Shaking himself mentally, he diverted his attention to the window facing the parking lot and spotted Laura coming around the side of the building.

Rounding the corner of the trading post, Laura saw the woman at the loom. The rug she had half done was exquisite. Laura stared at it, trying to recall the legends in the book on Navajos that Ada had given Peter last year for his birthday. She couldn't recall it all, just something about a god named Changing Woman who taught the art to another god named Spider Woman.

She walked closer for a better look. The woman

looked up from her work and smiled.

Laura moved closer. Silently, she watched the blur of the woman's fingers as she guided the shuttle back and forth, shifting yarn to follow the intricate design of the rainbow arched across the face of the sun. The colors, dazzling reds, oranges, whites and blacks, all deep and vibrant, seemed to have a phosphorescent quality. Near the edge of the rug, a small opening broke the border design. Laura thought about it for a moment, and then recalled the opening was the path left for the weaver's spirit to escape so as not to become forever imprisoned in her work.

Her attention suddenly captured by the design itself, Laura became conscious of the rainbow's strong resemblance to her pendant. She reached inside her shirt and extracted the piece of jewelry. It wasn't just similar—it was identical.

"Excuse me." She stepped in line with the woman's side vision. "Your rainbow is just like this one." She showed the woman the pendant. "Is this design of special significance?"

The woman smiled warmly. "The rainbow is the pathway of the Holy People from the Underground to the mortal world." She went back to work.

Laura watched silently until she felt Kaine standing beside her. Funny how she always knew when he was near without actually seeing him.

"*Ya tah hey*, Little Mother. Willoughby says your sister was in the canyons gathering her sheep from their summer grazing lands. Did she say anything about seeing a small boy?"

"*Ya tah hey.*" The woman never missed a beat with the shuttle. "There was a boy."

Laura came instantly alert. "Where? Where did she see him?"

Kaine took her arm and shook his head.

"But—"

He drew her to the side. "She'll tell us. In the meantime, don't interrupt. She'll consider you rude, and we won't learn anything."

Laura bristled at having to wait this out, but nodded.

"Little Mother, we believe the child belongs to this lady. He's been lost for three days in the canyons. Can you tell us where she saw him?"

The woman continued to slip the shuttle back and forth through the threads of her loom. The silence seemed to stretch on forever. Laura glanced impatiently at Kaine. He seemed undisturbed at the delay.

"It was a boy. He drank from the creek water in Canyon de Muerto."

Laura saw Kaine's jaw muscle tighten, but he said nothing. After a long pause, presumably to make sure the woman had finished speaking, Kaine spoke again. "How many days past did she see the child?"

"Two, maybe three. Her memory is not so good anymore."

"Thank you, Little Mother."

Kaine took Laura's arm and began leading her back toward the loaded car. Laura pulled loose, then turned back toward the woman. "Thank you," she called to her.

The woman stopped weaving, turned to Laura and smiled. "Walk in beauty, Little One."

Ada's words. Laura felt herself blanch. Her knees gave way. Had it not been for Kaine's supporting arm, she would have collapsed on the ground.

"What the hell's wrong with you?" Kaine steadied her with a hand to her elbow, then guided her the rest of the way to the car. "You okay?"

"Did you hear what she said?" Laura could barely get the words past her lips.

"Yeah. It's an old Navajo blessing. Comes from one of the Ways."

She clutched at the front of his shirt. "It's what Ada always said to me when I left the house. I thought she'd gotten it from a poem by Lord Byron."

"Well, hell fire, woman, that's no reason to pass out on me. That greeting is very common around here."

Laura glanced at the woman again and shook her head. He was right. She was making too much of it. Probably nothing more than coincidence or something Ada had picked up from one of her many *Native People* magazines.

Not until they were settled in the Rover and Kaine had started the engine did either of them notice they had an addition to the passenger list. A soft thumping from the backseat made them both turn around. Sitting in the seat, looking as if he belonged there, was the white dog that had been sleeping on the porch earlier.

"Okay, I don't know how you got in here, but you can't come with us," Kaine said, climbing from the car and opening the back door. As he reached for the animal, the dog bared his teeth and emitted a low growl. Kaine pulled back. He smiled and eased toward the dog again. "Now, come on, nice doggy. You can't stay there." Kaine reached again and this time, the dog's snarl told Laura that if Kaine got any closer, he might lose his hand. He pulled back. "I'll be right back," he told Laura.

Keeping a wary eye on the dog, she watched Kaine sprint back into the trading post and emerge several minutes later.

"Willoughby says it's not his dog, and he has no idea where it came from." He scratched his head. "Well, we don't have time to fool with him now. Let's leave him there and maybe when we stop, he'll jump out. If not, we'll let him tag along and when I get back, I'll see if I can find his owner." Kaine got back behind the wheel. As he reached to turn on the ignition, the dog stretched over the backseat and licked his ear. "Stupid mutt," he mumbled.

Kaine got the car back on the road, and Laura suddenly recalled his reaction to the name of the canyon where the woman's sister had seen the boy. That hadn't been her imagination. "Why did you look like that when she said the name of the canyon?"

"Like what?"

Plainly he was being evasive and not doing a really good job of it. "Don't play with me, Kaine."

He glanced her way. A playful smile curled his lips. "Lady, if I play with you, you'll know it."

She ignored the sexual innuendo and the way her pulse sped up and pressured him for an answer. "Why?"

For a long time, he concentrated with exaggerated intensity on moving the shifting lever from one gear to another. While the car cruised along in third gear, he finally answered. "It doesn't even bear mentioning, but Canyon de Muerto means Canyon of the Dead."

Under other circumstances, on another day, Laura could have admired the Arizona countryside as much as she had when she'd first seen it as she rode next to Kaine to their little house to start a life with him.

Today, however, she looked at this vast wilderness through the eyes of a mother and could see only the dangers it presented for a little boy all alone and scared. Today, she saw only the foreboding beauty of a landscape filled with high bluffs from which a child could tumble; deep slot canyons in which he could get lost; dry arroyos that could flood at a moment's notice and suck him down into the jaws of a watery death. What she should have seen as a breathtakingly beautiful blue sky looked to her like a large bowl turned upside down, trapping heat against the earth, heat that would drain Peter's strength, heat that could kill him. Then there was the threat of wild animals, lack of food and water and—

Kaine's hand covered hers. Laura jumped.

His fingers squeezed hers. "Stop thinking about it."

It was the very first sign from him that he felt one ounce of compassion for her plight. For that scant moment, he was the Kaine she'd married. She absorbed it like a dry sponge. Then his hand was gone as suddenly as it had come.

"So, what have you been doing with yourself in the last eight years?" he asked, keeping his gaze on the road ahead.

He hadn't said the words, but Laura could hear their echo in the silence. *What have you done besides sleep with some no-good guy who left you to fend for yourself and raise a kid on your own?*

"After she found me wandering in the streets, I went to live with Ada. She was very good to me." Laura smiled as the memories closed around her, removing some of the chill of Peter's disappearance. "She insisted that I go to college so I could support Peter and myself after he was born. She even helped me get the student loans to pay for it."

Kaine skillfully steered the Rover around another of the thousands of chugholes they'd been dodging all day. "So what did you decide to become?"

"A nurse." She glanced at his set profile. She knew Kaine could have cared less about her life after she'd left him, but she was grateful that he was making small talk to keep her mind from dwelling on Peter. "I work at the

Tucson Children's Clinic."

"Why'd you leave L.A.?"

"After Ada died, there was nothing there for me. She'd left me her house, but it wasn't the same without her. Too many memories."

His jaw tensed. "Yeah, houses have a way of doing that."

Out of nowhere, Laura felt a pang of guilt. She knew he was thinking of the tiny adobe house they'd shared for such a short time. She looked away.

"A friend told me about a job opening at the Tucson Clinic. I applied and was accepted. So I sold the L.A. house, and we moved to Tucson." She sighed. "What about you? What have you been up to?"

When Kaine didn't answer, Laura turned toward him. His dark-eyed gaze flitted between the road and rearview mirror. A concerned frown knitted his brows.

"What is it?" She turned in the seat to look behind them, but saw nothing but cactus, mesquite bushes and empty road.

"It's nothing."

She looked back at him and knew he was lying. He'd seen something that had alarmed him. But unless he chose to share what it was with her, Laura knew there would be no point in asking him about it. She checked on the dog that was stretched across the backseat sleeping peacefully, as if he belonged there. Then she turned to the front to stare out the windshield, but from the corner of her eye, she could see Kaine still checking the mirror periodically.

✤   ✤   ✤

A half-hour later, Kaine had stopped looking in the mirror, and Laura still had no idea what he'd seen. Finally, she'd dismissed it and once more immersed herself in thoughts of her son. She'd no sooner begun thinking about Peter when the dog let out a sharp bark from the backseat. Laura looked to where the dog was staring. In the distance, she noticed a child beside the road. Her heart pounded against her chest.

Peter?

She glanced at Kaine, who had begun slowing the car, obviously having seen the child as well. Both of them stared at the child, but as they drew closer and then pulled up beside him, it was obvious it wasn't Peter. Laura's heart ached, but she pushed her own pain aside and concentrated on the child.

Clothed in the traditional pants and shirt tied at the waist with a colorful swath of cloth, the Navajo boy sat cross-legged on the ground in front of a hogan that screamed poverty and was clutching his finger. To one side, a rotting car without wheels balanced precariously atop some cinder blocks. A few boards with rusted nails protruding from them lay around on the ground. He bit his trembling lower lip in a futile attempt to hold back the tears cascading down his brown cheeks.

Kaine began to accelerate. Simultaneously, the dog barked and Laura yelled, "Wait! Stop!" She wrenched open the door before the car came to a complete halt. After jumping to the ground, she hurried over to the child. The white dog padded along beside her. Squatting to his level, she reached for the boy's hand. "What's wrong? Did you hurt yourself?"

He pulled back, but there was no need for his answer. The boy had hit his finger with something and blood was collecting beneath the nail, turning it an ugly, dark purple. She glanced to the side and saw that the culprit was probably a large rock he'd been using to hammer a rusty nail into a board.

Peter had done the same thing the previous summer while building a tree house in the backyard, and she knew the procedure for treating it.

"Will you let me fix it for you?" she asked the boy.

He stared at her for a long time, his chocolate gaze assessing her, flitting to Kaine and then back to her. The dog chose that moment to bath the child's cheek with a wet swipe of his tongue. Hesitantly, as if needing that reassurance from the animal, he nodded and held out his hand.

"What are you going to do?" Kaine asked, kneeling beside her.

"I have to relieve the pressure under the nail. I need something that comes to somewhat of a point. Nothing sharp. We want to put a hole in the nail and release the blood buildup without hurting the flesh under it." She glanced around them, but saw nothing that would work to drill down through the nail.

Kaine thought for a moment and then said, "Hang on; I might have something that'll work in the Rover." He stood and hurried to the vehicle. In less than a minute, he was squatting next to her again. "Try this." He handed her a silver paperclip. "It was on some of the papers in that folder you gave me last night," he added in answer to her silent question.

She began bending it until one end extended beyond the rest. "We're going to need to heat it to make it work. Any suggestions?"

Kaine stood, drug into his jeans, and extracted a cigarette lighter. "How about this?"

"Perfect." Laura took the lighter and turned it over in her fingers. "Have you taken up smoking?"

He smiled down at her. Her heart felt as if someone had squeezed it. "No. But I have learned over the years that when a match gets wet, it's useless. On the other hand, a lighter may not light when it first gets wet, but once it dries out, it'll work as good as ever." He resumed his position next to her. "Comes in handy when you spend as much time in the wilderness as I do."

Laura took the boy's hand again. "When I tell you to, heat the paperclip until the end glows red." She turned to the boy. "This is not going to hurt. It will just feel like I'm pushing on your nail. Okay?"

The child nodded. The dog sidled closer to the boy.

"Heat the clip," she told Kaine. While he was doing as she'd instructed, she again addressed the boy. "You must try not to move. Can you do that for me?"

He straightened his spine and looked her directly in the eye.

"He won't flinch," Kaine said, handing her the hot paperclip. "To do so would shame him, brand him as a coward."

Laura took the clip and placed the end on the boy's nail. Slowly, she rotated it back and forth. The smell of the burning nail drifted up to her, telling her it was working. When it cooled, she handed it back to Kaine to heat again. Over and over they repeated the process. The boy never moved as much as a facial muscle.

Finally, she removed the paperclip for Kaine to heat it once more, and blood spurted from the hole in the nail.

Laura pulled a clean tissue from her pocket and dabbed gently at the pool of blood. "Does that feel better?" She really didn't need to ask. A wide grin split his face. The lines of pain around his eyes had disappeared. He nodded.

"What's your name?" Kaine asked, discarding the paperclip.

"*Naayéé neizghání*," the boy said proudly, his guttural pronunciation of the words sounding much like the old man in Laura's dream.

Kaine made an odd sound.

Laura looked at him. His expression was one of . . . stunned surprise. She opened her mouth to ask him what was wrong, but she felt something being placed in her hand. By the time she looked around, the boy had vanished and in her palm laid a small leather pouch, its drawstrings dangling through her open fingers.

Kaine nudged her. His gaze was fixed on the dog, which had walked a few feet in the same direction the boy had gone. "If we move quickly and quietly, maybe we can get in the car before he notices we're gone." He pulled Laura to her feet.

His movement had been unexpected, and she dropped the pouch. He waited while she retrieved it and then guided her to the car. As she climbed into the front seat, she caught movement behind her and peered over to see the white dog had once more sprawled his snowy body over the backseat.

✣   ✣   ✣

Kaine hadn't spoken for the last few miles, ever since they'd left the spot where Laura had treated the Navajo boy. The white dog was snoring softly in the backseat. She wanted to ask Kaine what had made him react as he had when the child told them his name. However, she remembered enough about her husband to know that he would offer the information when *he* was ready—and not a moment sooner. So, she contented herself with riding in silence and allowing her thoughts to wander to the lack of medical facilities available to these people. She wondered how many had died because they couldn't get to a hospital for help. They should, at the very least, have a clinic to go to.

They probably couldn't afford to build one, she decided. But if they did something like the craft fair she'd run for the Tucson clinic, they could support it. She'd seen the jewelry and rugs these people made, and there had to be a market for them.

A bead of perspiration trickled down her cleavage and drew her attention away from the clinic to the gathering heat of the day.

The interior of the car had grown warm and stifling. Dust filtered in through Kaine's open window and coated the dark brown dashboard in a fine beige powder. Sweat beaded her brow, ran down her neck, and stuck her hair to the exposed skin above her collar. Her clothes adhered themselves to her flesh, which only made it that much more uncomfortable.

Laura gathered her hair into a rubber band, and then ran her finger around her collar. Glancing at the dashboard, she read AC on one of the control knobs and wondered why he didn't turn it on before they suffocated.

"If I turn on the AC," Kaine said, startling Laura by guessing her thoughts, "you'll get used to it and then the heat in the canyons will be impossible for you to tolerate. I don't have time to nurse you through heatstroke."

"You won't have to nurse me through anything. I'm fine," she said stubbornly. "Just fine."

He looked at the dark circles radiating from her armpits and turning the khaki material to a deep brown, and a playful smile danced around his lips. "Right."

She'd been trying her damnedest not to let him know that she was finding the heat unbearable. Obviously, he still knew her almost as well as she knew herself. She prayed that his insights wouldn't extend to the direction of her son.

"You did a good job back there with the boy."

The compliment startled her. "Thanks. I've had lots of practice patching up little boys." She didn't look at him, just continued staring out the windshield and fingering the drawstrings on the leather pouch the kid had given her and tried not to think about how hot she was.

"What's in the bag?"

Laura held it up and looked at it as if she hadn't even been aware she was holding it. She shrugged, then pried it open and peered down into it. "Some kind of yellow stuff." She poured some into her palm and held it out for Kaine to inspect.

He exchanged hands on the steering wheel and used his free one to take hers so he could look closer at the yellow powder. It suddenly occurred to him that this was the first time *he'd* voluntarily touched Laura in over eight years. Tiny shivers danced up his spine. His fingers began to tighten. Forcing himself to concentrate, he loosened his hold and looked at the contents of her hand.

"Corn pollen," he finally said.

"Why would he give me corn pollen?" She squirreled up her nose. "And what's it for?"

Unable to stand the feel of her soft skin against his calloused fingers one second longer, Kaine dropped her hand abruptly and then gripped the steering wheel as if it would fly off at any moment. He really had no desire to discuss the beliefs of the Navajo, but it was infinitely better than thinking about Laura and how warm and soft her skin had felt.

"The Navajo believe that, among other things, corn pollen brings health and is used as a blessing in many rituals. That he gave you such a gift is a big honor."

From the corner of his eye, he saw Laura smile. Using her fingertip, she traced circles in the corn pollen.

He couldn't resist yanking her chain a little. "It's also used to promote fertility."

She made a face at him. "Funny, Cloudwalker. Very funny." But despite her seemingly casual dismissal of his words, she cast a nervous look at the corn pollen and then poured it back in the bag and shoved the bag in the pocket of her jeans.

As the day wore on and the sun traveled higher in the sky, the heat increased. Eventually, Laura knew she had to find some way to distract herself from the discomfort.

"So, you know my story of the last eight years, what's yours?"

Kaine dragged his gaze from the rutted, dirt road they'd been jouncing over for what seemed like days to Laura. He looked at her for a second and said nothing, but the slant of his eyebrows spoke volumes. He was telling her without words that he was not about to share any of himself with her.

Laura decided otherwise. "Come on. Fair's fair. I told you about me, now it's your turn." She adjusted her body on the seat so she faced him. "Are you still running off to Washington on a regular basis?"

His frown deepened. "No."

"Oh? I didn't think you'd ever give that up."

When she'd been with him, it had seemed to her that his entire life revolved around trips to Washington to lobby for the rights of his people. At the time, she'd resented every moment he was away from her. But that was when she was young, selfish about his time with her, self-centered and very much in love. And to her, that he chose to spend so much time away from her proved he didn't care about her, didn't love her.

Now, having seen the poverty and the lack of adequate education and medical facilities firsthand, she understood his fire to change the lives of his people to something better. Now she could look back on it and see that her selfishness had driven her to leave. She still believed he didn't love her, but she also was willing to concede that the isolation amid a culture she didn't understand and the lack of friends had added to her misery. But if she missed him that much, she should have gone with him. Maybe that would have saved their marriage. But it was too late for ifs and maybes.

"I stopped because it was past time for the younger men to fight for the People," he said simply. The straight line of his mouth and the pulsing jaw muscle told her this was not a subject he wanted to delve into.

The white dog emitted a low growl as if their tense tone was something to which he took offense. Both of them ignored him. Silence vied with the heat for space within the car.

It had been partially because of his frequent absences and partially because of his resistance to sharing himself with her that Laura had realized he never loved her as she had thought he did. It was because of that that she'd left carrying his unborn son. Now, he refused to talk about it? Anger pushed her on.

"You quit the trips to Washington, just like that?" She snapped her fingers. "No reason?"

He glared at her then back at the road. "I never said there was no reason."

"Then what made you give it up?"

He stopped the car abruptly. The dog sat up. If it hadn't been for the seatbelt holding her back, Laura would have been dumped on the floor. He turned to her.

"You're not going to let go of this, are you?"

The expression on his face made her pull back against the passenger door. But she stood her ground. She shook her head. "No, I'm not."

"Well then, here it is. After you left, my mother was diagnosed with cancer. I begged her to go to the Anglo hospital for treatment, but she refused, opting for the Ways of the People instead. So the *hataałii* came and sang chants over her, drew pictures in the dirt and then sang some more, but it didn't help. After weeks of arguing with her, I finally got her to go to the hospital in Phoenix. By that time it had metastasized. She died a month later." He turned away to stare beyond the windshield. "It was then that I realized that I was fighting battles to preserve a way of life I no longer believed in."

Laura's heart broke for him. Kaine and his mother had been very close. It must have nearly killed him when she died.

She laid her hand on his arm. "I'm sorry, Kaine."

He shook it off. "Yeah, so am I."

Jamming the car in gear, he stomped on the gas pedal. The car shot forward, bouncing and jouncing over the ruts in the road. Laura had to hang on the arm rest to keep her head from being slammed off the roof. The dog slipped and slid, trying to get his footing on the slick leather upholstery. After a few minutes, Kaine's anger seemed to have cooled, and the car slowed to the cautious pace at which he'd been driving before he stopped to tell her about his mother.

"If it helps," she offered, "given that the cancer was that far advanced, getting her to a hospital earlier would not have prevented the final outcome."

"It doesn't help," he growled. "And you can keep your medical opinions to yourself."

"Okay. Deal, if you tell me why that little boy's name bothered you."

"It didn't."

Laura turned toward his set profile. "You may be able to hide a lot from me, but I'm not stupid. I can tell when someone is shocked."

Kaine sighed impatiently and then glanced out the side window, then back to her. "*Naayéé neizghání* means Monster Slayer. He's one of the twin sons of Changing Woman and the Sun. It's nothing. Some Navajo mother named her kid after one of the legends. That's all."

That's all? Laura wasn't so sure. Too many things had been happening that they kept piling up as coincidence. She clutched the pendant through her shirt and almost as if someone had spun a kaleidoscope, the strange things that had happened in the past few days paraded before her mind's eye: the dream, the woman at the fair, the pendant, the weaver, the boy. It was almost as if the Navajo gods were trying to tell them something, maybe something to do with Peter.

When she said as much to Kaine, he jammed on the brakes again and then exploded. "For Christ's sake,

Laura, stop reading into every little thing. You're beginning to sound like—" He cut himself short. "It means nothing. They're just stories the Old Ones tell the children. Instead of thinking about that tripe, you'd be better off spending your time thinking about what's ahead, and how you're going to make it through it."

A loud *crack* drew their attention. They turned in time to see a white bolt of lightning slice through the clear blue sky.

"Really? And what do you call that?"

"Heat lightning," he said, but the lack of conviction in his voice told her he didn't believe it any more than she did.

H e'd lied. Flat out lied. Kaine had lived all his life in this part of the country and never, in all his thirty-three years, had he seen heat lightning in a *clear blue sky*. But, at the moment, he was at a loss for any other logical explanation for what had just occurred. He certainly didn't need to add to Laura's conclusions that something supernatural was happening to them.

Try as he might, however, he could not deny the goose-flesh that chased over his skin when he thought about some of the happenings of the last two days. Rather than delve into it, he directed all his thoughts and attention on the rough terrain they were driving over. Better that than getting caught up again in the mumbo-jumbo of the Navajo myths and legends.

If they continued at the rate they were going, they would be able to make it to the rim of the Canyon of the

Moon by early evening. However, he had a bunch of supplies sitting in front of the house he'd planned to repair, and first he had to make sure they were protected from the elements until he got back. Since it was on the way, it would only take a few minutes, and they could still get to the rim of the canyon by late tonight. Either way, they couldn't make the descent until sunup, so whether they arrived at the canyon's edge this afternoon or tonight made no difference.

Resolutely, he swung the Rover down a side road.

Laura straightened in her seat, rode silently for a time, and then looked around at the passing landscape. "Where are we going?"

Kaine didn't answer. He didn't have to. They'd just emerged from behind a bluff into the yard of the house they had once occupied as man and wife. He heard Laura's soft intake of breath.

"I have to cover those things up in case it rains while I'm gone." He motioned to the lumber, bags of cement, and other building supplies piled in the front yard.

"What are they for?"

He took a deep breath. "I'm fixing the house up to sell." Without another word, he climbed quickly from the Rover.

Laura watched him and then directed her gaze to the small, ramshackle house. He was going to sell the last connection, or so he believed, to her. The very idea of someone else living in their little house, shot a sharp pain through her heart.

Driven by the ache throbbing inside her, she slowly slipped from the car, crossed the overgrown yard, and stepped onto the front porch. To her surprise, the white dog trotted along beside her. A board squeaked beneath her foot, and she smiled. She'd always used that board to let her know when Kaine had come home. Her pulse quickened with the memory of what usually happened after one of his prolonged absences.

Inside, the smell of disuse, dust, and painful memories assailed her. She walked through the living room, where they had cuddled before a blazing fire for warmth on a cold winter's night, and into the kitchen where she'd lovingly prepared his meals.

She chuckled. Back then, she'd had a tough time boiling water without scorching it. But having to fend for herself after her parents had turned her away, soon taught her that, to survive, she could learn to do many things she'd never had to do before, withstand many hardships she'd never dreamed she'd have to face.

Outside, she could hear Kaine throwing a tarp over the building supplies. She continued her walk down memory lane and went into the small room Kaine had used as an office, a room she had avoided during their marriage because it held all the reminders that Kaine belonged more to his people than he ever would to her.

How selfish you were back then. If only . . .

Before it could take form, she shook free the thought.

Taking a deep breath, she stepped into the room. The late-afternoon sun streaked across the sand-colored walls. Detritus that had blown in through a broken window crunched noisily beneath her feet.

A sharp bark from the white dog drew her attention. He was staring at the wall. She followed his gaze. A lone beam of light spotlighted a picture hanging askew on the wall, a picture that Laura had never seen before.

It was of a natural, sandstone arch that spanned the width of a canyon. Though everything around it was brown and barren, plants, flowers, and bushes flourished on the banks of the stream that meandered beneath it. Written on the border of the picture, in Kaine's scrawling script, was the word NONNOSHOSHI.

"It means *rainbow turned to stone*," Kaine said from just behind her.

She jumped, but not entirely because he had surprised her by joining her, quietly and unexpectedly. The pendant inside her shirt suddenly burned against her skin. She grabbed it.

"Why have I never seen it before?" she asked, trying to ignore the heat of the pendant in her palm.

Kaine stepped around her, ripped the picture from the wall and glared down at it. "I put it up after . . . after, to remind me of all the time I'd wasted fighting for a people who would rather cling to old lies than embrace the modern age." He laughed derisively. "It was one the few things I was able to lobby for successfully and get it declared off limits to the Anglos."

"It's beautiful. But why make it off limits?"

"It's considered to be sacred. The Navajo believe that the rainbow is the connection between the mortal world and the afterlife. It's the bridge the gods use to pass between the two worlds." He balled the picture in his hand, threw it to the floor, and walked out of the room. "That's if you believe that nonsense."

When had he become so cynical? This was definitely not the Kaine she'd known, not the Kaine who would have walked across hot coals to protect the rights of his people. The same Kaine who had studied to be one of the holy men.

The white dog nosed the balled up piece of paper toward her. Laura picked up the crumpled picture, smoothed it and studied it. The pendant immediately cooled. Comforting warmth spread through her. She wasn't sure how or why she knew it, but she was positive in the depths of her soul that this bridge had something to do with where they would find Peter. However, she was not going to mention this to Kaine. She'd had more than her share of blowups from him for one day. She folded it and then slipped it into her pocket.

"Anytime you're through strolling down memory lane, we need to get going. I want to make it to the canyon rim before dark, and we need to leave now," Kaine called from outside the house.

"We better go," she told the dog. His tail fanned the

air as he followed her out of the room.

Unwilling to give him any reason to regret bringing her along, Laura hurried to the Rover and opened the back door for the dog to jump in. Before she got in, she cast one last longing look at the house that should have been the place they began their life together and instead had spelled the end of it.

It didn't occur to her until they were driving away from the house that she'd never entered their bedroom. She glanced sideways at Kaine. It was good that she hadn't. That room held too many memories, more than her suddenly aching heart could stand.

✦   ✦   ✦

They'd made much better time than Laura had expected, and by the time they reached the rim of the canyon, purple, orange and pink streaked the evening sky. In a few minutes it would be so dark, Laura wouldn't be able to see her hand in front of her face. Having been raised in a brightly lit city, the total and complete darkness was one thing she'd never gotten used to about this country. When the sun sank behind the buttes, it got pitch black almost instantly.

While Kaine gathered wood for the fire, she spread the sleeping bags out on the flat rock on either side of where he'd lain out a fire ring. Then she got out their eating utensils and rummaged around in the box of supplies until she found a can of beans, a cooking pot, a can opener, some coffee, and a metal coffeepot.

By the time Kaine walked back into their campsite, his arms loaded with the few pieces of wood he was able to find, she had coffee grounds and water in the coffeepot, the beans in the saucepan, and she was sitting on the sleeping bag petting the dog and staring out at the deep purple shadows creeping over the vast wasteland.

For a moment Kaine was stunned by the picture she made. Laura had taken the rubber band from her hair, and it cascaded over her shoulders like black silk. The sinking sun highlighted it with streaks of gold. Her profile was serious but breathtaking. His footsteps faltered as he tried to get control of his rioting emotions.

God, but she was beautiful in a way no other woman had ever been to him. As the sun sank lower and shadows played over her features, he recalled the times they had sat on their porch and watched the end of the day together. She'd always been chilly and had cuddled close to his side, taking the warmth from his body into hers. Her silky hair had tickled his cheek, and the sweet smell of her shampoo had filled his nostrils until his senses were saturated with nothing but Laura. He remembered the rush of need to protect her, to love her, to be with her forever; and how he'd scooped her into his arms and carried her to their bed.

In response to the waves of memories, his body came alive as it hadn't in a very long time. His groin began to ache, and his heart beat a thunderous tattoo against his chest. The wood slipped from his arms and landed at his feet with a clatter.

Laura turned toward him, her eyes misty. "You scared me," she said, but her body language said differently, and her voice held no fear. It was filled with the same despair that he felt coursing through him.

He tore his gaze from her and began arranging the wood in the fire ring. Her hand closed over his arm, sending shards of desire racing through his aroused body.

"You've been driving all day. Let me do that."

Rather than prolong the emotions erupting under her touch, he pulled away and left her to finish the fire. He scooted back onto one of the open sleeping bags and watched her. The dog settled next to him, resting its chin on his knee. He stroked the soft fur absently. Since the Laura he'd married had as many outdoor skills as a house cat, he knew it would be only minutes before she yelled *uncle* and asked for his help.

To his utter and complete surprise, it wasn't long before she had a blazing fire going in the fire ring and the pot with the beans sitting on it heating for their supper. She stirred the pot periodically, to keep the beans from sticking, then removed it from the fire and replaced it with the coffeepot. After dividing the beans between the two metal plates and dishing up a smaller portion for the dog, she handed Kaine his.

"You've acquired a few skills since last I saw you," he said, shoveling a forkful of beans in his mouth.

"I didn't have a choice," she said around a mouthful of food. Then she swallowed. "Peter was . . . *is* in Boy Scouts, and I had to help him earn his badges. Building a fire was among them."

That was true, but by the time Peter was in Scouts, she already knew how to build a fire. But she was not about to tell him that she'd first learned how to keep from freezing to death on the streets of Los Angeles. It would just give him one more thing to gloat to her about.

"So what other accomplishments do you have that I don't know about?"

His question seemed innocent enough, but she could hear the underlying sarcasm. Would there ever come a time when he stopped hating her? She wasn't sure which was worse, the man who had kept himself hidden from her during their short marriage or this stranger who looked at her with such contempt.

It seemed like Laura had just closed her eyes when Kaine was shaking her awake. She sat up, rubbed her hands over her face, yawned and looked around the nearly empty campsite. He'd already put everything they wouldn't be taking with them in the Land Rover and had two backpacks filled and sitting by the ashes of last night's fire. Beside them were the coffeepot, one cup, and the white dog, his blue eyes centered on her, his tail swishing back and forth creating a fan design in the dirt. She eyed the coffee longingly.

"I left some coffee for you," he said, gesturing toward the pot, a faint smile teasing at his mouth. "If memory serves, you don't function until you've had at least a cup of caffeine injected into your blood stream, but make it fast." He glanced at the eastern horizon filled with the pink glow of the rising sun. "I let you sleep so we're late getting started."

Eager to get on the way to locating Peter, Laura slid quickly from her sleeping bag, adjusted her wrinkled clothing and headed for the nearest large rock to answer the call of nature. Back at the campfire, she filled a plate with water for the dog, then poured the dark coffee in the cup and drank eagerly, relishing the way her body responded to the stimulating caffeine.

When she'd drunk three-quarters of the life-giving brew, she began brushing the tangles from her hair. As she picked up the rubber band to secure it in a ponytail, she noticed Kaine studying her, his dark gaze raking over her with an assessing intensity that made her skin tingle. "What?"

He continued to stare for a moment, then shook his head and picked up the backpacks. "Come on. Let's go."

Still puzzled about why he'd been staring at her, she took the backpack he handed her and slung it over her shoulders. The weight dug into her skin and she had to lean forward to keep from tumbling over backward.

✤ ✤ ✤

Kaine kept his silence while he led Laura and their ever-present companion, the white dog, along the rim of the canyon, his mind busy trying to erase the memory of the way her blouse had pulled tight across her breasts while she'd brushed the snarls from her hair. But when he succeeded, they were instantly replaced by memories of another time, memories of sitting on the bed after making love and combing the brush through her hair while he let the silky strands slip through his fingers like dark, moonlit water and fall over her naked skin.

His hands tightened on the straps of the backpack. His breathing occurred in quick gulps, and not because he was finding the going particularly rough. He was in top physical shape, and he'd hiked these canyons too many times for that. It was the damned woman walking behind him playing hell with his libido. With concentrated effort, he flushed her from his mind.

He trudged along, his sharp gaze on the rough terrain. The heat of the sun, as it rose higher in a startling blue sky, began to beat down on them. How long would Laura be able to stand it before she asked him to stop? And why did he care? It was her decision to tag along, not his.

He stopped next to a large outcropping of rocks that looked ironically like a giant baby had been playing with blocks and piled them haphazardly and then crawled away, leaving them to topple at any moment. Kaine turned to Laura. Her flushed face glowed, sweat beaded her brow and stained her blouse.

He frowned. "You okay?"

Laura looked at him, and he could read the stark determination in the mask she'd lowered over her expression. She could be dying, and she would never admit it to him. That was fine with him. He had neither the time nor the inclination to baby her through this. She'd made her decision, now she could live with it. Still he could not totally erase the concern gnawing at his gut.

"I'm fine."

"We're going to start down now. Stay close to me and watch your footing. Don't step anywhere you don't see me step. These rocks look like they'll hold you, but they can roll from under you in a second. And," he motioned toward the drop over the side of the rim, "it's a long way down."

She glanced over the edge of the steep wall that plummeted thousands of feet down into the gorge, swallowed hard, then looked back at his stoic face. She fought down the stab of regret. There had been a time when he'd spoken to her in soft, loving tones and not the cold, emotionless, matter-of-fact way he did now, as if he were instructing one of the tourists he'd led through the canyon country.

"Ready?"

Laura adjusted the straps of the backpack. "Lead on."

✤ ✤ ✤

The trail wound horizontal to the rim like a snake, but at a precarious downward angle that was, at times, so steep Laura and Kaine had to hang onto the rocks lining the path to keep from plunging forward or over the side. They squeezed their bodies in and out of tight places, and clambered over and around boulders that looked as if they would plunge down into the canyon if she so much as leaned against them.

The only one of them that seemed to be tackling the trail with ease was the dog. At times Laura could see nothing more than his shadow weaving in and out of the landscape. Then he'd suddenly reappear in front of her, as if checking to see that she was okay, then he'd disappear into a crevice again, only to appear again a few feet beyond them, ears perked, tail wagging.

Hours had passed, and it seemed as if they had barely made any progress on getting closer to the canyon floor. The sun had risen over the rim and the heat wafted over her, stealing her breath and draining her strength, but she pushed on, determined not to slow them down, and tried not to think of Peter facing the same treacherous terrain. Far below them a stream snaked through the bottom of the canyon, meandering from side to side, tantalizing her with the promise of its cold, refreshing water. The echo of the rushing water seemed to fill the canyon, so close, yet so very far away.

The backpack straps bit into Laura's tender skin like two knives. She shifted them, only to find that moments later the irritation had begun a new.

Suddenly, she slammed into something solid and unmoving. Concentrating so intently on where to step, she hadn't noticed that Kaine had stopped directly in front of her.

"Let's take a break. Here," he said, handing her a canteen.

She dropped to a rock and drank greedily from it.

"Hold it." He took the canteen away. "If you drink it all now, we'll have nothing before we get to the bottom."

The dog appeared out of nowhere and settled at Laura's side. She smiled and ran her hand over its head. "It looks as though, whether we like it or not, we have a permanent companion."

Kaine poured some water into his palm and held it out for the dog to lap up. "Looks that way."

"He should have a name." She thought for a bit and mentally tried names like Snowball, Whitey and Ghost, but discarded them all. Then she thought about the way he drifted in and out of her line of sight. "Shadow, I think." The dog's sharply pointed ears perked at the sound of the name. "I think he approves. Okay, Shadow it is."

Laura continued to pet Shadow and thought about how much Peter had always wanted a dog, but they'd never been able to have one. A pet took care and what with her job and his school, neither of them would have been home enough to see to it that the dog got the care and attention it would need.

She regretted that decision now. A boy should have a dog. They could have made time. *She* should have made time. Funny how tragedy brought to mind all the regrets for things left undone. Laura had a pile of them that she'd never really given much thought to before now: not making more time to be with Peter, not making his favorite peanut-butter cookies more often, not . . . she glanced at Kaine. Not telling Peter about his father and giving him the opportunity to meet him.

"Why the long face?" Kaine was studying her with furrowed brows.

Laura shook her head. "Just wishing I'd done some things differently with Peter when I had the chance."

He dropped down on the ground beside her. "Like what?"

"Like getting Peter a dog when he asked for one. Every boy should have a dog." Her voice cracked, and she looked up into the clear blue sky while she blinked back the tears that came with the realization that she might never have a chance to do all the things she'd planned for Peter.

Kaine's warm hand covered hers. "I'm sure you did what you felt was best for the boy." He stood. "Besides, who's to say that you won't still have time to become a Supermom, if that's what you want?" He held out his hand and drew her to her feet. "Don't count the kid out yet."

For a long time they stood almost chest to chest, hands remaining joined, looking into each others eyes. Was there a chance, she wondered as she looked at her reflection in the depths of his eyes, to change other things she now regretted doing?

Kaine was vaguely aware of Shadow nudging the back of his legs, as if pushing him closer to the woman whose full mouth had captured his attention. Laura's face swam before him. Her warm breath fanned over his skin, tempting him, inviting him to do things he knew he shouldn't even think about. The need to feel her lips beneath his swelled inside him like a growing storm. All he'd have to do is lower his head a few inches, and he could taste her lips. Just a few inches. Just—

Kaine dropped her hand as if it had burned him and then abruptly took a couple of steps back. "It's getting late," he said hoarsely. "We need to get going if we're going to make the halfway camp before sundown."

He'd trudged a few feet down the narrow path that overlooked a sharp drop of over eight hundred feet, before he finally heard Laura's footsteps behind him. What the hell had he been thinking? What would kissing her prove besides that the old passion which had blazed between them could be easily rekindled? And then what? More sleepless nights trying to wipe her from his head after she took her kid and walked out of his life again? More days when her image hovered on the edge of his mind, just waiting to slip into his conscious thoughts to torture him?

You're a freaking masochist, Cloudwalker. When will you learn that she doesn't want you? How much pain will it take for you to finally get that through your thick skull?

Giving no thought to how it would affect the woman behind him, Kaine picked up the pace and hoped it would drive the image of her sweet mouth from his thoughts.

✤   ✤   ✤

Before they even got to it, Laura could hear the sound of water plummeting over rocks. The reverberation was like music to her ears. Looking down, she could see it wasn't just the echo of the stream crisscrossing the canyon floor. The sun glinted off its smooth surface and there was no sign of the white caps of churning water. Nothing that could account for the rumble she heard.

She searched the area above and around them and saw nothing there either. It was somewhere ahead. She ignored the pain in her shoulders and hurried along the rock-littered path as fast as she could, the sound drawing her like a magnet.

Just as they rounded a large boulder the same deep orange color as the sun that was slowly sinking into the western sky, she spotted it, a waterfall cutting deep into the canyon wall and flowing into a pool below it. The pool, swollen by the water, overflowed and plummeted down another waterfall to the canyon floor. In sharp contrast to the barren landscape they'd passed through for the last eight hours, vegetation flourished in abundance all around it. Air cooled by the water rushed at her, instantly stealing the day's heat from her skin.

"It's beautiful," she said, her gaze glued to the spectacle that seemed so out of place, yet so welcome, in this arid wilderness.

"It's called *tikan tó*, sweet water." Kaine stood close behind her, close enough that she could feel the heat emanating from his body. She wanted to move away, but found that her heart had rooted her to the spot. "We'll camp here tonight." He swung his backpack from his shoulders and set it near a half-circle outcropping of rocks forming a natural shelter to the side of the clearing. "Why don't you take a dip and cool off, and I'll see if I can find some firewood."

The thought of immersing herself in that cool water made Laura want to swoon, but not wanting to look too eager, she just shrugged and slid her fingers under the backpack's straps. "Maybe later."

As she lifted the weight from her shoulders, an involuntary cry of pain escaped her before she could even think about stifling it. The material of her blouse had adhered itself to the open blisters on her shoulders. She glanced down and could see dried bloodstains on the khaki material.

"Wait!" Kaine commanded. He dug into his backpack and pulled out one of the tin coffee cups. Filling it with water from the pool, he began pouring it slowly over the material.

The water felt delicious as it trickled over her shoulders and down between her back and breasts. A first it stung her raw skin, but gradually, the pain disappeared and blessed numbness took its place. She closed her eyes and absorbed the heavenly relief.

Then Kaine's hand slipped inside the collar of her blouse.

Her eyes shot open, and her whole body tensed.

"Easy," he said. "I'm just trying to loosen the material from your skin."

The pain from the blisters quickly took second place to the little slivers of fire his touch sent dancing over her skin. His breath fanned her cheek, and the smell of fresh air and sunshine emanated from him like an intoxicating aphrodisiac. Laura fought to keep from throwing herself in his arms. Instead, she closed her eyes again.

Then his hand slipped from inside her blouse, and before she could open her eyes, he was on the other side of the small clearing fumbling with their backpacks, as if putting them in exactly the right spot was more critical than breathing. Without looking back at her, he headed into a crevice between two boulders and disappeared.

Laura stared after him for a while, trying to recover from the first time the man she loved, the man she'd never stopped loving, had really touched her in over eight years. Forcing her legs to move, she pulled a bar of soap, a towel, and clean clothes from her backpack, and then found a large outcropping of rocks behind which she could undress. Laying her clean clothes on one of the rocks close by, she striped off her dirty clothes. The cool air coming off the water washed over her skin and helped ease the desire that had tangled in a knot in her belly.

She glanced at the horizon and decided she had about an hour more of sunlight. Hurrying to the pool, she waded in. At first the water sent shivers over her naked flesh, but as she acclimated to it, it warmed to a very comfortable temperature. Laura sunk below the surface so that only her head was visible.

Shadow came to the water's edge, checked to see where she was, then took a long drink and laid down to watch her as she bathed the grime from her body.

She just finished rinsing her hair when she noticed Shadow had gotten to his feet and was fixed in the direction of the spot where she'd left her clothes.

"What is it, boy?" she called. He ignored her, his gaze still trained on the same spot. "What do you see?"

Her nerves tensed. She followed his gaze, but could see nothing out of the ordinary. Perhaps it was an animal or maybe Kaine coming back with the firewood. Unwilling for him to come back before she got out of the water, Laura waded from the pool and grabbed her towel. Picking her way through the rocks, she slipped behind the biggest boulder where she'd left her clean clothes and began to quickly towel herself dry.

Shadow joined her. She noted the dog's hair was standing on end in a ridge down his back from his head to his tail. A low growl gurgled up from deep in his throat. His sharp eyes were fastened on a spot behind Laura. She spun around, and her gaze met one of the most grotesque sights she'd ever seen in her life.

A long piercing scream cut through the stillness. Not until she heard Kaine running toward her and calling her name did she realize it had been her scream. Frozen in place, she could only stare down at the animal laying several feet from her.

Since its hide had been totally removed, she had no

idea what kind of animal it was; only that it was big, very big. It would have taken something equally as big or bigger to bring it down. There was just enough sunlight left for her to be able to see the blue veins beneath the pink flesh of the bloody carcass, and the few tufts of dark hair that still clung to it. The vacant eyes bulged in their sockets and stared sightlessly into the gathering night.

Her stomach lurched, and her knees threatened to buckle, but she couldn't tear her gaze from the dead animal. Her head had grown light, and she was sure she'd pass out any second, then—

"What the hell—"

Kaine's voice came from behind her. Without thinking, she spun around and buried her face in his chest. His arms closed around her. She clung to him with all her strength.

"Shit," he murmured above her head.

Laura looked up at him. "What?"

"Skinwalkers," he said, this time his voice was louder and from his tone, there was no mistaking that whatever skinwalkers were, they were not good.

"What are skinwalkers?" Her body still shook, and her voice quivered, but slowly she was managing to get a hold of herself and calm down.

"They're what the Navajos call men who skin animals and then wear the skins."

Laura didn't swallow this as a full explanation. She'd felt Kaine's body tense and heard the tone of his voice when he'd spotted the dead animal. She suddenly recalled the way he'd kept checking the rearview mirror in the car. Maybe it was because he was still holding her as he'd never let her go or because he kept scanning the falling darkness as he talked, but she felt certain there was a whole lot more to this than he was telling her.

"What does this mean, Kaine?" She stared up expectantly at him.

He avoided her eyes, released her, scooped her clothes off the rock and handed them to her. "Get dressed."

Laura looked down at herself and then blanched. She'd forgotten that the only thing covering her was a woefully inadequate towel. Still she didn't relish the idea of being left alone with the animal carcass. "Why won't you answer me, and where are you going? You're not leaving me here alone, are you?" To her utter astonishment, her voice had risen giving away the fear still coursing through her.

"Relax. I'll be right here." He pointed to the edge of the cluster of boulders surrounding them. "When we get back at the campfire, we'll talk." He took a few steps away from her and then turned back. "Oh, and don't button your blouse."

Her mouth fell open.

"I want to put some salve on your shoulders."

"But—"

Kaine shook his head. "Are you afraid I'll ravish your body?" He laughed bitterly. "Or maybe you're afraid I won't." He studied her surprised reaction for a time and then turned his back, leaving her with her mouth hanging open.

❖   ❖   ❖

As he stood facing the rocks, Kaine took a deep breath and leaned against the solid sandstone. His skin still tingled from the feel of Laura's nakedness pressed against him. He realized that what he'd said had a crude edge to it, but from the look on her face, it had, as he had hoped it would, served to divert her attention from her discovery. He rubbed his palms together and pushed Laura to the back of his mind.

He couldn't think about that now. He had other problems, big problems. That animal's carcass was fresh. That meant someone had been watching them and dumped it there for one of them to find, and probably while Laura had been bathing. Why? The first thing that came to mind was it had been used as a scare tactic because someone didn't want them here.

How would anyone know where they'd be? Even Willoughby and his wife hadn't known their exact destination, just the general direction they'd be traveling. But anyone who lived out here would know what routes they'd use to get into the canyon. There weren't that many access trails and almost from the time they'd left Willoughby's, he'd felt like they were being followed, but had dismissed it after he hadn't seen any signs of it. He should have paid more attention to his gut instincts and would from here on out.

He thought about what lay before them. Tomorrow, they would descend onto the canyon floor and follow the stream to the area where Peter disappeared. Between here and Canyon de Muerto they'd pass through nothing but rocks and river. Or would they?

Directly in their path was the area that Oates and Longtree said the ground-pickers were ravaging—the Rainbow Arch. Could the carcass just be something the pottery thieves had concocted hoping to scare Kaine away by using the myths of his people?

He almost laughed at the idea. Any one of his people would have turned tail and ran at the sight of the dead animal. But of all the people who would not be scared off by a dead animal carcass, it was him. If grown men wanted to walk around in the skins of dead animals for whatever reason, that was their business. If they decided to use it to frighten him or Laura, then it became his business, and they would suffer the consequences of their folly.

But, when Laura stepped into his line of vision, clutching her blouse closed in front of her, face white, eyes large and frightened, he knew that, as far as she's concerned, they'd already accomplished their plan. Laura was terrified. She had enough on her mind with Peter's disappearance, and he had to find a way to make this whole thing sound plausible and harmless, and then he'd hope like hell he was right, and it was harmless.

Chapter 8

Kaine fumbled through his backpack and finally found the small tin of homemade salve he'd been searching for. Opening it, he went back to the fireside and knelt behind Laura.

"What is that?" she asked looking down at the foul smelling, pea green substance and curling her nose.

"It a salve my grandfather taught me to make from herbs and cactus sap. It smells like hell, but it works."

Without further explanation and very carefully, he eased the material of her blouse from her shoulders. She jumped at his touch.

"Did I hurt you?"

She shook her head. "No."

When she offered no further explanation for her reaction to his touch, he was left to wonder if it had affected her as much as it had him. Had she felt that bolt of fire running through her veins and the heavy thumping of her heart?

Taking a bit of the salve on his fingertips, he got ready to apply it to her blistered skin, but he stopped. His breath caught in his throat. On each shoulder was a bright red circle the size of a half-dollar. The skin had been rubbed off it until only raw flesh remained. To have reached this point, she must have walked for hours with the pain of the straps digging into these sensitive wounds.

He didn't have to wonder why she'd done it. He knew. He'd made it perfectly clear from the beginning that he was not about to coddle her in any way, that she was on her own and it was up to her to keep up with him. She would never have admitted to any discomfort or anything else that would have prompted him to berate her for being too soft to be here.

The Laura he'd married would have moaned and groaned about the heat and the dirt and the long walk over rough terrain. But not this new woman she'd become, not the woman who'd given birth to a child and raised him on her own, not the woman who'd gone nose to nose with a six-foot-plus Indian and threatened to follow him into this wilderness come hell or high water, and not the mother who would subject herself to any hardship to find her son.

"I'm going to put the salve on," he warned to give her time to fortify herself. "I'll try not to hurt you."

She said nothing, just bent her head to the side to allow him better access to her shoulder. Her unspoken trust warmed him in places that had been cold for far too long.

A movement on the far side of the clearing caught Kaine's attention. It was Shadow. Though the big dog didn't seem upset, he paced back and forth around the perimeter of the campsite as if standing guard over them. Kaine smiled.

When his fingers touched Laura's skin, he felt the heat coming from the blisters. But he felt more than that. As if a fine thread had sprouted from the wound, something pulled at Kaine's insides, as if sucking him into a deep abyss. He pulled away.

"What's wrong?" Laura half turned her head, trying to see him.

"Nothing," he said quickly. "Just sit still." He took a deep breath and waited for his insides to right themselves, then began again to apply the salve. This time nothing happened.

Must have been my imagination.

"That feels wonderful," she said, sighing and throwing her head back. "The pain is gone. You should sell that stuff to a drug company."

He snorted cynically. "Yeah. We could call it *Cloudwalker's Magical Cure-All*, and I could travel from town to town hawking it." He tapped the top of her head lightly. "Let me get the other one."

Obediently, she tilted her head the other way and fell silent.

He'd just about finished slathering the healing salve

over her flesh when he found he didn't want to stop touching Laura. Before he could stop himself, he was kneading the flesh beyond the wound, letting his finger tips glide over her silky shoulders and down her arms. Her skin felt so smooth, so soft, so damned inviting.

He leaned forward and inhaled the essence of her freshly washed hair. He lowered his head and pressed his lips against the cool skin at the base of her neck. She groaned and tilted her head farther, silently inviting him to continue. He didn't need a second invitation.

Sitting flat, so that her body fit snuggly into the "V" of his legs, he pulled her back against him, encircling her upper body with his arms. For a time, he sat very still, eyes closed, just holding her and savoring the feel of her. But very quickly, the need to do more than just hold her overcame him.

He slipped his hands inside the open front of the blouse she'd used to cover herself while he administered to her blisters. Her warm breasts nestled into his palms as if there had never been a time when he had reached for them only to find thin air. The stiff peaks pressed against his palms like two red hot coals.

Laura groaned and twisted in his arms until she was on her knees before him. She reached down and drew his shirt over his head. The night air cooled his hot skin. She smiled at him and leaned forward until her bare breasts skimmed over his flesh, leaving behind a trail of heat and desire so intense it stole his breath away. Kaine's groin tightened painfully.

He pulled her to him, flattening her chest to his. The sensation of her naked flesh on his caused a painful contraction in his loins. His mouth unerringly found hers. Her lips had already opened to him, and he took advantage. His tongue dove deep inside, tasting her sweetness. With his pulse throbbing in his groin and his heartbeat pounding in his ears, Kaine swung her around so she was draped over his lap.

He ran his hand up her leg and then cupped the valley between them. Heat seared his palm. Moistness seeped through the thin material of her khaki shorts. She wanted him as much as he wanted her, and his whole body sprang to life with the thought.

The years of separation melted away. He was holding his wife again.

Laura squirmed against Kaine's hand, frustrated with the barriers between her and the culmination to the building heat inside her. She wanted more. She wanted it all. She wanted Kaine, inside her. She hadn't felt this alive in a long, long time, and she hung onto the pleasant sensations pumping through her like a lifeline. Her senses sang with desire, and her mouth sought his again. She nibbled hungrily at his lips, sucking them into her mouth, and then laving them with her tongue.

She locked her arms around his neck, pulling him as close as she could manage. It had been so long, so very long.

"Laura." Her name tore from his lips, the sound

imbued with a desperate need, the same need she was experiencing.

His hand snaked between them, and she felt the waistband on her shorts loosen. The soft *whirr* of the zipper sounded like a clap of thunder. Kaine's warm hand slid slowly and tantalizingly over her belly. She held her breath, waiting for the first touch of flesh on flesh.

A piercing bark from the other side of the clearing broke them apart as if they were guilty teenagers caught petting by the cops. Laura fumbled with the zipper and the button on her shorts and hauled her blouse around her nakedness. Kaine jumped to his feet, pulling his shirt on as he went.

Shadow stared into the darkness, his tail still, the hair on his back showing the same raised ridge it had when Laura had found the carcass. His white, bared teeth gleamed in the moonlight.

"What is it, boy?" Kaine whispered, creeping across the clearing to the dog's side.

Shadow continued to stare into the night, a low, menacing growl rolling up from deep inside him. He took a step toward a large crevice between two boulders. Whatever was causing him to react was in there. Laura watched, her breath caught in her throat, hoping Kaine would not go in there to see what it was.

Kaine returned to the fire and dug into his backpack. He extracted a flashlight; and, though Laura only caught the glint of the fire off a small part of it, what she knew was a gun. The hollow sound of Kaine cocking the gun echoed around the campsite.

She snagged his sleeve as he swung around toward where Shadow stood. "Please be careful."

He gave a brief nod, then handed her the gun. "Use it if you have to," he said, then hurried off and disappeared inside the black crevice.

The gun felt cold in her warm hand. She glanced down at it. Laura hated guns. She'd seen too many people carried into the emergency room with holes blasted in them to have any love of the weapon, but she wasn't stupid either. She knew without a moment's doubt that if the need arose, she'd use it to save Kaine's or her life.

Long moments ticked by. Ears alert to any sound, she kept her gaze trained on the spot where Kaine had disappeared. Her own breathing echoed in her ears, along with the frantic beat of her heart. Sweat beaded her cold brow. A cool breeze chilled the exposed flesh of her midriff.

Not until that moment had she consciously thought about her state of undress. Laying the gun in her lap, where she could easily grab it, she buttoned her blouse. As she did so, her mind wandered to what had just taken place here. She'd come so close to giving herself to Kaine. Would she have been able to go through with it?

She'd never know, but one thing she did know was that it wouldn't go that far again, not as long as her secret stood between them. She could never make love to Kaine until he knew who Peter was, and she was not sure she could risk telling him that.

The crack of a twig pulled her instantly from her troubled thoughts. She pointed the gun in the direction from which the sound had come. Her finger trembled on the trigger. Her hands gripped the butt so hard her fingers ached.

Then she saw Shadow, his tail waging, followed by Kaine, emerge from the dark crevice.

She ran to them. "What did you find?"

"Nothing," he said too quickly and not looking at her.

"I don't believe you. Please, don't baby me. I want to know. Whatever it is presents as much danger to me as it does to you. I *deserve* to know."

Kaine sighed, walked to the fire, added a log and then turned to her. "All right. I found footprints."

"What kind? Man? Animal?"

Silence hung above them for a long moment. "Both," he finally said.

"Are you sure it's not just Shadow? He's been all over here since we made camp."

"No, it wasn't Shadow. The prints were too big." Kaine avoided meeting her eyes.

He didn't want to tell her that the prints he found were not just any man or animal. The man's prints had gone so far then turned into animal prints. They were being followed by skinwalkers.

"Whatever it was, it's gone, so we might as well get some sleep." He grabbed the sleeping bags and spread them beside each other next to the fire.

"Shouldn't one of us stand guard in case they come back?" Laura looked around her as if expecting something to jump from the shadows at any moment.

"Do you think anything could get past him without us knowing it?" Kaine motioned toward Shadow.

As though the dog understood what Kaine had said, Shadow jumped to his feet and began patrolling the perimeter of the campsite.

✜　✜　✜

Despite Shadow's constant vigilance, neither of them slept well, and Laura was up and moving around preparing breakfast before the sun topped the canyon walls. After they'd eaten and Kaine had applied more salve to Laura's blisters, she filled their canteens from the pool, while Kaine broke camp and packed everything for the start of the last half of their trek to the canyon's floor. Shadow wandered back and forth between the two of them.

Laura handed the canteens to Kaine, who packed them away and then stood. "We better get going so we can make it all the way to the bottom before sundown. Because of the high canyon walls, darkness will come faster while we're down there, and I don't want to be on the trail then."

She didn't need him to explain why. If whoever or whatever was tracking them, darkness would be the time to strike; and if they were on the narrow trail, they'd be sitting ducks.

"Kaine, why would someone be following us?"

He glanced at her and then shook his head. "Not a clue, but I'm sure they'll let us know soon enough."

Laura shivered. It was not what she'd hoped he'd say. She wanted to hear that it was probably just some animal looking for a meal and that, because of Shadow, it would eventually lose interest in his intended prey or that some tourist had wandered into the area where they were. That someone or something out there was stalking them formed a ball of terror in her stomach. Se swallowed and pushed it out of her mind.

"Then let's get moving." Laura walked over to the backpacks and looked at hers with hesitation.

Even though the blisters looked remarkably better, the thought of putting the backpack on her shoulders almost brought tears to her eyes. She started to pick hers up, and Kaine's hand closed over her wrist.

"I'll take the backpacks. This part of the trail is steeper and the pack can throw you off balance if you're not used to it." It sounded good, but the real reason was the guilt eating at him for having picked up the pace yesterday with no thought of her. Bottom line was he felt responsible for the blisters she'd sustained.

"No, there's no need for you to carry my stuff. You have enough to carry with your own stuff. I'll be fine. I can't ask you to carry both packs just because of my blisters."

He swung on her. "Did I say it was because of your blisters? I told you, it's for safety reasons. I'd do it if you didn't have blisters." He hauled both packs up and hung one off each of his broad shoulders. "Besides, if you get infected, I'll have to nurse you through it, and I don't have time."

Kaine knew he was being a bastard, but he didn't know how else to control the feelings that had been given life last night, feelings he'd kept hidden for years. Feelings he thought had died long ago.

✤　　✤　　✤

That night there was no cool, spring water to sooth Laura's aching body. Where they'd emerged at the base of the canyon's steep parapet, the river's rapids beat angrily against the rock walls and, had she tried to swim in it, the swift current would have sucked her under. So she settled for a few splashes of water on her face from a cooking pot she'd lowered into the river. Truth be known, she was too tired to do more than that anyway. The last half of the descent had been more rigorous than the first, and she could do no more than think longingly of the time when she could lay her exhausted body down for the night.

She and Kaine said very little while they prepared a quick supper, cleaned up, and crawled into their sleeping bags. Shadow stationed himself between them. It took minutes for Laura to fall asleep, but not before she heard the soft snores coming from Kaine's direction. She smiled sleepily at the sound that had grown so familiar to her during their marriage, the sound that had lulled her to sleep on many nights, the sound that . . .

✦   ✦   ✦

Shadow's deep growl cut into Laura's slumber. Without opening her eyes, she reached out and stroked the animal's soft fur. "Shhh, Shadow. You'll wake Kaine."

"Kaine's already awake," came a whisper from right behind her.

Her eyes popped open. "What are you—?"

Shadow growled again. His body tensed beneath her touch. His haunches bunched, ready to spring.

Kaine's face came closer to hers. He slipped his hand over her mouth. "Shhh. Don't move."

Instinctively, she looked toward where Shadow's sharp gaze was directed. Her heart stopped. Kaine removed his hand. An icy chill snaked down her spine. She pressed back against Kaine.

"Oh my—"

"Shhh," Kaine admonished softly.

Just outside the circle of light cast by the dying fire she could see no less than six very large, very shaggy animals that resembled huge dogs, but weren't like any dog she'd ever seen before. Their coats were unkempt and four of them were on all fours while the other two stood unsteadily on their hind legs. Slowly, the ones on all fours prowled back and forth just outside the weak circle of light from the dying fire. Though the beasts made no move to advance on them, the predatory prowling back and forth continued nonstop, and their satanic, red-eyed gazes never left the object of their attention—Kaine, Shadow, and her.

Shadow growled again. Laura hooked her fingers in the heavy, white coat to prevent him from lunging at the strange animals watching them so pointedly.

She turned halfway to better see Kaine, and then whispered, "What are they?"

Never taking his gaze off the strange animals, Kaine shook his head. "I'm not sure."

Suddenly, the biggest of the animals started toward them, each step measured and cautious. Two very large fangs protrude from its top jaw. From the angle of its head and by following the line of its evil gaze, Laura felt like it was looking directly at Kaine.

Kaine felt her push closer, as though using her body to protect him.

Shadow sprang to his feet, his paws planted wide in anticipation of an attack. His low growl had become a feral snarl. His top lip pulled back from his teeth; salvia dripped from his lips. The threatened animal stepped back.

Another of their number separated from the pack and slowly advanced on them. Though smaller than the other, this one seemed bolder, more eager to challenge Shadow. Kaine read in the dog's stance what he was going to do.

"No, Shadow," he said, his voice barely audible. The only sign the dog showed of having heard Kaine's command was a slight twitching of his ears.

"Can you reach your gun?" Laura asked.

He'd thought about that, but he'd foolishly left his backpack too far away for him to grab it without calling attention to himself and risking one of these beasts charging them.

"No."

"Are they wolves? Maybe coyotes," Laura whispered.

"A coyote's and a wolf's eyes glow yellow. I've never seen any animals like this before."

What he didn't tell her was that he'd never *seen* them, but he'd heard stories about them from the old ones all his life. For a man who no longer believed in the teachings of his heritage, he was finding it very hard to accept that he was now face-to-face with what looked very much like one of their myths he'd heard from the elders around a campfire.

Skinwalkers.

The animal took another step toward them, its eerie eyes still centered on Kaine. It took one more step, and Shadow lunged. The rest of the pack came alive and counterattacked. But Shadow skirted them and dashed off into the darkness, the strange animals following behind him.

Kaine scrambled to his feet and grabbed his backpack. Gun and flashlight in hand, he turned toward where the animals and Shadow had disappeared. Before he could take a step, sounds of growling, snarling, and scuffling came from behind the rocks. A series of pain-filled *yipes* followed quickly and then more growling and snarling, then more howls of pain.

Shadow? He couldn't tell. He took a step forward, but Laura sprang to her feet and stopped him, her fingers bunched tightly in the material of his shirt sleeve.

"You can't go out there. They'll tear you to pieces."

He looked down at her. "If I don't, they'll kill Shadow."

"We just have to hope that Shadow can hold his own." Worry for the dog's welfare choked off her voice.

"Against six huge animals?" Kaine couldn't believe how fond he'd become of the dog in such a short time.

Laura looked up at him, but said nothing. She didn't have to. He could tell by her expression that she knew. If he didn't go to help him, one dog could not hope to win against that pack, no matter how valiant his heart was. Shadow would probably die.

As if she had come to the same conclusion, she released his arm. "Be careful."

A few days ago, he would have laughed at anyone who said that to him. After all, taking chances had become a way of life for him. But now, since Laura had come back into his life, he'd developed a fondness for living that he couldn't explain.

"I will," he said, and he meant it.

He had no idea what was happening between him and his estranged wife, but he did know he wanted to see it to its conclusion, whatever that might be. He couldn't do that dead.

As though someone had thrown a light switch and turned it off, the snarling and howling suddenly stopped. The deafening, ominous silence hung over the campsite like a mourning shroud. Both he and Laura stared expectantly at the spot where Shadow had disappeared from sight. They waited, their nervous breathing and the rumble of the river currents the only sounds in the inky night.

Something moved in the darkness. Kaine waited, straining to catch the appearance of those shining red eyes again. His grip tightened on the gun. Beside him, Laura bent and picked up a piece of wood and then dropped it on the hot coals of the fire. The dry wood caught instantly and flared brightly, sending light to all corners of the campsite.

Not far from the boulders ringing the camp was a mound of something white.

"Shadow!" The word burst from both of them in unison.

They rushed to the dog's side. Laura ran her hands over the dog, searching for wounds, waiting for her fingers to encounter a wet spot of blood. But she found neither. If she hadn't heard the commotion coming from the other side of the boulders, seen those huge animals, heard the yelps of pain, she would have sworn that Shadow was simply tired.

"I can't find any broken bones or open wounds. Nothing," she told Kaine, her hands still busy checking the dog for injures, as if trying to disprove what she'd said. How could Shadow have encountered those fearsome beasts and come out of it without a scratch?

Kaine reached past her and picked up the dog, cradling him close in his arms. He carried Shadow to the fire and gently placed him on one of the sleeping bags.

"Look him over again." He moved to the side to give Laura room.

She squatted down beside Shadow and repeated her examination. Shadow shifted his head and looked her directly in the eye and lifted his chin, throwing his head back to reveal his neck.

After running her hand over the dog's face and ears, she moved on to his neck and then stopped. Laura leaned forward, closely inspecting the area below the dog's chin.

"What do you see? Is he hurt?" Not waiting for her to answer, Kaine leaned forward to see what had snagged her attention.

"No, he's okay. I just don't recall seeing this before." She moved her hand to reveal a section of golden fur about the size of a small orange that looked very much like a sunburst.

Kaine had played with the dog and petted him often enough in the last two days that he should have noticed the differently colored patch of fur. "Maybe he laid in something."

"Maybe," she said, but she didn't sound convinced. Then she seemed to rouse herself from thought. "I'll get him some water."

She went to where their cooking supplies laid and

picked up a canteen. When she tried to open it, she found the cap had been screwed on too tight for her to remove it. She struggled with it, trying over and over to budge it, but it was on there solid.

"What's wrong?" Kaine had come to stand beside her. Seeing her dilemma, he took the canteen and turned the cap easily.

Just then, a *whoosh* of warm air came from behind them. They turned quickly. Shadow had vanished.

Chapter 9

The sun was already turning the horizon a deep pink when Kaine returned from searching for Shadow. Laura laid aside the gun he'd left for her in case the animals returned and looked at him expectantly.

"Well?"

"I couldn't find any sign of him." He shook his head and ran his fingers through his hair. "No prints, nothing." He flung himself down beside the fire and poured a cup of hot coffee from the pot nestled in the glowing coals.

"Dammit, Kaine, he can't have vanished," she bit out. "Dogs don't just disappear like that." She snapped her fingers. "He *has* to be out there somewhere."

Kaine sipped the hot coffee, swallowed hard, and then sighed tiredly. "Laura, I'm as fond of that dog as you are, but we have a choice, search for Shadow or search for Peter. We can't look for both."

The question was moot. Of course, Peter would take precedence over a dog. Still, Laura could not help hating the additional ache in her heart left by the absence of the animal that had been their constant companion for days, the animal that had taken on a pack of . . . of whatever those ghastly animals were, to protect her and Kaine.

She glanced at him, certain her answer was written in her eyes, but she said it anyway. "Peter, of course."

He nodded and shoved himself to his feet. "Good. Get everything else packed up, we'll be leaving in fifteen minutes."

To stay sane while Kaine had been off looking for Shadow, she'd packed almost everything, but it grated on her raw nerves to have him throwing orders at her as if she were his own personal lackey. However, she didn't have the energy to fight him, so she did as he'd instructed.

❖   ❖   ❖

Thankfully, the following day the rough terrain had spread out into an alluvial plain created by the silt deposits of the now slowly moving river. The topography had leveled out so they were no longer climbing up or down over boulders and rocks. But Laura's tired body protested even the easier path.

Since the night Shadow had disappeared, she'd had a hard time sleeping, certain that if she closed her eyes, those horrible animals would come back. And this time, there would be no dog to chase them away.

By the time they stopped to eat on the second day after the appearance of the skinwalkers, she was sure she could not have taken another step. Kaine still carried his backpack and hers, but she was exhausted. She kept her complaints to herself. Actually, she'd hardly said two words to Kaine—or he to her. She wasn't sure why he wasn't talking, but she knew what her own problem was. On top of her exhaustion, she was shouldering the heavy burden of guilt for having snapped at him when he'd come back empty-handed from his search for Shadow. It wasn't his fault he couldn't find the dog.

He'd also done what he could to make this whole ordeal easier on her: carrying her backpack; and although he had relegated the task of applying the salve to her blisters to her, they had improved due mostly to his help. Despite having said nothing to indicate it, she knew he was taking special pains not to push her beyond her endurance, even when she never complained.

She took a swallow of tepid water from the canteen. "Kaine, I'm sorry I've been acting like such a spoiled brat the past few days. I know you did all you could to find Shadow." She handed the canteen to him. "I don't know what got into me."

He looked at her thoughtfully. "Well, let's see." He screwed the cap back on, laid the canteen down, and then held up his hand and ticked off his fingers one by one. "Your son has been lost out here for almost a week; you're being subjected to a way of life that's totally foreign to you; in the last few nights, you may have managed to get a total of four hours sleep, and you've had to do all this while being forced into the company of a man you can't stand the sight of. I'd say you have good reason to be a bit out of sorts."

She stared at him for a long time, and then slowly shook her head. "I never said I couldn't stand the sight of you." *On the contrary,* she thought, *I'm in love with you, I've always been in love with you, and since this may be the last time I see you, I'm savoring every moment.*

She waited for Kaine to make some sarcastic remark, but none came. Instead, he held her gaze for a long time. But try as she might, she could not read anything in his dark chocolate eyes that would tell her of his true feelings.

When he made no move to look away, and she began to fear he was reading far more than she wanted him to know in her eyes, she glanced up at the sky. "There was one thing you left off your list."

"Oh?"

She looked back at him, this time certain that her eyes reflected nothing but her determination to get an answer to a question that had been nagging at her since the day they'd help the young Navajo boy.

"I'm being kept in the dark about what's going on."

"Going on?" He didn't meet her eyes, which told her she'd been right. There was a lot more to this whole situation than he was talking about.

"Yes, *going on*. Ever since we stopped to help that boy with the injured thumb, things have been happening that you are aware of, but that you aren't talking about. I want to know what they are. I deserve to know." He opened his mouth, but she stopped him with a raised hand. "No more half-truths, please, and no more fragments of information. I want to know it all. I have enough to worry about with my son; I don't need to be wondering what all this other crap is about."

For a moment, Kaine resembled a trapped animal. He shifted uncomfortably under her scrutinizing gaze. Then his whole body seemed to relax, as though getting it out might prove a huge relief.

"Before I tell you, you have to understand that I never kept it from you because I didn't trust you or because I didn't want to tell you. I didn't want to say anything because I figured you had enough on your mind without me adding to it." He laughed without humor. "I also thought you'd think you'd hired a basket case to help you find Peter." Taking a deep breath, he leaned forward and rested his elbows on his knees. "This may sound totally off the wall to you, but here it is." His chest heaved with a deeply drawn breath. "The night you came to ask me to help find Peter, after you left, I had a dream."

The word *dream* brought Laura instantly alert. Her own dream came vividly to mind. His next words answered her question.

"My grandfather, Brother To The Owl, came to me

in that dream, along with a Navajo Holy Woman called Changing Woman." Kaine studied Laura as he spoke, waiting to see one flicker of doubt from her. He found none. Her expression was impassive, but her attention remained riveted. "It was Changing Woman who told me about your friend Ada Dooley." The friend's name brought the first subtle change to Laura's face, a lifting of the corner of her mouth in a half-smile. "Changing Woman's Navajo name is *Asdzaa Dootlijii*."

He paused, waiting for Laura to think about what he'd just said. When she sat straighter and her eyes widened, he knew she'd seen the same subtle similarities he'd detected between her friend's name and the Navajo Holy Woman's.

"You mean . . ."

"I don't know, but other things that happened only make sense, if that's true. The boy you helped. His name being the same as that of the twin son of the Holy Woman seems just too coincidental to have any other explanation."

"What about the corn pollen he gave me?"

"I haven't figured that out yet, but I'm sure it works in somehow. But the lightning bolt we saw that day . . . it's said that the twin, Monster Slayer, was given a lightning bolt by his father, The Sun." He cleared his throat. "Then there's Shadow—"

"Shadow? You think the dog is part of this . . ." Looking bewildered, she stopped speaking and studied the flat water's edge where they sat on rocks, as if somewhere in the scrub grass or the rocks peppering the banks of the river lay the answer she sought. "God, I don't know what to call it. Magic? Supernatural? Otherworldly events?"

He shook is head. "I don't know either. But *weird* comes to mind."

"Kaine, please don't think I'm laughing at you, because I am well aware of how serious this is. It's just so—"

"Unbelievable?"

She nodded. "Is there more?"

He nodded. "The Navajo believe that Changing Woman is synonymous with life. She's the measure of time. She grows to maturity and old age only to endlessly repeat the cycle. She has four stages: Whiteshell Woman, Turquoise Woman, Abalone Woman, and Jet Woman. The stages of her life are depicted by the color of the clothes she wears."

Again, Laura sat straighter. This time her complexion blanched. "Ada always wore white. Always. I used to tease her about it. I even called her my Guardian Angel because of it."

"This may seem like a silly question, but bear with me. Were there any other women in your life recently who wore all white?"

Laura searched her memory, but could find nothing. She was about to shake her head no, when she suddenly recalled the woman at the bazaar, the woman who had given her the pendant. "There was one woman. At a hospital fair. She was Navajo, and she'd been dressed totally in white." She reached inside her blouse and pulled out the pendant. The sun glinted off the colored stones forming the rainbow. The centerpiece of the necklace lay comfortably warm in her palm. "She gave me this and then vanished, a lot like Shadow did. She was there and then she was gone."

Rather than looking relieved, Kaine looked more and more agitated with each fact they uncovered. He stood and walked to the river's edge. Bending down, he picked up a handful of small stones and began throwing them, one by one, into the slowly moving water.

She went to stand beside him. "How does Shadow fit in?"

"What color is Shadow?"

She was stunned. "You don't mean that Shadow is—" It was too wild to even put into words.

Kaine turned to face her. His expression told her he was as serious as death. "Changing Woman has the ability to take any form she wants."

Laura was speechless. Shadow? Then she remembered the splash of gold on the dog's chest. "The woman at the fair, the one in white, she wore a pendant shaped like the grinning face of the sun. That marking on Shadow's chest looked like a sunburst." She frowned. "Kaine, what does all this mean?"

He remained silent for a long time. Then he turned to her. "My grandfather told me in my dream that the *hozho* of the People has been disturbed and that I had to step into the eye of the dream because time was running out." He paused again. "I think he was telling me that I've disturbed the balance, and it's my responsibility to find a way to restore harmony to the Diné'."

For a moment, Laura digested what Kaine had just said and then something occurred to her. What if the old man in her dream was also his grandfather? What if . . . ?

"Kaine, what does *Sa?ah naghai bikeh* mean?" She wasn't at all sure that she'd come close to pronouncing the difficult Navajo words correctly, but from the look of shock on his face, she was sure he'd gotten the gist of them.

"Shit! Where did you hear that?"

"Before Peter went missing, I had a dream, too. There was an old man in it, an old Navajo who seemed to be angry with me for something. Back then, I didn't know who it was, but from your description of your dream, maybe he was your grandfather." She didn't tell him that he and Peter were also in the dream. That would just open another can of worms, and she didn't need that right now. "So, what does it mean?"

"Loosely interpreted, it means *the balance of life has been disturbed*. And that's the basic message my grandfather and Changing Woman had for me, too." He ran his hands through his hair and stared up at the towering canyon walls. "Damn!"

Kaine's expletive barely penetrated the tangle of thoughts racing through Laura's head. She dropped to a large rock near her before her knees gave out. This was insane, just a series of coincidences, things that could be easily explained. But how? Then something came to here.

My God, does all this have something to do with Peter?

She wanted to ask him, but refrained from doing so because she was terrified of where it would lead. It was just too soon to tell him who Peter really was. *Way too soon.* She wasn't ready to face his reaction to it—or his condemnation of her. Not now. Not when they relationship seemed to be slowly mending.

But thinking of Peter also brought to mind the dangers he was facing alone. Like those beasts that visited their campsite. The skinwalkers. Were they stalking Peter, too? She wasn't sure if the thought of Kaine saying *yes* or her not knowing was worse. Finally, she forced the words through her lips.

"What about the skinwalkers? What do they have to do with this? Are they after Peter, too?"

Kaine came to her, squatted down and took both of her hands in his. "I honestly don't know. That's the one thing I haven't figured out in all this. I do know that the Navajo believe when the *hozho* is disturbed it brings evil with it."

That wasn't what she wanted to hear. She needed assurances that Peter was safe, that those beasts were not stalking her son for their next meal.

Suddenly the exhaustion of the last few days, the fear in her heart for her son, and the love she carried secretly for a man who would soon hate her coalesced, and she felt her throat tighten. Before she could stop them, tears rolled down her cheeks, accompanied by deep, heart-wrenching sobs that felt like they were being torn from her very soul.

Kaine said nothing. He merely enfolded her in his arms and pulled her to the ground to straddle his lap.

"I never should have let him go with Anne. He's too young. You must think I'm a terrible mother." She wrapped her arms around Kaine, buried her face in his neck and let the tears come.

He let her cry it out, and then, when her sobs turned to hiccups, he murmured into her hair. "I could never think of you as a bad mother. In fact, I always believed that you'd have been one hell of a mom to our kids, if we'd had any."

She sniffed loudly and leaned back to look at him. "Really?"

He chuckled. With the pad of his thumb, he wiped the tears from her cheeks. "Yes, really."

Once the tears were gone, he continued to caress her face. They stared deep into each others eyes. Kaine could see himself reflected in their sea-green depths, as if he was inside her, part of her. A wild heat started in his belly and shot to all parts of his body. Their faces were very close and her lips, swollen by her tears, were so damned tempting. He ran his thumb over her bottom lip. She opened her mouth a sliver and sighed deeply. His pulse raced out of control.

"God, you are a witch," he whispered, a hair's breadth from her mouth. "What would you do if I said I need to kiss you more than I need my next breath?"

"This." She pulled him closer and covered his mouth with hers.

That the hot Arizona sun was shining down on them, that it was broad daylight, that their lives had become a tangle of inexplicable real and unreal happenings vanished from Kaine's mind. Every sense he possessed centered on the woman in his arms: her hot mouth; her silky soft skin; her luscious lips, salty from tears; her curves molding to his hardness, as if they were made to fit together like puzzle pieces.

Eight years of starving for her mushroomed inside him as though a flower had opened its heart to the sunlight. Every inch of him burst to life. Every nerve tingled. Every beat of his heart echoed through his head.

He lifted his head slightly, a mere breath of air separating their mouths. "This could lead to other things, you know."

"I . . . know," she mumbled, interspersing the words with quick nibbles at his lips.

"And you don't have problem with that." He drew her bottom lip into his mouth and tasted it.

Her answer was to slip the top button of his shirt through the hole, then the next and the next. He smiled at Laura.

The warmth in his face flooded Laura. She grinned

back at him and spread her fingers across his chest. His flesh was tanned copper from the many hours he'd spent under the desert sun, but it was smooth, flawless, and it quivered beneath her fingertips. When he had reached his senior years, she had no doubt the man would die handsome. And just as sexy.

Suddenly, a thought occurred to her, and she stopped. Looking over her shoulder and then scanning the area, she bit her lip. This was going to sound really strange, but considering the events of the last few days, reasonable, she thought.

"You don't suppose that your grandfather and that woman are watching, do you?"

Kaine blinked. "What?"

"Well, think about all the stuff that's happened. It's not such a stretch of the imagination, is it?"

Kaine laughed delightedly. "God, but I love you."

The bushes rustled behind them. They froze.

Chapter 10

In the end, the noise in the bushes proved to be nothing more than a brightly colored turquoise bird. It was, however, enough to dispel the sensuous mood that had overcome them.

Kaine stood, brushed the soil from his clothes, assisted her to her feet, and picked up her backpack. "We should be going. The sun will go down early, and we still have a long way to go to our next camp."

When he realized his voice betrayed the desire still coursing through him, he cleared his throat. Taking his gun from the backpack, he tucked it into the waistband of his jeans and then slipped the backpacks over each shoulder. "I don't want to be on the trail after dark." Before heading off down the path running along the river, he glanced at Laura.

She had no desire to be out there in the open either,

but she was still recovering from not only their physical encounter and her self-imposed seduction of Kaine, but also what he'd said. *God, I love you.* Had he been serious—or had it just been a throwaway line to express the humor he was feeling at the moment?

She stared thoughtfully at his back, and then quickly hurried after him. Would she ever be able to truly read what went on below his stoic surface?

The turquoise bird, which had been perched on a nearby rock, flew low ahead of them.

✢   ✢   ✢

Later that day, when the sun was kissing the canyon rim, Kaine finally stopped. "We'll camp here for tonight. We'll soon be at the Rainbow Arch. Day after tomorrow, at the latest. That's just below the spot on the upper rim where Peter vanished."

Those were the first words he'd spoken to her since they'd started out again. Laura's heart skipped a beat. At last, they could begin the actual search for Peter. Her son hadn't been far from the surface of her thoughts, but those thoughts now shared space with a myriad of questions about his father. But, as always, rather than voice them and risk his cold replies or his sarcasm, she shoved them to the back of her mind.

Instead of speaking, Laura nodded and unfurled their bedrolls near where he was digging out a hollow of ground for the firepit. Their routine had become so set by this point that they could do it by rote.

The river, which must have swollen beyond its banks from the spring rains, had deposited an array of driftwood along the edge. Once Kaine had the firepit ready, he collected an armload of it, brought it back, and piled it beside the pit.

While he laid the fire, Laura waited. Finally, she could stand neither the nagging questions nor the dead silence any longer.

"May I ask you something?"

Without looking up, he nodded and continued laying small pieces of wood and twigs, the base for what would become their cooking fire and heat against the cold desert night.

"After all you told me about the legends of the Navajo the other night, you still don't believe any of this has anything to do with the supernatural, do you?"

For a moment, she thought he wasn't going to answer, and then he turned to her, skepticism was written all over his features. "There's a lot of stuff that happens in life that we can't explain. That doesn't mean it's supernatural. It just means it's . . . unexplainable."

He went back to lighting the fire. After he'd added the larger pieces of wood, he drew the lighter from his pocket and ignited the twigs at its base. Flames caught on the kindling, then grew until the bigger logs caught and the fire blazed brightly, sending its light into the rapidly darkening corners of their campsite.

Deep inside Laura, she knew he didn't totally believe what he'd just said. If he did, he would have downplayed it the other night when he told her about Changing Woman and her twin sons and all the rest. And that's not what she'd detected in his words, his voice or his body language. He may not *want* to believe any of this, but he did.

Just then, the bird that had been following them all day twittered loudly and tumbled from the branch to the ground with a muffled *thud*. Laura ran over and picked up its limp body and cradled it in her palm. She stared at the tiny turquoise breast. It wasn't moving.

"It's dead," she said, awe filling her voice. "How could it have been sitting on a branch one moment, then dead the next?"

Kaine came to her side. "Let me see it," he said and took the bird from her.

The bird laid very still; not a feather twitched, nothing to reveal any sign of life left in the tiny body. Kaine stared down at it for some time, and then he stroked the bird's chest with the tip of his finger. Suddenly, its wing twitched, and then its leg; it flipped over in his palm, looked at both of them, and flew away.

Laura gasped. "How did you do that?" She stared in awe at the bird as it disappeared behind a large rock.

"Do what?"

"That. The bird was dead. Something you did revived him."

Kaine shrugged. "I didn't do anything. It was probably just knocked out and need time to come around." He went back to stoking the fire as if what had just occurred was as common as the sun rising in the morning.

She followed on his heels, coming to stand beside him. "I don't believe you. Something just happened that brought the bird back to life, something wonderful and inexplicable. Something to do with your touch."

He swung around to look at her. "You'd be better off grounding your thoughts and concentrating on finding your son, than reading something into everything that happens around you." He frowned. "Now, let it go and get some food started. We need to get to bed so we can get an early start tomorrow. We've wasted enough time on nonsense."

Wasted time? Nonsense? Is that how he viewed what happened between them today? A nonsensical waste of time? Her heart contracted in her chest, and she bit back tears of disappointment. Well, at least she had her question answered as to whether he meant it when he'd said *I love you*. She had to stop fantasizing that there could ever be anything more than anger and resentment between them.

✤　　✤　　✤

"Laura."

Someone was calling her, but whom? It had to be Kaine. Laura stirs in her sleep. "Can't we sleep just a little longer?"

"*Laura.*" This time, the voice is sterner, more insistent.

Knowing he wants to leave early, she gives in to his commands and struggles free of the cotton wool of sleep. Forcing her eyes open, she can see not Kaine scowling down at her, but a halo of light coming toward her. She blinks against the searing brightness. A beautiful woman steps from the light. She is dressed in clothes the color of the bird Kaine had saved.

But as Laura watches, the color of her clothes begins to swirl, transforming to an iridescent material that catches the rays of the light, making the fabric come alive and shimmer like the surface of a pond bombarded with raindrops during a summer sun shower. The dancing array of colors reminds Laura of the abalone shells that she and her best friend had collected at her parents' California beach home.

Abalone! *Is it. . . . Can it be. . . .*

"Who are you?"

The woman smiles. "You know who I am, child. Why do you waste words on things that mean little and leave the important questions unasked?" She comes forward and stands above Laura.

Laura tries to rise from her sleeping bag, but her limbs won't obey her commands. Her brain still befuddled with sleep, she tries to focus in on what the woman is saying. "I don't understand. What questions do you mean?" She shakes herself. *I can't believe I'm having a conversation with someone in a dream. Kaine was right. This supernatural stuff is taking over her brain.*

The woman steps closer, her expression stern and foreboding. "Do not allow your trust in what cannot be explained waver now, Laura. Kaine will soon be tested by the evil ones, and he will need your strength. He has lost his faith in the Ways of the People. He has lost faith in himself and his powers, even when the proof is put before him." Suddenly a bird appears on the woman's shoulder, a bird exactly like the one Kaine had saved. "If you truly wish to find happiness for either of you, you must help him find his faith again before my last lifecycle ends. You must restore the hozho *of the People."*

"How?"

"Do as you have always done. Love him above all else. Remain at his side as his wife." Her features soften. "Tell him the true identity of the boy."

A shiver of terror races over Laura. Tell Kaine who Peter really is? Risk losing her son and whatever feelings Kaine has for her beyond his anger?

"But he doesn't want my love. He shares nothing of himself with me. How am I to know what to do? How—"

The woman holds up her hand to stop Laura's protest. "Listen," she says. "He plays the native flute, the music of the people. It is through his music that you can read the words written on his spirit."

Laura listens to the plaintive notes coming from somewhere beyond her dream. They ring with sorrow, with pain, with need that comes from the soul, with a hunger for happiness. Had she done this to him when she'd left him eight years ago? If she had, then she is certain his pain is her fault, how will she ever heal his emotional wounds?

"Laura, do not be blinded to all else by your emotions. His music does more than speak of what lies hidden inside him. It calls out to the evil ones, the ones who covet his power over nature and man. It is drawing them to what they want most. You must not allow that to happen."

"But how can I stop them?"

"You will know how when the time comes. Walk in beauty, Little One." And the woman vanishes.

✦   ✦   ✦

Laura bolted upright and looked frantically around her. No bright light blinded her or filled the campsite. No woman stood before her. For a moment, she thought she heard the fading strains of flute music as it echoed around the canyon walls, but quickly decided it must be nothing more than the winds whistling through the slot canyons.

She glanced into the darkness beyond the circle of firelight. Her breath caught painfully in her throat. Staring back at her from the inky darkness, malevolence evident in their glowing, red eyes, was the pack of skinwalkers. And this time there was no Shadow to chase them away.

Laura glanced toward Kaine's sleeping bag, it was empty. Icy-cold terror shivered over her entire body.

Squinting, her blood rushing at panic speed through her veins, she scanned the darkness, trying in vain to catch a movement or a sound that would betray Kaine's whereabouts. When she detected nothing, a cold sweat broke out across her forehead. Chills of stark fear shivered down her spine. She clutched at the sleeping bag, pulling it higher against her quaking body, as if by doing so she could use it as a barrier to protect her from the slowly advancing beasts.

A sound from her right drew her attention. Kaine stood just inside the circle of light looking more the savage than her parents could have ever stamped him. His bare, glistening chest rose and fell rapidly. The firelight bounced off it, making him look like a bronze god of war. His bare feet were planted far apart in a stance of defiance. In one hand he held a flute, in the other was a gun, aimed at the leader of the pack, a large, ugly beast whose fangs dripped saliva and whose nasty snarls filled the night air.

When Laura looked back at the pack, she realized that the animals' attention had shifted from her to Kaine.

He is showing them the way to what they want most.

Changing Woman's words played through Laura's head. It suddenly struck her what the woman had been trying to tell her. The skinwalkers wanted Kaine.

Terror such as she'd never known engulfed her. Her stomach heaved. Sour bile filled her throat, and she had to swallow to keep its meager contents where they belonged. Without thinking, she bolted to her feet.

"No, Laura. Stay there."

"But—"

"I said stay there. They want me."

Her gaze fell on the flute clutched in his hand. *It calls out to the evil ones, the ones who covet his power over nature and man*, the woman had said. Cold dread settled over Laura.

"Why? Why do they want you?"

"Because they know that I can—"

His power over nature. A flashing image of Kaine and the bird came to her. "Because you heal animals by simply touching them?"

His gaze darted to her for a split second. Having waited for his chance, the largest of the beasts launched himself at Kaine, catching him off guard. The report of the gun going off split the night. But the bullet missed its target and the gun was knocked from Kaine's hand by the beast's weight. The weapon skittered across the hard-packed earth and stopped several feet beyond where Kaine struggled with the skinwalker. Where the firelight bounced off it, Laura could just see the gun's handgrip.

Kaine had the beast by the throat and was squeezing, keeping its dangerous fangs from finding his flesh, but the claws of each paw flailed at him, tearing his skin from shoulder to elbow. A strangled cry of pain rent the night. It was not an animal, it was Kaine. Laura's knees threatened to buckle. Her stomach churned as blood turned Kaine's upper torso bright red. Every time the beast clawed at him, Laura could feel the agony of Kaine's pain streaking through her, as if the animal tore at her flesh.

She had to do something to stop it, but what? Then she remembered the gun. If she could just get to it.

Thinking only of saving Kaine, Laura ran toward where she'd spotted the gun. As she did so, she was very aware of the other skinwalkers standing by, but none of them seemed interested in her, only the struggle between Kaine and their leader. To her horror, they were beginning to advance slowly, their fangs dripping with the anticipation of joining the fray. If that happened, she would never be able to save Kaine. They'd tear him to shreds before she could shoot them all.

Blocking out the sound of the fierce snarls, Kaine's cries of pain, and her own fears, she snatched up the gun and whirled on the combatants. Hands shaking, she cocked it and pointed it at the two struggling figures. They twisted and turned, making a clean shot impossible for someone with no shooting experience. She stepped closer, hoping to improve the accuracy of her shot. Her hand trembled. She bit her lips and forced herself to hold steady.

What if she hit Kaine? She glanced at the remaining skinwalkers. They were edging ever closer. Soon, they would attack. She'd have to do it soon or lose her chance. But could she?

Adrenalin pumped through her like water over Niagara Falls. This was the man she loved, she had no choice. Locking her knees so they wouldn't give out, she took a deep breath and held it. Then willing her hands not to shake, she took careful aim at the big, hairy head of the animal fighting with Kaine and squeezed the trigger. The reverberation bounced off the canyon walls before fading into the night.

The kick from the discharge had thrown her hands upward, but the bullet had hit its mark. The beast's head snapped to the side then fell limply forward. Its paws slid slowly down Kaine's chest as it slipped from his loosened grasp into a heap on the ground.

The rest of the skinwalkers stopped. Stunned that their leader was dead and perplexed at what to do now, they looked at Kaine; then, by unspoken consent, they turned and ran into the night.

Laura dropped the gun and ran to Kaine, who had collapsed to his knees.

"Nice . . . shot," he said. His face twisted with the pain his words must have cost him.

"I probably would have been better off if I'd shot you instead. At least then I wouldn't have to worry about you getting yourself killed again." She regretted the words the second they'd passed her lips. That had come from the anger at him for risking his life and the fear that she wouldn't be able to save him speaking, not her heart.

"If you'd . . . killed me . . . you'd . . . miss . . . me."

Miss him? My God, how could he joke about it? He'd nearly—

She cut her thoughts short, unwilling to even consider it.

"Shh. Let's get you over to the fire so I can look at

your wounds. Can you help me?"

He nodded and used the little strength left in his legs to raise himself far enough to drape his arm around her shoulders. Together they staggered to the fire. She eased him down on his sleeping bag and then dug through the backpacks for the first-aid kit and one of the canteens.

Kneeling beside him, she poured water on a gauze pad from the first-aid kit and swabbed at the blood pouring from the jagged, raw gashes on his arms and chest. But the blood was erupting from the open wounds faster than she could clear it away. If she didn't get it stopped, he'd die from loss of blood.

His eyes were getting glassy. Shock was setting in.

Laura leaned over him. "Kaine, talk to me. Why in hell did you play that damned flute if you knew it would bring them to us?"

"Stupid. Forgot . . . flute music . . . calls them." His words were so faint she had to almost put her ear on his lips to hear them.

When she turned away to get fresh gauze, his hand gripped her arm with surprising strength.

"Get out . . . of canyon. Go. Leave . . . me."

Laura looked him in the eye, swallowing back the tears gathering in a hard knot in her throat. "I'm leaving this canyon one way, with my son and you by my side." But deep inside her logical medical training told her that if she couldn't staunch the flow of blood soon, the only thing she'd be doing is burying him.

Use the corn pollen. Remember what he told you. It has healing properties.

The voice of the woman from her dream played through her head. Not stopping to question this newest strange occurrence, Laura snatched up her backpack and rummaged through it. In frustration, when she was unable to locate the leather pouch in the tangle of her belongings, she turned it upside down. Its contents tumbled over the ground. Pawing through them, she finally located the small, leather pouch the boy had given her.

She opened it and poured half the contents into her palm. But what did she do with it?

Sprinkle it over the wounds and then cover the pollen with your hands.

Laura did as the woman instructed. The coppery smell of Kaine's blood drifted up in a cloud around her. The warmth of his skin seemed to burn her palms, but she kept them in place. Then she felt pressure on her hands, as if another pair of hands had covered hers.

Suddenly, excruciating pain shot up her arms, filling her body. It radiated out to all her extremities, nearly doubling her over with the force of it. She cried out in abject agony. It felt as if her skin had been peeled away and her entire body had been laid raw. Still, though she tried to pull away, the phantom hands kept hers firmly in place over Kaine's wounds. The pain ravaged her, throbbing through her veins and then, as if by magic, seemed to pass out of her and into the still night.

She repeated the process on each gash, until corn pollen had been applied to all of them. Totally exhausted, she sat back and looked down at the man beside her.

Kaine laid deathly still, his breathing shallow. The blood, mixing with the yellow pollen, turned a deep orange.

Long moments passed while Laura stared at Kaine's chest. To her utter shock, it began to rise and fall in a smooth, rhythmic cadence as opposed to the erratic breathing she'd seen a few moments ago.

He was alive!

But beyond the fact that his respiration had regulated, and he was still alive, she couldn't believe the condition of his wounds. What moments ago had been raw, bleeding, gaping slashes in his flesh were now clogged with coagulating blood and the angry red coloring of the skin around each wound had disappeared. His wounds seemed to be healing before her eyes. She'd never witnessed anything like it in all her years in medicine.

In awe, she picked up the pouch of corn pollen and stared at it. How could something she'd used to make muffins have the power to do this?

"I told you it had healing powers."

Laura spun back to Kaine. He was sitting up smiling at her.

"You should lie down," she protested. "You've lost a lot of blood. You're too weak to sit up yet."

"Do I look weak?"

She had to admit his color was good and the lines of pain had disappeared from his face. "Kaine, I don't understand any of this." She proceeded to tell him about the dream, then about Changing Woman guiding her through healing him with the corn pollen. "But, there's one thing that still puzzles me. She said that the skinwalkers covet your power over nature and man."

Kaine looked away from her, his expression tense. A deep frown marred his normally smooth forehead. His lips tightened into a stubborn line.

Anger bubbled up in her. Obviously, he was not thrilled about having to share any of this with her, but she was not going to settle for his evasiveness this time. She wanted answers, and she wanted them now.

"After what I just went through, what you just went through, I think I deserve a straight answer. What haven't you told me about all this, about you?"

He pushed himself to his feet. She expected him to weave with the weakness left by the loss of blood, but he stood steady and straight and miraculously, seemed to grow even stronger with each passing moment.

"When I was a child, I found that, simply by touching

them, I could heal animals. My mother's father," he went on, inexplicably reverting to the Navajo custom of not speaking the name of the dead, lest you summon their evil spirit, "the *hataałii* of our people, recognized it in me early on. As I grew older, he began teaching me the Ways and ceremonies of the Navajo, how to use my power to help the People." He propped his back against a rock and stared off into the inky night. For a long time, he said nothing. "Some say I would have been more power-ful than him in time." He turned to look directly at her. "They want that power. It would serve them well in heal-ing their own."

Laura waited, sensing there was more to come.

"I lied to you, Laura." He took a deep cleansing breath. "My grandfather wasn't the one who did the *sing* over my mother the night she died."

Silence punctuated by the voices of nature ate up the night. A coyote howled in the distance, reminding Laura of the skinwalkers and sending shivers down her back. The soft night breeze carried in its arms the smell of earth parched by the relentless sun. Behind them, the babble of the slow moving water underlined the stillness.

Laura waited patiently for him to continue. This was the very first time Kaine had shared anything of himself with her, and she was not going to miss one word.

"It was me. I did the *sing*. I did the sandpainting. I laid her pain-wracked body in the middle of the painting. I did the chants and the prayers. I was the one who failed her. I was the one who let her die because I relied on myth and magic and not real medicine."

Laura wasn't sure which had been worse to bear, the painful cries that had issued from him during the fight with the skinwalker or the pain filling his voice now. She rose and went to him. Silently, she encircled him with her arms. Gently, she laid her head against his scarred chest.

"You did what you could, Kaine. When cancer claims a body, especially at the stage your mother had progressed to, there is little anyone can do. It makes no difference if it's *bilagáanaa* medicine or the Navajo Ways." She leaned back and stroked his cheek. "The prognosis is the same. You can't—"

He shrugged away and turned his back to her. "Please, don't say I shouldn't blame myself, because I do. Aside from the fact that I hadn't developed far enough, learned enough to do a *sing* on my own, I knew that my touch only worked on animals. It had never worked on humans. But I did it anyway."

Laura followed and stood in front of him. "Look at me." He reluctantly raised his gaze to meet hers. "Why didn't you call your grandfather?"

"He was away in the mountains performing a Blessingway."

"So what choice did you have? Should you have stood by and do nothing?"

He shook his head and broke eye contact again. "I tried to, but I couldn't."

Laura's heart twisted in her chest. She had never before seen her strong husband so filled with defeat. This was the same man who fought relentlessly for almost a decade for Navajo rights, the same man who did hand-to-hand combat with a huge, hairy beast moments ago.

"Of course you couldn't. She was your mother. You loved her. You would have done everything in your power to save her, but, Kaine," she took his chin and made him look at her, "*it was already too late.*" Hoping to penetrate his blanket of self-blame, she emphasized each of the last five words and then repeated them. "It was too late."

Kaine stared at her for a few moments; then he shook his head, walked away, and collapsed onto his sleeping bag. Laura looked around as though searching for the answers that would convince him he was blameless in his mother's death. Her gaze fell on the spot where the dead skinwalker had fallen. She gasped. The body was gone. In its place was a pool of some kind of black liquid.

"Kaine, look at this."

He sat up, then obviously seeing the distress written on her features, hurried back to her and examined the puddle. "It's his blood. Black because of the evil that fills them. If we leave it, it will contaminate everything around it, and it will draw them back here to feed off it. Get the pouch of corn pollen."

While Laura retrieved the small leather pouch, he knelt and started digging a hole in the hard-packed ground with a stick. When she got back to his side, he was chipping away the earth all around the puddle, then shoving it into the hole. Once he'd removed all trace of the skinwalker's blood, he covered it with corn pollen and shoved the dirt over it, then stamped it down firmly with the heel of his boot.

Kaine handed the pouch back to her and met her gaze. Her face had lost its color, and she was frantically searching the darkness with terrified eyes.

"Laura?"

She swung toward him. "Will they go after Peter?" Her voice was almost a whisper, but so imbued with fear for her son that it tore Kaine's heart wide open.

"No. They won't go after your son. I told you, they want me." He wasn't at all sure that was entirely true, but he couldn't think of any reason, when there were no blood ties between him and Laura's son, that they'd take Peter over him. Even if that were not true, he wouldn't tell Laura and add to her already out of control anxiety.

"Come on. You need to get some sleep." He slipped his arm around her and guided her back toward the fire. Her entire body quivered against him.

"I don't know if I can sleep," she said, her gaze still darting around, searching for the evil that waited just inside the concealing shroud of darkness.

Even though Kaine knew he probable wouldn't get any sleep with Laura so close, he knew what he had to do. He cupped her chin and raised her face to his. "Can you sleep if I hold you?" She paused for a fraction of a second, and then nodded.

Stepping away from her, he unzipped both sleeping bags totally, and then zipped them together to make one big bag. She watched him silently.

When he'd finished, he turned to her and held out his hand. Laura took it and let him lead her to the combined bags.

Minutes later, snuggled against his body spoon fashion, his arm draped over her waist, Laura felt calmer and safer and waited for sleep to come. But it didn't; nor, as time passed and her body began to react to Kaine's closeness, did she think it would.

Her breath began to come harder. Blood pounded through her veins. Squeezing her eyes tightly shut, she willed the sensations to go away and be replaced by peaceful, safe sleep. But they didn't.

She was far too aware of the man tucked in behind her. His arm lying over her waist was like a branding iron reminding her of how many nights she'd lain in her lonely bed wishing for just one more chance to feel him close to her. His body pressed against hers brought to life all the longing, the emptiness she'd lived with for eight long years. His warm breath feathering her neck fanned the dormant fires of passion she'd held at bay for too long.

Then Kaine's fingers began to gently massage her side through her shirt. She fought the tingling that radiated from his touch. How she wanted to turn into his arms and allow him to make love to her. But she couldn't, not as long as the secret of Peter lay between them.

Determined to clear the air and rid herself of the secret she'd carried like a large rock strapped to her conscience, she turned to face him. "Kaine—"

Before she could say more, his mouth covered hers. Desire washed over her like a tidal wave hitting a beach. All thought of anything but Kaine instantly vanished from her mind. She could only feel. His hands stroked over her sides, and then moved slowly, tantalizingly up to cup her breast. His leg slipped between hers to massage the heat building in her lower body.

She prayed for sanity, but it didn't come. In its place came a rush of passion, a need so deep and intense she could not deny it. She wanted Kaine as much as he wanted her. She was tired of fighting the feelings that had lived inside her, imprisoned in her soul for far too long. His touch had cracked the ice surrounding her heart and the warmth of his passion spread through her at an alarming rate.

A groan issued from her, and her hands slid over his naked chest, amazed that all that was left of his wounds were scarred ridges. She found the tiny nubs of his nipples and rolled them between her thumb and forefinger in imitation of what he was doing to her. Her breath caught in her throat. When she could breathe again, his name slipped from her on a sigh of pure pleasure, but she held back. She could not let this happen without clearing the air between them. She had to tell him about Peter.

"Kaine."

"Yes, babe?" Because he was busy nuzzling her neck and sending spasms of desire coursing through her, his voice was muffled. He raised the hem of her blouse and buried his face in her cleavage.

"I need to tell you something."

Lifting his head, he gazed down at her. "Okay." Gently, as he unbuttoned her blouse and each button slipped from its buttonhole, he laved her newly exposed skin.

Laura's body arched of its own will. Her thoughts jumbled together with sensations that tore into her logic, leaving behind only the naked need she felt for Kaine.

Oh, God. I can't think. I can't breath. I can't—

She fought the tidal wave of sensuality drowning her, but her emotions were rioting out of control. She could do no more than concentrate on the insatiable longing radiating through her. It had been so long, so very long since she'd felt his touch, tasted his skin, been devoured by his kisses.

Kaine was battling with his need to take Laura. He was so hard the pain of it nearly drove him crazy. But he couldn't, wouldn't rush this. He wanted to savor every touch, every kiss, every moment.

He looked down at her. The moonlight bathed her skin, turning her to a silvery, shimmering wanton, and God, but he'd dreamed so often of this moment he was afraid the alarm would go off, wake him up, and rob him of it again.

With infinite care, he lowered his mouth to hers. The

memory of its softness in no way lived up to the reality of the hot satin of the real thing. As with the first time he'd kissed her, he played with her lips, nipping and nibbling, tasting and teasing, withdrawing and waiting for her arms to circle his neck and drag him back. When they did, he swept her closer and heard her moan out his name as she captured his mouth and stilled his tormenting love play.

Her body molded to his, branding him for all time with the imprint of the cushion of her breasts, the jut of her hipbone, and the flat plain of her stomach.

Opening her lips, she invited him to explore deeper. He enthusiastically complied. His groan vibrated through him like a guitar string. She tasted of sweet stuff and sunshine, of hot desert days, and cold desert nights, of crackling lightning and wild, stormy winds.

Laura moaned with frustration. His slow seduction was out of sync with the blood racing through her veins with a feral intensity. She wanted Kaine, wanted him now, wanted him without the barrier of clothing, wanted to feel the smooth flesh stretched over his entire muscular body against her naked skin, the hard length of his legs and thighs.

"Easy, baby, easy," he crooned, taking her hands in his, knowing the need driving her matched the one driving him. Warily he held back, aware, despite her reckless display of passion, that she wasn't nearly ready yet. He wanted her wild and begging for him. He battled for control of the demand burning inside him, knowing he could end up consumed in its flames. "There's time."

But there isn't time. Only a handful of days. What had seemed to be an endless eternity a few days ago, when they embarked upon this journey, now seemed a pitifully inadequate period of time in which to fill herself with Kaine.

He unzipped the sleeping bag and pulled her to her feet. She followed mindlessly. The light from the full moon bathed them in shafts of silver radiance.

Keeping his arm around her, Kaine positioned her in front of him, faced her into the moon's light, snaked his arms around her waist, and then slipped his hands over her breast and peeled her blouse from her shoulders, down her arms, and off.

As fingers of hoary light danced over their entwined bodies, he began to slowly massage her engorged nipples and explore her naked flesh. Inch by inch, Kaine continued to memorize her. Then he stepped in front of her and gripped the waistband of her jeans, unzipped them, and peeled them down her legs.

"Step out of them."

She obeyed.

With a quick jerk, the jeans were off and lying on the ground beside them. Kaine devoured her nakedness with his eyes while he caressed her flesh, exciting, titillating, arousing her to heights she'd never known.

"Turn with your back against me."

She did as he instructed.

With excruciating care, he surrounded her with his

embrace and cradled her breasts, lifting them, offering them to the full moon. Laura sucked in her breath and molded her back against him.

"Close your eyes. Imagine the feel of the sun on your skin," he murmured in her ear, his hands smoothing over her. "Absorb it. Use it to warm you when you're alone and cold."

Laura let his words drift over her, remembering each and every sound.

"Smell the perfume of the night-blooming cactus on the breeze. Let it bring the peace of being one with all that's around you."

Doing as he instructed, Laura knew a serenity like none other she'd ever experienced before. It sank into her soul and spread throughout her body.

"Absorb the colors of the earth. Memorize them to call forth when the night hides them in shadow and your world grows dark."

From the far reaches of her mind, Laura understood what Kaine was doing. By using the Navajo tradition of becoming one with all around her, he was preparing her for their inevitable parting. But before she could tell him it didn't have to be that way, he moved his hands over her aching breast and captured a swollen nipple between thumb and forefinger. Laura moaned and closed her eyes.

"No," he commanded softly against the skin of her temple. "Open your eyes. Watch. Watch while my hands worship your beauty."

She did as he asked, finding herself mesmerized by the sight of his long brown fingers kneading her aching flesh.

Kaine fought to control his growing need, fought to keep from throwing her to the ground and hiding himself in her fire. Grasping his control by the throat, he felt like a dam with the mighty river straining to break through the tiniest crack.

It didn't aid his battle in the least when she twisted against him in response to his rubbing the hardened peaks of her breasts in circles against his palm. Nor did it help when she doubled her effort and swayed back more, grinding her body into his groin.

Every muscle and nerve in him stretched to its limit. He closed his eyes and sucked in deep, calming breaths. When a semblance of order had been restored to his chaotic emotions, he ran his palms over her taut stomach.

"Watch, Laura," he coaxed, his hand skimming her abdomen with feathery caresses.

Her sharply inhaled breath went through him like a hot knife. Deliberately he trailed his fingertips over her stomach, taking pleasure from the sensation of the satin-smooth skin beneath his touch. Kaine followed their progress in his mind's eye and had to remind himself to breathe.

Moonlight trickled over Laura, transforming her skin to glittering alabaster. Her body became a sensual collage of shadow and light—a living, breathing, erotic work of art.

"I always thought you should wear nothing but the

moon," he whispered hoarsely, tracing the outline of a slash of light across her navel with his fingertips.

Laura's gaze followed the slow progression of his finger and shivered when it delved into the dimple of skin just below her waist, then moved lower. All day, the desert sun had warmed her flesh, but nothing in comparison to the fire Kaine kindled with his amorous ministrations.

He began stroking the soft pelt of black hair covering the juncture of her thighs. The wild drumbeat of her blood pounding in her temples nearly drowned out her moan of pleasure. Then his palm cupped her intimately. She squirmed against the hard length of him pressing against her buttocks.

Impatient to feel her newly freed body against his with no barriers, she spun in his arms. She leaned forward and traced patterns over his chest with her lips. The smooth skin, now devoid of any trace of his fight with the skinwalker, reminded her of newly tanned suede. His stomach contracted and quivered as her tongue drew wet circles around his tiny nipple buds.

She looked up at him. A muscle twitched in his jaw. His eyes blazed with dark velvet flames. His lips parted slightly, allowing the breath he'd been holding to rush from him. The knowledge that she had produced this reaction in him made her bolder.

A bit mad with desire, she kept her eyes trained on his face and slipped her fingers inside the waistband of his jeans. Kaine stood still as a statue, squeezed his eyes shut, bit his bottom lip, and groaned softly—all the while enduring her sensual, tormenting exploration.

Pleased with the result of her byplay, Laura lowered the zipper slowly. A smile spread across his lips at the same moment her eyes widened in surprise at the brush of coarse hair against her fingers. Kaine wasn't wearing underwear, and he was thoroughly enjoying her shocked discovery of that fact.

Laura hooked her fingers in his belt loops, squatted, and stripped his jeans to around his ankles. Her hair brushed his groin. He sucked in a sharp breath. She smiled smugly. Wanting to enjoy her triumph, she glanced up at him and, instead of staring into his dark eyes, came face to face with his rampant arousal.

Her mind turned to scrambled mush. Her breath remained trapped somewhere between her lungs and her throat. Jelly invaded her knees. Her heart pounded against the wall of her chest. Just as she felt herself nearing collapse, Kaine's strong hands grabbed her under the arms and drew her to her feet.

She'd barely had time to catch her breath before his mouth descended on hers in a scorching kiss. She could never remember kissing a man who did it with such thorough intent. Kaine kissed her as if his very life depended on sucking all the nourishment he could from her mouth. Their entwined tongues imitated the age-old motion of the mating ritual, darting, withdrawing, thrusting.

Groaning, she leaned against his nakedness, feeling

the pressure of his aroused heat nudging her belly. His hands captured the globes of her buttocks, lifting her into the cradle of his thighs and then lowering her slowly, excruciatingly slowly.

Laura stepped a bit away and let her gaze wander over him. Such a beautiful specimen of the male animal, all bulging muscle and smooth skin, a flesh-and-blood Michelangelo statue. An abundant thatch of blue-black fur formed a "V" at the base of his flat stomach, from which protruded the visual proof of his state of excitement. Corded muscles rippled with strength down the length of his legs. For all his blatant masculinity and hard plains, she knew he moved with the fluid, deliberate, tomcat-like grace of a well-honed athlete.

Their naked bodies glowed, haloed in the silvery rays of the moon, brought her to a fever pitch. She was sure she couldn't stand any more, but she was wrong. Kaine dropped to his knees and rained kisses over her stomach. Leaving behind a trailing path of moisture to be cooled by the night air, he laved his way from her navel to her collarbone.

"Kaine!" His name left her lips carrying a desperate plea.

"Enough sightseeing," he growled. He swung her into his arms, carried her to the sleeping bag, and placed her on it.

For a moment, Kaine could only stare down at her, hypnotized by her exquisite body. His hungry gaze traveled the length of her, stopping briefly to appreciate the swell of her engorged breasts, the hourglass curve of her waist, the downy hair concealing the core of her femininity, and the luscious legs that never seemed to end. At that moment, he understood fully what it meant to *walk in beauty*. Laura did it daily, inside and out, without giving it conscious thought.

"Kaine?"

He blinked and took the hand she offered, allowing her to pull him down beside her. He lay back and pulled her close. "I can't get my fill of looking at you." Rolling toward her, he closed his lips over hers before she could reply.

Laura wrapped her loving arms around him, holding on with all her strength. She surrendered to the flood of passion being generated by his hand finding the moist heat between her thighs. She wiggled closer. The savage sensations buffeting her were overwhelming. One second she wanted him to stop the exquisite torture, the next she wanted it to go on forever. Finally, she settled on one word that said it all.

"Please."

His voice was as breathless as hers when he answered. "Soon, baby, soon."

His head dipped, and his mouth captured the turgid peak of her breast, then he covered the swollen mounds with light, biting kisses. As his lips worshipped her breasts, his hands and fingers danced over her squirming body, touching, probing, exploring hidden creases and leaving a path of fire in their wake.

Only when he was satisfied that she could stand no more did Kaine lower himself gently between her separated knees and enter the haven of her body.

Laura's eyes snapped open. She'd forgotten the size and strength of him. Her fingers dug into the muscles of his back, muscles hardened with leashed strength. Feeling untamed and wildly out of control, Laura wanted Kaine to feel the same. Urging him on with her hands and body, she told him of her need. He thrust into her with the intense power of a desert storm.

Together they rode the whirlwind of sensation, climbing higher and higher on the boiling air around them. When Laura was sure she'd die from the building tension, it exploded in a shower of light and sensation, tossing them over the edge, leaving them trembling with the force of the aftershock.

Filled with the wonder of what he'd just taken part in, Kaine struggled to breathe. Never in his life had he experienced anything that equaled making love to Laura. It went far beyond any fantasies, into a world most men only dream of exploring.

Rolling off her, he gathered her pliant body close.

Laura labored to catch her breath. She clung to him and let the moment stretch out, needing his closeness, needing to keep this fantasy from ending. And fantasy it was because as the afterglow of their passion diminished, a new need assailed her, the need, now that sanity had returned and she could think clearly, to hide from what she knew she had to do. If they were ever to pass beyond the physical need to a deeper understanding and love of each other, she had to clear the air between them.

The thought that she was about to destroy the best thing that had happened to her in the last eight years quickly robbed her of the joy of the past moments. She took a deep, shuddering breath.

"You okay?" he murmured close to her ear.

As the moment of truth came ever closer, she hesitated to say what she knew she must, wanting to scream to the heavens that this wasn't fair. But, in her heart, she knew she'd perpetuated this lie, and she had to make it right.

"I'm fine," she lied, her voice lacking conviction.

With the tip of his finger, Kaine tilted her head back from his shoulder to look into her eyes. "Why do I hear a *but* hanging on the end of that?"

With every moment she allowed to pass, her resolve grew weaker. But with every day that passed without him knowing, Kaine would hate her more. She couldn't put it off any longer.

"I have something to tell you."

Searching frantically for the words to tell Kaine that he had a son, Laura sat up and pulled her knees beneath her chin. Was there an easy way to say this? Was there a painless way to tear out Kaine's heart? In the end, she knew that she had to just say it before her courage deserted her. To continue to keep it hidden only made it harder on both of them. She took a deep breath and blurted it out.

"Peter is your son, Kaine."

For an eternal moment, Kaine said nothing, made no movement. With her back to him, she couldn't even read his expression.

The night closed in around her, suffocating her. The Earth seemed to have paused on its axis, waiting for him to react. The sounds of the night creatures had stopped. Even the intermittent breeze hid somewhere beyond the canyon walls. Laura held onto the frail, if unreasonable, hope that his unbroken silence meant he was taking the news better than she'd expected.

Kaine bolted upright, grabbed her shoulders and turned her to face him. His fingers bit hard into her flesh. His face, even in the moonlight, had lost some of its color. The only expression on it was anger so intense that it made Laura flinch away.

"What do you mean Peter's my son? How can that be?"

"It's true. I was pregnant when I left you." Laura took a deep fortifying breath. She made no move to pull away. Somehow, she felt she deserved the pain. "I was so excited when I found out. I couldn't wait to tell you. I waited for you to come home, and waited and waited, but you never came."

"I did, eventually," he bit out.

"*Eventually*?" Laura's long unresolved anger washed away her fear, her trepidation and came to her defense. "How long was I supposed to wait, Kaine? You see, I had no idea exactly how long *eventually* was? Is it a year, a week, a month? Never?"

He shot to his feet and stood before her, hands on his hips, feet spread, anger shooting from his eyes. He was still naked and looked pure savage to the bone. "So, you just walked away?" he ground out.

His nakedness reminded her of the beauty that they had just shared. Her heart felt as though it had been torn from her body and trampled upon. She threw his jeans at him, pulled the sleeping bag around her own nakedness, and stood to face him. "No, I didn't *just* walk away. It was the hardest decision I've ever had to make."

He pulled his jeans on, zipped them, and looked back at her, his intense anger still evident in every line of his face and body. "Tell me something, Laura, how *hard* was it to decide not to tell me about my son?"

There was no point in trying to make him understand the hell she'd gone through wanting to run back to him, but knowing he didn't love her, wanting to tell him the news of his child, but wondering if he'd even care about a child that would forever connect him to a woman he didn't love. Connected by their child, but with a gulf so deep and so wide separating them that they would never be able to bridge it.

The chasm of loss that opened inside Laura swallowed her anger. "Kaine, can't we talk calmly about this and put the anger aside? Can't we find someway to forgive each other . . . for Peter's sake?" *And ours*, she added silently.

"Forgive you? Talk calmly?" He paced back and forth and ran his fingers through his hair, agitation evident in each movement. "First off, you've robbed me of my son's childhood. You've robbed him of a heritage he should be proud of."

"No. I never did that. Ada taught Peter all about the Navajo and their beliefs and Ways. He knows who he is, where his roots originated, Kaine. He's your son in every sense of the word."

"In every sense except knowing me, talking with me,

sharing his life with me." Kaine stared at her, and then threw his head back as if to find his thoughts in the star-studded sky. "You have no conception of what you've done, do you?" He looked back at her, his eyes glowing with barely controlled anger. "You've just lost your son."

She stared at him dumbstruck and then his words sank in.

My God, he's really going to take Peter from me.

"No! I can't lose him. He's all I have."

"You should have considered that before." His voice held not one ounce of compassion. "Who else knows I'm Peter's father?"

She frowned. "Just Ada and my friend, Anne Yatzee. Why?"

"Two total strangers knew before I did. Nice, Laura."

"Anne was my friend when I desperately needed some-one to talk to. I'm not sure I would have gotten through the time after Ada's death without her. And no matter what you say, Kaine, Ada or Changing Woman was *never* a stranger to you. She's been part of your life since the day you discovered there was something wonderfully dif-ferent about you."

He turned away from the truth of her words and the plea in her eyes. He didn't give a damn that other people knew he was Peter's father before he did. Yes, it stung, but right now, he had other concerns that trumped that one by a mile. Her words had brought to mind all the things that had taken place over the past few days. It sent a foreboding chill coursing through him.

Because of her selfishness, Laura may well have signed Peter's death warrant, *his son's* death warrant. If the skinwalkers found Peter before they did, and they knew that Peter was his son, they would kill Peter believing he had inherited his father's powers as Kaine had inherited his grandfather's. Oddly, by keeping her secret, Laura just may have saved Peter's life. Then again, if at least one of the other two people that knew were skinwalkers, and if the skinwalkers were still after Kaine, it might mean that they had not yet found Peter. They might still have time to find Peter, and protect him.

If they found his son, the thought of what the beasts would do made Kaine shudder. His blood turned icy cold. He knew the process well. They would kill the boy and then grind his bones into corpse dust to sprinkle on the wounds of their fellow beasts.

"Did Peter ever show any signs of being able to do things that . . . that other kids couldn't?"

"You mean did Peter have any powers like yours?"

He nodded.

"No, not that I'm aware of. Why? And why did you ask about Ada and Anne? What do they have to do with this?"

"I just wondered how much my son had inherited from me besides his bloodlines." Thank goodness, it had, as it sometimes did, seemingly skip a generation, leaving Peter free of the powers that would attract the skinwalkers.

But it also made him vulnerable. If they found him, real-ized who he was and that he had no power, and then they would kill him anyway. Either way, their son was in mor-tal danger.

As angry as he was at Laura for keeping this secret from him for eight years, for robbing him of his son's first years, for allowing him to think he had been fathered by some stranger who impregnated Laura then deserted her, he could not tell her that the skinwalkers might be stalk-ing Peter. Not even he could be that cruel. Besides, if they were to find Peter in time, he didn't need a hysterical mother holding him back.

"What about Anne and Ada?" Laura asked again, rousing him from his thoughts.

"Nothing. I just wondered how many people had the privilege of knowing something you didn't see fit to share with me." He grabbed the combined sleeping bags and un-joined them, tossing one her way. Re-zipping his own, he spread it out and climbed inside, turning his back to her.

"Kaine?"

"Go to sleep, Laura."

When Kaine shook Laura roughly awake, she felt as if she'd just closed her eyes, but obediently crawled slowly from the warm sleeping bag into the cool morning air. Though the sky overhead had lightened with the rising sun, daylight had not yet reached into the narrow canyon. Deep shadows still sprawled across the rusty ground. The chill air trapped between the stone walls seeped into her bones and made her shiver. The fire had gone cold and no coffee waited to stir her awake. The knapsacks sat at Kaine's feet, packed and ready to go. He stood over her like avenging angel.

"Let's go."

Laura pulled herself to her feet, stared at his set profile for a moment, and did what she had to do to get ready to leave. Only minutes later, she was trudging over rocks and boulders, as they climbed higher and higher along the canyon wall.

"Why are we going up?" she called to his stiff back.

"This part of the terrain is full of slot canyons," he explained without stopping or turning back to her. His tone had again become the impersonal one he'd use when addressing a tourist. "I heard thunder in the distance this morning and if it rains, there's the danger of a flashflood. We need to get above the flood line." He pointed at a dark, horizontal mark in the canyon wall above them that evidently had been made by high water. Then he went silent again.

The pace Kaine set was rigorous and faster than any they had kept since starting out. Between the extra physical activity they had undertaken last night, and the lack of sleep or any breakfast, Laura was finding it difficult to keep up. A few times, Kaine disappeared from her line of vision, and she had to hurry to make sure she didn't lose him.

Periodically, she heard the rumbling of thunder growing closer and closer and was reminded of Kaine's words about the danger of a flashflood. She trusted his judgment, but had to wonder why, when the thunder was miles away, they had to worry about flooding where they were. She glanced up.

The canyon had narrowed a lot since they'd set out that morning. At this point it wasn't more than ten feet to the other wall. What she could see of the sky above them was pure blue, not a cloud in sight. When she looked back at the trail ahead of her, Kaine had disappeared again, and she had to put all thought of the distance storm out of her mind and concentrate on putting one tired foot in front of the other to catch up.

By the time they stopped to eat lunch, Laura was ready to sell her soul to the devil for a moment's rest and some food.

"This will have to do," Kaine explained, handing her a package of trail mix and a slice of beef jerky. "We don't have time to build a fire or to engage in a long, leisurely lunch, so eat fast. We're still too far below the flood line."

If Laura hadn't learned anything else in her time on this journey, it was that an object that appeared to be just a few moments away could take hours to reach; and that it might not be possible to do so by traveling in a straight line. They'd stumbled along a horizontal trail that either rose or ascended slowly along the face of the canyon walls. Sometimes the trail was clear and easygoing, but mostly it was littered with boulders that had to be skirted in a wide arc—or they had to pass through crevices so constricted that Laura had to turn sideways to make it through them.

Amazed that she could still read Kaine's thoughts to a certain degree, she realized that something more than a possible flashflood was bothering him. He was tense, jumpy. As he ate, his gaze darted around them, as if searching for something . . . or on guard against something.

It couldn't be the skinwalkers. He'd said they only travel and attack under the cover of darkness. What did he see out there—or not see—that she was not aware of?

She found herself also glancing around in search of whatever it was Kaine expected to find. Her gaze stopped on a crevice in the canyon wall behind them that she hadn't seen when they first sat down.

Towering about five feet above them and no more than a few feet wide, its walls had been worn smooth by the wind. They swirled with the hues of the canyon—various shades of brown, orange, and rusty red, as if an artist had stirred his paints in a bowl and then painstakingly applied the resulting mixture of colors to the sandstone. It made her want to run her hands over it to see if it was as smooth as it looked.

"It looks beautiful, but it's as treacherous as a rattle snake."

Kaine's voice roused her from her contemplation of

the slot canyon. She shot him a curious look. "Why?"

As if on cue, thunder rumbled much closer this time.

Kaine jumped to his feet. "If that turns into what I think it will, you'll soon see." After grabbing their backpacks, he vaulted to his feet and began to run.

He looked back in time to see Laura just standing there. "Move!" he bellowed, hoping to jar her from her stunned state.

Seconds later, a muffled rumble too close to be thunder came from above. It grew louder by the second, until it echoed around the canyon and filled his ears with the noise. He looked up in time to see a cascade of muddy water carrying logs and other debris pouring from the slot canyon above their heads. It was headed straight at Laura and gaining speed as it cascaded down the walls.

"Run, Laura!"

Kaine watched in horror while Laura remained rooted to the spot, transfixed by the surging water. Then she seemed to arouse and started running toward him. Again she stopped, backtracked and fumbled with something on the ground. Her foot slipped, and she sank to her knees. Her gaze flew to him.

"My foot's stuck." Panic filled her voice.

He darted to her. Reaching out, Kaine snatched her foot free and ignored her sharp cry of pain. He scooped her into his arms and headed for a large rock to take cover—just as the water descended upon the spot they'd occupied moments before.

He clambered over the rough surface and onto another rock balanced atop the first one, putting them well beyond the flow of the storm's water. But they couldn't stay there. The water would collect in the narrow canyon and fill it fast. They needed to be higher.

"Can you walk?"

Laura tried to put her weight on her injured ankle and grimaced. Tears filled her eyes. "No."

Kaine slung the backpacks onto either shoulder and then lifted Laura in his arms. She clung to his neck. He glanced back at the water gathering in the canyon. It was rising fast. Logs and tree limbs and other debris swirled in it like a giant, boiling pot of mud. If anyone caught in it didn't drown first, they'd be beaten to death by whatever the floodwaters had collected on their way here.

"Hang on," he instructed and began climbing higher.

Laura could feel his bunched muscles straining to carry his added burden. His breathing was labored. Sweat broke out on his forehead and trickled down his neck to be absorbed in the collar of his shirt, causing an ever-widening dark patch to appear on the material.

She could feel Kaine's pace slowing. His muscles must be screaming. How long could he keep up the pace, bear the weight?

She looked back over his shoulder. The water was within feet of them. Would this be how they'd die, together, drowned in water so thick with mud it had the consistency of brown pea soup? And if they died what would happen to Peter?

Then, as suddenly as it had started, the slot canyon stopped spewing water into the gorge. Miraculously, the water level began to slowly recede.

"It's stopping," she said.

Kaine placed her on the ground and bracing his hands on his knees, bent double, trying to catch his breath. When his respiration had turned to a semblance of normalcy, he turned to Laura.

"Why in hell didn't you run when I told you to?" His breathing was becoming less forced.

"I lost this." She held up her hand. From it dangled a pendant. The sun caught and glittered in the polished silver and the rainbow inlays. "Changing Woman gave it to me at the fair."

Kaine had all he could do to keep from screaming at her that she was putting way too much credence on the myths. There was no solid proof that any of this was connected to a supernatural world. No sooner had the thought passed through his mind than another followed on its heels.

Fool. Why must you see to believe, Kaine Cloudwalker? Will you wait until my lifecycle is over and you've lost everything before you believe?

Kaine shook away the voice. Laura was infecting him with her crazy belief in the Navajo gibberish. He turned to where she had collapsed after their escape from the flood.

She was slumped against a boulder. Her eyes were

tightly closed; one hand clutched her ankle, and the other clutched that damned pendant. Pain had stolen the color from her face. At first, he thought the pain in her ankle, the adrenalin rush brought on by their dash to safety, and their close call with the floodwater had drained her of all strength. Then he noticed the stream of blood running down her cheek.

Quickly, he tipped her head back and looked at her face. A long, ugly gash marred her forehead. She must have hit her head when she fell. The cut wasn't bad, but because it was a head wound, it bled profusely. He fished into the backpack and extracted the first-aid kit.

Encircling her with his arm, he pressed her head into the crook of his shoulder and applied the gauze pad against the gash until the bleeding stopped. As he held her, he gazed down at her. His heart twisted. What if he hadn't been able to pull her to safety? What if he'd lost her again, but this time for good?

Though it didn't remove it completely, the thought served to take some of the sting from finding out that Peter was his son. It seemed that no matter what this woman did, he could not totally rid himself of her. She remained inside him like a festering sore that shot pain through his soul whenever he came too close to her and opened a gaping hole when she wasn't. But, hands down, the pain of not having her at all was infinitely worse.

"What happened to my head?" she asked, feeling at the spot from which a sharp pain radiated on her forehead.

"You must have hit your head when you fell."

She suddenly realized his arm was wrapped tightly around her, and her head was resting against his shoulder. Was there a chance that he'd forgiven her? Though she knew she should, she didn't move.

"I'll bandage it and wrap your ankle and then we need to move on."

Kaine straightened her, removed his arm from around her, and found the gauze and tape to cover her wound; then he wrapped an elastic bandage around her ankle.

"Can you put this back on for me?" Laura held up the pendant.

Kaine took it and felt the comforting warmth that seemed to radiate from it up through his fingers, stealing away the anxiety of having almost lost Laura to the flood and then seeing her wounded. He dismissed it as being a result of the warmth of her skin still on the metal. Inexplicably eager to get it out of his grasp, he fastened it around her neck.

When he'd finished, he stood. "Let's go."

"Thanks." Laura pulled herself to her feet with the help of his outstretched hand. Then she looped her arm around his waist. He balanced her with his arm around her, and they started off down the path, looking, she was sure, much like they were entering a three-legged race.

✤   ✤   ✤

For the rest of the day, even after she protested that she could walk on her own and he released her, Kaine moved at a slower pace, making it easy for Laura to keep up with him. When the late-afternoon sun began painting long, dark shadow-fingers on the progressively narrowing canyon, he stopped to make camp. Without the sun, the air became chilled very fast, and Laura grabbed her sweatshirt from her backpack and slipped it over her head.

"We'll probably reach Rainbow Arch by later afternoon tomorrow." Kaine didn't look at her when he spoke. Nor did he say what she knew must be on his mind. Her injured ankle would slow them down. She'd inadvertently done what she had pledged not to do when they started out on their trek. Going back for the pendant had been foolish, but she couldn't leave it behind. Now, not only they, but also Peter, would suffer for her foolishness.

Kaine spread the sleeping bags on either side of the firepit, in which a blazing fire shot sparks toward the heavens. Outside the fire's illumination, dark shadows surrounded them, blinding them to what lay beyond their vision. Laura sidled closer to the firelight.

Kaine's cold demeanor made her almost afraid to ask. "What happens when we reach the arch?"

"We start the real search for your . . . our son."

His words went through her heart like a sharp knife. A muffled noise from somewhere beyond the lighted campsite made her jump and stare into the inky night. Shivering and trying to keep her overactive imagination at bay, she eyed the sleeping bags. "Kaine?"

"Hmm."

"Do you think the . . . the skinwalkers will come back tonight?"

"They might. There's no way of knowing for sure."

Unsure of what kind of reaction she'd get from him, Laura hesitated to ask what was on her mind. But her fear of the shaggy beasts that had torn Kaine apart overcame her trepidation of his reaction.

"I know you're very angry with me, but I'd sleep much better if we could . . ." She glanced at the sleeping bags, then at Kaine.

Without speaking, he strode to the firepit and moved the bags so they were aligned parallel to each other on one side of the fire.

"Thanks." She flashed him a weak smile.

He ignored her.

✦   ✦   ✦

Laura had only been asleep for what seemed a short time, when she awoke. She had the strange sensation she was being watched. Slowly, she opened her eyes a slit. Standing over her was a large, black, hairy animal. It was close enough that she could feel its warm breath fanning her face.

Laura tensed, waiting for the animal to spring. Her heart stopped beating. Her hands clutched at the inside of the sleeping bag. She wanted to scream, but her voice was trapped inside her constricted throat.

Suddenly, the animal bent toward her. Her eyes flew wider, and she sat up. Before she could pull away, it licked her cheek. The animal was on eye level with her. Its black coat would have blended in with the night except for the sunburst of white on its chest. If it had been a white dog, she would have sworn it was. . . .

"Shadow?" she whispered.

The dog's tail began to beat the air furiously, and it licked her face again, then turned and raced away, blending into the darkness.

"Kaine," she cried, shaking his shoulder.

He came awake instantly and bolted upright. Automatically, he scanned their surroundings. "What? Is it them?"

She laughed. "No. Shadow's back . . . sort of."

"Shadow? Sort of?" Again, he scanned the campsite as far as the meager firelight would allow. "I don't see him. Are you sure you weren't dreaming?"

"No. He licked my face. It was him, but he's black now."

"Black?" Anxiety rather than the surprise or disbelief Laura had expected filled Kaine's voice.

As if to give validity to the claim, the black dog came bounding out of the shadows. In his mouth, he carried something red and white. He dropped it on Laura's sleeping bag.

"Oh, my God!" She felt the blood drain from her face. Her hands began to shake uncontrollably.

"What? What is it?" Kaine grabbed the piece of cloth, shook it out and held it up to the firelight. It was a small boy's polo shirt.

"It's Peter's," Laura whispered.

Chapter 13

Kaine's gaze flitted from the shirt to the dog. He was finding it harder with each passing day not to give Laura's theories about Changing Woman credence. Telling himself it was all her imagination wasn't working anymore, if it ever had. He couldn't deny the truth of his own abilities to heal animals. There were a great many people who looked at that with skepticism.

But if he was so good at healing animals, why hadn't he been able to save the life of one of the people he'd loved most in this world? Why hadn't he been able to save his mother? If there was a logical explanation hidden somewhere in the Navajo Ways, he'd missed that lesson.

"What do you think it means?" Laura asked, her gaze glued to the shirt Kaine held, tears choking her voice.

He handed the shirt back to her. She placed it against her cheek and rubbed the material against her skin, as though by doing so, she could conjure Peter from wherever he was.

"It means I have to get my head out of my ass and start paying attention to the signs."

A beginning, he told himself. Reading the signs didn't mean he had to believe the rest of the mumbo-jumbo. Reading the signs didn't mean he would trust the life of a loved one to a few words sung over them and a picture drawn in the sand.

"We better get some sleep," he said and drew her down to the sleeping bag. She didn't resist. When she was supine again, she tucked Peter's shirt beneath her face. "Relax. You need sleep, and so do I. Shadow will keep watch until morning." The dog barked, as if to verify his promise. Kaine could feel Laura's fear in every tense line and muscle of her body. He drew her, sleeping bag and all, against him. Leaning close to her ear, he cradled her in his arms and whispered, "He's mine now, too. I won't let anything happen to him. You don't have to do it alone anymore. We'll find him together."

✤　✤　✤

The next morning, Laura didn't need Kaine to wake her. She'd been unable to close her eyes all night for worry about their son. How easily that rolled off her tongue now. Besides, she didn't want to leave the safety of Kaine's embrace. But she had to wonder if the change in Kaine the night before would last and did it mean he'd forgiven her for keeping her precious secret from him?

The sun was low enough in the morning sky that the canyon had not yet been blessed with its warmth and light. Cold air lay against the ground, sending icy chills through Laura. Shadow lay where he'd been all night, at their feet, his ears perked and twitching with the slightest sound.

Careful not to wake Kaine, Laura slipped one arm from the sleeping bag, grabbed a log from the stack Kaine had placed near the fire, and threw it onto the glowing embers. Moments later it caught, and she added another log until the warmth from the blaze eased the chill from the air, and she could climb out of the sleeping bag.

Shadow escorted her to a nearby rock and waited until she was ready to return to the fire. As quietly as possible, she prepared a pot of coffee and set it on the fire to brew. While it cooked, she curled up beside Kaine on her sleeping bag.

Careful not to wake him, she shifted her head slowly to see the face of the sleeping man. His lack of eye movement told her his slumber was deep. Taking advantage of his oblivious state, she enjoyed her view. His black hair, mussed from a night's sleep, lay in scattered disarray over his forehead. His full lips, slightly parted, allowed a soft whisper of air to escape with each deep breath he took. His free arm was bent at the elbow, his hand palm-up beside his cheek.

He's beautiful, she thought, drinking in the picture

of him at peace, his tanned face relaxed, his wide brow smoothed over. The temptation to press her lips to his nearly overwhelmed her, but she feared waking the sleeping savage. Lying here beside a man who could devour her with his seductive charm awoke a need in Laura that cried out to him in silence. And even though everything in her yearned to kiss him awake, if the change in him last night had only been brought on by sympathy, then she'd rather not know.

"See anything you like?" His sleepy question startled her.

Her gaze darted to his eyes—soft, dark, sexy, and filled with a silent invitation. She could see her reflection in them, as if she was trapped forever inside this man, and she was beginning to believe that was more truth than fancy. His full lips curved in a half-smile. Her insides did a flip and then tried in vain to right themselves.

"Uh...." Laura fought to find an excuse for what she'd been caught doing, but none came. "I was just . . . just—"

He reached for her. She tried to pull away, but her strength was so pitiful compared to his. "I know what you were doing, and I liked it. I like having you look at me, imagining what it would be like to have me inside you again." He pulled her down and captured her mouth with his.

When he finally released her, she was breathless. Thoughts swirled through her head like a child's kaleidoscope, changing and shifting form and logic. His velvety gaze assessed her reaction, held her prisoner, daring her to deny what she'd just felt in his arms.

The *hiss* of coffee hitting the fire's hot coals broke the spell. She sprang to her feet.

Kaine chuckled softly and rolled to his back and watched Laura prepare coffee for both of them. The morning breeze lifted her long, loose hair from her shoulders and blew it behind her like a raven's wing in full flight. She hadn't changed clothes from the ones she'd slept in, merely retied her blouse beneath her breasts. When she raised her arms, the movement pulled the hem up, exposing the flesh he'd explored so many times and ached to taste now. Her face glowed with the heat from the fire. And those criminally long legs of hers still went on forever.

God, but she is lovely!

A cautious reminder to keep a distance between them followed immediately. *Like you did last night?* he reminded himself, disgusted with his show of weakness. But he also remembered the feel of her curvaceous body snuggled into the cradle of his hips.

Stop it! Comforting her is one thing, but letting her climb inside your skin again is another. There's no room in your life for the complications she can bring, the hurt, the pain knifing through a heart too broken to fight back.

Still. . . . He squashed the notion before it had time to mature into another gut-wrenching vision and turned away.

One bruised heart in a lifetime is enough for any man,

even a dumb Indian.

He took the cup of coffee she offered him and sipped cautiously at the steaming brew.

Laura stood in front of him, silhouetted by the few rays of light seeping over the canyon rim. He couldn't see her eyes, but knew they were centered on him. He could feel there intensity go straight to his heart. Letting his gaze travel over her, he memorized the curves and valleys of her body. With her hair tangled by the wind and her lower lip caught between her teeth, she looked the way she must have looked when she was twelve and the only thought in her head was getting money for a weekend movie with her friends. How he wished he'd known her back then.

Kaine wanted to reach out to her and pull her into the safety of his arms, to promise her nothing would ever hurt her again as long as he had a breath of life in him.

The thoughts careening through his mind and the raw-boned terror they produced in him were the only thing that stopped him. He'd done the stupidest thing he could have under the circumstances. But then, he conceded, only a dumb Navajo with no regard for his heart and its safety would fall in love all over again with the one woman who couldn't or wouldn't share his world, a woman who had kept the birth of the only child he may ever have from him.

He'd be a fool to even think they could have anything together again. There were just too many hurts, too many lies standing between them. He couldn't risk the hurt again.

Shadow came to stand beside him. He looked into the dog's eyes. *They are far too intelligent for any animal,* Kaine thought.

Suddenly, words he'd pushed from his thoughts came hurtling back through his memory.

"The fool stays awake, afraid to dream and risks nothing. In the end, he has nothing. The wise man welcomes sleep and risks all by stepping into the eye of the dream. When he emerges, he brings with him wisdom, strength and a full heart. Step into the eye of your dream, Kaine Cloudwalker, before it is too late."

Followed quickly on the heels of the words were reminders. Shadow, whom Laura believed to be Changing Woman in animal form, had first appeared to them as a white dog. Then there was the turquoise bird that Kaine had healed, and by doing so revealed his gift to Laura. Laura had told him about a dream she'd had the night before last in which Changing Woman's clothing had transformed into an abalone-colored dress. And now, Shadow was back, black as jet, the final phase of Changing Woman's lifecycle.

Had he already waited too long? Had his stubborn temper and injured feelings already cost him everything?

Shadow's piercing bark startled Kaine from his thoughts. The dog was standing before him holding Peter's shirt in his teeth.

✣　　✣　　✣

Laura spent the next day trying to force all manner of gory scenarios that involved Peter from her mind, but with little success. Although she kept pace with Kaine, who moved at a speed to accommodate her injured ankle, her mind was not on the increasingly precarious trail or the canyon that had become more a wide crevice than any canyon she'd ever seen, but on her son.

Had the skinwalkers found him? Was that why his shirt was left behind? Was Peter alive? How long ago had Peter been here? Had they carried his dead and maimed body off somewhere where she'd never find it?

Questions with no answers tumbled through her thoughts. With each one, she became increasingly more desperate and her despair of ever finding Peter grew by leaps and bounds. The one thing that kept her from screaming out her fears and anxieties was the pendant she kept clutched in her hand. Its comforting warmth calmed her as much as any mother who had lost her only child could be pacified.

By the time Kaine took their first break, Laura's despair felt like someone had placed one of the boulders from this desolate country square atop her shoulders. She dropped heavily to a rock protruding from the side wall of the canyon. Clutching her hands in her lap, she lowered her gaze to them and fought to clear her mind.

Shadow came to sit beside her. Occasionally, he

nudged her arm with his wet nose, as though trying to rouse her from her lethargy. Absently, she stroked his dark fur.

"Laura, what is it?"

Kaine's voice roused her from her dark thoughts. She glanced at him, bit her lip and shook her head, afraid to put her fears into words.

He sat beside her and encircled her slumped shoulders with his arm. "Talk to me."

"It's all so hopeless," she finally managed to get out, controlled tears making her voice tight. "Just look around." She waved her hands to encompass the desolate but beautiful landscape. "It's full of crevices and cliffs and all kinds of places Peter could be. We could walk right past him and never see him." Her shoulders sagged. She'd never felt so totally without hope in her life. "We'll never find him, will we?"

"Yes, we *will*," Kaine said, squeezing her shoulder reassuringly. "We *will* find him and soon. You can't give up hope. You've been stronger than any woman I know until know. Don't let go of that strength. Don't give in to your doubts and fears. Don't underestimate yourself."

Laura looked at him through the glaze of moisture that had gathered in her eyes. Did he really see her as strong? At the moment, she didn't feel anything like the woman who had stood up to the Navajo Tribal Police Lieutenant or to her angry estranged husband. She felt more like she'd been caught in a stampede of enraged buffalo intent on pounding her into the ground.

She smiled weakly. "You're a fine one to be telling me not to doubt myself." She pushed a lock of hair off Kaine's forehead, and then trailed her fingertips over his high cheekbone.

How much of him is in Peter! The same jet-black, straight-as-an-arrow hair; the same high cheekbones of his ancestor; the same dark eyes with tiny flecks of amber dancing through them like playful stars in a night sky. Will I ever see them standing side by side? By cheating Kaine of his son's childhood, have I robbed him of the opportunity to know him forever?

"Stop it." Kaine shook her. His voice was stern but compassionate. "We'll find him. You have to trust me on that. He's *our* son, and we'll find him together and bring him home. You can't let any other thought take precedence over that. *We* will *bring our son home.*" He cupped her face in his palms. "I want to meet my son, and I will not let anything happen to him before I do."

Kaine's words bit deep into Laura's heart. She had been so unfair to him by not letting him be part of Peter's life.

She stared deep into Kaine's eyes. "I am so very sorry for keeping Peter from you. I was wrong, and you'll never know how deeply I regret it." A lone tear trickled down her cheek. "Please forgive me and please don't hate me, Kaine."

If Kaine's heart had been cast in steel, at the look of total remorse in Laura's eyes, it would have split open like a newborn bird's egg. He pulled her into his arms and cradled her head against his wide chest. "I was hurt and angry because you kept it from me. I still am to a certain extent. I wanted to hurt you back, to make you suffer the way I had in those few minutes after you told me I had a son. But since then, I've realized that being angry at you was not going to bring back the eight lost years." He pushed her away from him and held her at arm's length so he could look into her eyes. "But even amidst all that anger and thoughts of revenge, I have never, ever hated you."

He released her and stood. While she tucked Peter's shirt into her backpack, Shadow bounded to his feet, tail wagging, ready to set off again.

Kaine held out his hand. "Come on, let's go find our son."

For the most part, Laura felt better for the rest of the day, but she still couldn't totally dismiss the worries she carried with her constantly for Peter's welfare. She was a mother, after all. No mother who loved her child could forget to worry when her child was missing.

But she had another problem plaguing her as well. *Kaine.* If she thought she had trouble reading him while they were married, it was nothing in comparison to reading him now. His changed attitude earlier and his stiff-backed attitude now were in complete opposition to each other. One minute he was treating her with compassion and understanding and the next he was virtually ignoring her.

Shadow had wandered off somewhere, leaving them to the solitude of the bleak landscape and the heat of the scorching sun. She sighed.

Because she was so deep in thought, she noticed too late that the terrain had become littered with small rocks that shifted under her feet. Her injured ankle twisted, and she cried out in pain. Favoring the sore ankle threw her balance off. She pitched sideways toward the side of the trail that bordered the crevice far below.

Strong hands grabbed her arm and hauled her back to safety. "You have to pay attention to where you're walking, Laura, especially with that ankle." Kaine's tone was sharp, his brow furrowed in anger.

He grabbed one of the backpacks and took from it a coil of thick rope that had been fastened to the shoulder braces. Leaving several feet of rope between them, he fastened one end around her waist and one end around his. The rough sisal scratched her skin through the material of her shirt, but at least she felt better about maneuvering the trail.

Without another word, Kaine picked up the backpacks and started off down the trail. When the rope grew taut and jerked her forward, Laura had no choice but to follow.

Even though the pace he set was slower to accommodate her and her injured ankle, it was by no means easy.

The trail got worse with each step. The rocks had gotten bigger and finding a place to step more challenging. Several times she stumbled and pulled on the rope attached to Kaine. He'd stopped and waited for her to regain her footing, but without a word or a hand to help her.

When he'd turned away, frustrated and feeling rather helpless, Laura resorted to the childish revenge of sticking out her tongue at his back. It didn't make the going any easier, and it wasn't nearly as satisfying as giving him a good swift kick in the ass would have been, but it did make her feel a bit more in control of her situation.

Long shadow-fingers reached down into the crevice like an unseen demon as the sun headed toward the western rim of the canyon. Laura's nerves tightened. With darkness came the possibility of the reappearance of the skinwalkers. She found herself approaching each darkened jut in the rocks holding her breath. Still Kaine pushed on.

He'd said they'd reach the Rainbow Arch this afternoon, but because of her being unable to keep a faster pace, it looked as if that possibility had flown the way of the eagles that soared high above them. There would be still another day before they could start their search for Peter in earnest.

Laura was once again immersed in morose musing about her son's fate, when the rope at her waist was jerked forward. She looked up to see their backpacks lying in the middle of the path. Then, a split second later, she was hurtling toward the drop-off that plummeted several hundred feet to the canyon below. Her forward momentum stopped abruptly when her body became wedged between two boulders on the very rim of the drop, just in time to see Kaine plunge over the edge.

"No!" Though she was too far away to be able to do anything, she reached out and caught thin air. Her scream echoed around the stark walls of the canyon, mocking her with its feeble attempt to stop his fall.

By stretching over the boulders imprisoning her, she could just make out his body suspended below her. Ironically, he was swinging back and forth at the end of the rope he'd used to keep her safe. He was hanging onto the rope and looking up at her. Her wedged body was all that was keeping him from dropping to his death. If she slipped through the gap between them, they'd both plunge to their death.

She braced her feet against the rocks. "Kaine, can you hear me?" she called.

"Yes," he said, but his voice sounded strained and seemed so far away.

"Hang on. I'll try to pull you back up."

"You can't. I'll be too heavy for you."

She knew he was probably right, but she couldn't give up. She *had* to try. She could *not* lose Kaine and Peter. She couldn't.

"Let me be the judge of that." The control in her voice surprised her.

Wrapping the taught rope around her hand, she bit back the pain of it cutting into her skin and taking a deep breath pulled with all the strength she could muster. The muscles in her shoulders screamed and burned like fire. Still she continued to pull. Sweat beaded her forehead.

Deep inside her, panic bubbled up. She was not going to be able to do this. She just didn't have enough strength in her slight frame to pull a six-foot-plus man straight up the sharp side of a cliff.

"It's no use, Laura." Kaine's voice drifted up to her, confirming her worst fears. "If you stay hooked to me, I'll pull you over, too. I'm going to cut myself lose."

"No!"

"Listen to me," he cut in, ignoring her anguished cry, his voice stern. "You have to go on. Find Peter and take him home. You can do it. Just continue to follow the trail you're on. It will bring you to the Rainbow Arch. Keep Shadow with you. If he is who we think, I'm sure he'll help show you the way; and he will protect you."

"No, damn you, you can't do this. I love you. You can't leave me. I won't let you." Summoning every ounce of her depleted strength, she gritted her teeth and began pulling frantically on the rope. "I won't let you do this." Blood droplets formed where the rough fibers cut into her skin. Tears cascaded down her cheeks.

Kaine's voice drifted up to her. "Walk in beauty, Little One."

Then the rope went limp.

Chapter 14

Laura leaned forward, straining to see where Kaine had fallen, but her view was blocked by the uneven side walls. She grabbed the rope and pulled it up, knowing he was gone, but needing proof. When she finally pulled the end over the edge and held it in her hand, she could only stare at the evenly cut fibers. He'd intentionally sacrificed himself for her.

Kaine was gone. She couldn't believe it. She couldn't let herself believe it. But reality set in. There was no way Kaine could have survived the fall to the canyon floor.

Without Kaine's weight to hold it in place, her body dropped free of the boulders. Feeling as if her very soul had been ripped from her body, Laura slid to the ground. Shadow nuzzled her cheek. She wrapped her arms around him and sobbed helplessly into his furry neck.

❖　　❖　　❖

Laura had no idea how long she sat there crying into the dog's fur, but when she finally ran out of tears, night had fallen and everything around her was as black as pitch. She wanted to just lay there and wait for death to claim her as well. Leaving Kaine eight years ago had nearly killed her, but to lose him this way . . . She bit back a sob and squeezed her burning, swollen eyes closed.

When she opened them, Shadow was sitting nose to nose with her, his eyes glued to hers.

You must not give up. The child needs you. You must go on.

The words came from inside her head, yet, somehow, she knew Shadow was transmitting them to her as surely as if she'd heard them leave his lips. The pendant warmed against her cold skin. She grabbed it in both hands.

Suddenly, though her heart felt wrenched from her body, and she suspected she would never again feel whole, Laura knew she had to go on. She was the only thing that stood between her son's survival and his death. She may have lost Kaine, but dammit, this savage land would not claim her son as well.

As if reminding her of his presence, Shadow nudged her arm. She smiled weakly and patted the dog's head. "Okay, boy. I know what I have to do."

On her hands and knees, she crawled in the direction of where she thought Kaine had dropped the backpacks. When she'd found them, she dug inside for the flashlight.

A wash of relief came over her as she clicked the button and light sliced through the all-encompassing darkness and bathed her and Shadow in a secure circle of illumination. As though the light had also illuminated the dark corners of her heart, Laura felt an immediate lifting of her spirits.

She'd survive. She'd find Peter, and she'd survive. She'd tell him about his father and how hard he looked for him and how much he wanted to meet him. Tears stung her eyes again. She blinked them back. There was no time for weakness now. Later, after she'd found Peter and they were home, she'd let the hard truth of losing the man she loved seep in, but not now.

How ironic life was, she thought, swallowing her tears and summoning a stiff backbone for what lay ahead of her. *What was the old dog saying? Be careful what you wish for?* Well, she hadn't wished for it, but she had sworn to find Peter alone if she had to and here she was, alone with only her instincts for survival to guide her. But she had made it alone on the streets of L.A., and in many ways that had been much more dangerous. The one difference, she reminded herself, was that there had been no skin-walkers in L.A.

It was too late to look for firewood, and her chances of finding any on this barren trail were about as good as finding a steak dinner. She located a deep notch in the wall, snuggled into it with Shadow beside her, and threw a sleeping bag over them for warmth.

As she sat there, she thought back to the night she and Kaine had made love and the words he'd whispered to her as they stood clothed in nothing but the silvery rays of a full moon.

Imagine the feel of the sun on your skin. Absorb it. Use it to warm you when you're alone and cold.

Laura repeated the words in her mind until the chill left her body and warmth coursed through her blood.

Smell the perfume of the night-blooming cactus on the breeze. Let it bring the peace of being one with all that's around you.

Breathing deeply, Laura centered her thoughts on the waxy, creamy-white flower. Although she knew no vegetation grew nearby, she could smell the exquisite perfume of the flower that lived but one night and died with the morning light. A breeze caressed her cheeks and her fears rode the wind with the perfume and evaporated into the night.

Absorb the colors of the earth. Memorize them to call forth when the night hides them in shadow and your world grows dark.

Closing her eyes, Laura conjured up the brilliant colors of the earth with the sun blazing down on it. In her mind they glowed like the lights on the Las Vegas Strip and then she opened her eyes and looked around, the dark shadows seemed to have grown lighter and less menacing. She smiled, thanked Kaine silently, closed her eyes again, and laid her head against Shadow's broad, furry back as if it were the pillow on her bed at home.

✤   ✤   ✤

Morning brought with it the reminder of Laura's loss. Knowing she could only carry one of them, she sorted through the backpacks, taking only what she would absolutely need and leaving the rest behind. When she'd finished, she still had to struggle to get it off the ground and onto her shoulder, so she set it down again and took more from it.

While she sorted through the items, she found Peter's shirt. Her resolve to stay strong wavered, and she buried her face in it for a moment before she gave herself a stern shake and stuffed it into the backpack. Then to firm up her resolve, she grabbed the extra sleeping bag. If . . . no, *when* she found Peter, he'd need some place to sleep.

Finally satisfied that the weight was something she could manage, she slung the backpack onto her shoulders and began her trek down the trail toward the Rainbow Arch. While she walked, she munched on a piece of beef jerky, not because she was hungry but because she knew part of her being successful was to keep up her strength—no matter how her stomach rumbled in revolt at the food. Periodically, she fed some to Shadow, who trotted along in front of her.

By the time the sun was overhead, dispelling the sheltering shadows with its heat and eating up the cool air from the night before, fatigue had set in—and with it came doubt.

Could she do this? A girl born and raised in the city? A girl who'd already run away from this harsh, inhospitable wilderness once? And what if she found Peter and he was sick or injured? How would she get him back to civilization and medical help?

She stopped in the path, suddenly weighted down by so many negative thoughts that her shoulders slumped, and her feet refused to move any farther.

Shadow stopped, too. He turned to her, his dark eyes burning into hers. He barked sharply, took a few steps farther down the path, turned back to her, and barked again.

Feeling somewhat reassured by the dog's unspoken faith in her, she reminded herself that she was a nurse. She could tend Peter if he was hurt and they'd stay here until he could travel. If necessary, they'd eat what they could find along the trail, but they *would* make it. They *would* make it for Kaine.

"Okay, I get the message. Let's go."

Laura checked her watch. It was around three o'clock, which if she'd been judging by the dark gathering in the canyon, would have not been her guess. The sun was dipping behind the canyon rim again and aside from the bright blue sky above, the canyon seemed to have entered into the twilight hours of the day.

Rounding a tall chimney-like sandstone column, she stopped. The trail had deteriorated into a deep gorge, bridged by some flat rocks over a sharp drop that ended in a dry water hole fifty to sixty feet below. Shadow was standing in the middle of the flat rocks looking back at her expectantly.

She glanced over the edge and swallowed hard. "I'm coming," she said. "I just need to muster a little courage."

Heights had never been a strong point for her and up until now, she'd always just blinded herself to her surroundings and followed in Kaine's footsteps. A sharp pain pierced her heart, and she forced her thoughts back to the problem at hand.

"Just don't look down," she told herself, even as she took her first step onto the flat rocks, and her knees threatened to turn to water. "Don't look down. Don't look down."

The rocks were slick with the blown sand that had accumulated on them. Anxious to get this over with, she walked a little faster, and then her foot slipped. Her heart jumped into her throat, and her knees went weak. She held her breath and threw out her arms to regain her balance and right herself. Slowing her pace considerably, she moved forward.

"Don't look down." She repeated the singsong mantra over and over until she found herself on the other side of the gorge and her feet thankfully back on solid ground.

Shadow dashed to her side and licked her hand.

"Yeah, I'm pretty proud of me, too," she told the dog,

patting his large head.

But Shadow gave scant time for congratulations and was quickly padding off down the path again. Laura took a deep breath and followed the dog.

"Slave driver," she muttered, adjusting the weight of the backpack to a more comfortable position.

The steep path, which had turned her calf muscles into two tightly drawn knots, seemed to have taken a blessedly downhill turn. Unfortunately, while not having to make that steady upward climb, it was now smooth and more like a child's playground slide than a mountain trail. The same sand that had accumulated on the flat rocks had also gathered here, making it slick and the footing precarious.

It seemed no matter how carefully Laura proceeded, unlike Shadow's surefooted steps, she slipped and slid. The grade of the path became steeper and harder to navigate. No matter how gingerly Laura placed her feet, they threatened to upend her at every turn.

She stepped on a small rock, and her feet were swept from beneath her. Before she knew what was happening, she was airborne. Almost in slow motion, or so it seemed to her, she rose in the air and then came down hard on her back. The backpack took the biggest share of the impact, leaving her uninjured, but gasping for the air that had gushed from her lungs.

Swirling and turning, flipping end over end, she slid down the path like a penguin on an ice slide. She reached for anything to stop her speedy descent, but there was nothing to grab. She tried to flip over, but the backpack kept her from doing so. Like a turtle on its back, she was left to ride it out and hope for the best.

Then she collided with something solid and rolled sideways, coming to rest on her back and looking up at one of the most remarkable things she'd ever seen.

Above her, stretching across one hundred feet from canyon wall to canyon wall, was a massive sandstone bridge shaped exactly like a rainbow. A perfect match to the photo that had hung in Kaine's office at their old house. She'd made it. She'd found the Rainbow Arch. Despite everything that had happened that day and the previous days, her heart sang. For the first time since she'd gotten that terrible phone call from the NTP, she felt that Peter was within her reach.

"Hang in there, Peter. I'll find you, sweetheart. I'll find you just as I promised your father I would."

Slipping the backpack from her shoulders, she blinked away happy tears and then managed to get to her feet, which sank into the wet sand bordering a small stream that flowed beneath the arch. On either side of the stream, vegetation flourished, flowers bloomed in a myriad of bright colors and perfumed the air around her. Yucca plants towered above her, the plumes of their white flowers blowing in a soft breeze. Pieces of driftwood deposited by the flashflood littered the ground.

She sighed. She'd be able to wash for the first time in

days and even start a fire to take the chill from the night and shed a circle of secure light around her and Shadow. She looked around for the dog and found him lapping thirstily from the stream.

Hope filled her soul and brought a smile to her lips. Maybe she could do this after all.

✤   ✤   ✤

Later, bathed, shampooed and in clean clothes, Laura gathered firewood. Hot food would taste almost as good as her bath in the chilly stream had been. It felt so good to be clean again. She thought back to the last time she'd been able to bathe her entire body.

It was the night at the falls. The night she and Kaine almost made love, the night the skinwalkers appeared for the first time. Thoughts of the hairy beasts prompted her to scan the area around her nervously and washed away any mournful thoughts about her husband that fought for recognition in her mind.

Laura shook away the thoughts of Kaine. She could not allow herself to mourn now. The time would come, but not now. There was little light left in the canyon and the shade caused by the wide stone arch overhead didn't help. She had to get the wood and get a fire started before complete darkness veiled the landscape.

She picked up a particularly large log and stacked it on the growing pile in her arms. About to walk away, she caught site of something black and white peeking from beneath a rock. Curious, she set the wood down, rolled the rock away and dug the object from the ground with her one of the sticks.

It was pottery, black and white pottery with a strange design on it. In the same hole, she found several more pieces. When she'd laid them in a small heap, she noted one larger piece at the bottom of the cavity. Taking a stick, she pried it from the ground.

She'd found a shallow bowl which seemed to be intact except for a hole in the bottom. Turning the bowl over in her hands, she scanned the pictures that had been painted on its sides. They were a combination of geometrical shapes and animals ranging from frogs to rabbits and turtles.

The tingle of recognition skirted up Laura's spine. She searched her memory. Laura had seen this type of pottery once before in some paperwork Kaine had brought back from one of his trips to Washington, D.C. It was Mimbres pottery, very rare, very valuable, and very far from New Mexico, where it was normally found. The intact bowl with the *kill-hole* was used for burial. Unless the seller and/or the buyer had a special permit to harvest it, it could mean jail time and hundreds of dollars in fines. Because of its pristine condition, this piece was probably worth thousands of dollars to a collector.

So what was it doing here? Had someone stashed it under the rock to be collected later?

Well, whoever it was, she was not about to let them

steal a part of her son's and husband's heritage. She rolled the rock back in place, carefully collected the smaller shards and put them in the bowl, then placed it beside her backpack and returned for the pile of wood.

The damp wood made it hard to get the fire to catch and keep burning, but eventually it did. She lay back on her sleeping bag and gazed up at the black velvet sky studded with glittering stars. Shadow curled close to her side, and she ran her fingers through his fur.

"Looking at that beautiful, peaceful sky and listening to the absolute silence out here, you'd think everything was right with the world," she told the dog. His ear flicked in response.

"But you and I know that nothing will ever be right with my world again."

A lone tear trickled down her cheek and into her hair. Shadow licked it away and then laid his head on her shoulder.

Laura woke to the sun beating down on her and the eerie sensation that she was again being watched. Thinking it was Shadow, she yawned and rolled to her side.

"I know. I overslept," she said, not opening her eyes. "If you just let me sleep a bit longer, I promise I'll get up, and we can be on our way."

"I'm afraid that's not going to be possible," said a male voice from somewhere above her.

Laura bolted upright and squinted against the bright sunlight. She could just make out the silhouetted outlines of two men, one slight and the other much larger. Shading her eyes with her hand, she was able to make them out more clearly.

"Who are you? What do you want?" Laura threw a nervous look at the backpack a few feet from her where the gun was safely tucked away, but the smaller of the men was between her and it. Backing up, she clutched the sleeping bag around her.

"We should be asking you that," said the bigger of the two.

Both men moved to the other side of her, and she was finally able to see them clearly. They were both clean-cut and dressed similarly in jeans and T-shirts and navy windbreakers. The big man was definitely Caucasian and the smaller one, with his high cheekbones, black hair and coppery skin, had strong Native American bloodlines.

"I'm Special FBI Agent Oates and this is Jim Longtree from the Bureau of Indian Affairs." Oates flashed a badge at her so quickly she didn't have time to really get a good look at it. "You have some questions to answer."

Laura stood very slowly, unwilling to give Oates any reason to pull the gun that peeked from beneath his windbreakers. "I don't understand," she said, her nerves showing in the quiver in her voice.

"How about this?" the man called Longtree said, holding out the bowl containing the pottery shards.

"Oh, they aren't mine. I found them over there." She pointed at the rock under which the shards had been hidden.

"What did you plan on doing with them?" Oates circled her, making her nerves jangle even worse.

"Nothing. I mean . . ." What had she planned to do with them? Maybe take them to the nearest NTP office? She swallowed hard.

Longtree picked up the backpack. Laura held her breath. If she was being grilled this bad over a few pieces of pottery, she couldn't imagine what he'd say if he found Kaine's gun.

"What's your name?"

"Laura. Laura Kincaid." She answered him without taking her gaze from Longtree and the backpack.

"And exactly what are you doing out here in Canyon Country all alone?" She breathed a small sigh of relief. Longtree had lost interest in the backpack for the moment.

"My son. He's lost. I'm looking for him."

"Alone? Without a guide?"

Laura nodded at the young BIA agent.

"And I assume you have a permit to be here. This is reservation land. No one is allowed in these canyons without a Navajo guide or a permit." Longtree stepped closer. "This place especially is off limits to any tourists."

"I . . . uh . . . I had a Navajo guide, but he—"

"Who?" Longtree demanded before she could finish.

"Kaine Cloudwalker."

Oates gave a derisive laugh and exchanged a we-got-her look with Longtree. "Try again. We happen to know Cloudwalker is on vacation."

She shook her head. "No. He was supposed to go to go on vacation, but I asked him to help me find Peter."

"Lady," Oates said, advancing on her, his florid face breaking into a sarcastic smile, "I think you need to come with us so we can sort this out."

Panic took root inside her. If she wasted time going with them and explaining all this, Peter could die. She shook her head furiously and stepped back. "No, I can't leave. My son. You must understand. I have to find Peter. If I go with you, it will be too late." She took another step back, but came up short against something solid and definitely male. Longtree had slipped behind her and grabbed her arms.

"What we understand is that you are in possession of illegally obtained Indian artifacts," Oates drawled. "That's a felony, and you are under arrest."

"No! Please! You have to let me go," she cried, struggling to get away.

"We don't have to do anything," Oates snarled.

She wasn't sure if she heard the *click* first or felt the cold metal against her skin first as Longtree slipped handcuffs on her wrists.

Chapter 15

"If I were you, I'd take those cuffs off the lady."

Kaine?

Laura's head snapped toward that deep, familiar voice. He was muddy and bruised, and his face and arms were covered with small scratches. The lines around his eyes and mouth made him look tired enough to sleep for a week. But he was *alive*. And to her broken heart, he looked like Zeus standing atop Mount Olympus.

Her face transformed into a wide grin. Kaine didn't see it. He was too busy glaring at Jim Longtree. "I don't think you want me to repeat myself, Jim."

Caught off guard, Longtree's grip on her loosened. She broke free and ran into Kaine's waiting arms.

"Don't you guys have anything better to do than harass my wife?" Although his words sounded casual, she could feel the bowstring tension in his body.

"Wife?" Longtree said, his mouth gaping open. "I thought you were divorced."

Kaine ignored Longtree.

Oates swiped at his forehead with a white handkerchief. "Wife, huh? How do we know you're not in on this with her?"

Laura looked at Kaine. His eyes had turned a dangerous, dark black, his brow furrowed, and his jaw muscle worked furiously. Anyone who knew him would have run for their life. Oates evidently had no idea he was looking death in the face and stood his ground.

"Because there's nothing to be *in* together. If my wife says she found the pottery, then that's exactly how it happened."

Oates leaned down and picked up the bowl that Longtree had dropped before he handcuffed Laura. "Then you won't mind if we take these."

"Be our guests." Kaine grasped Laura's arm and walked her toward Longtree. "I believe these belong to you." He turned her back to the young Navajo and pointed at the handcuffs.

Without a word, Longtree released the handcuffs. Laura cuddled back against Kaine and rubbed at her wrists. The cuffs hadn't hurt, but having her hands confined had been the most helpless feeling she had ever experienced, and she was more then glad to be free of them.

Longtree looked at Kaine. "Because I know you to be an honest man, I'm going to take your word for this,

Kaine. But if I find anything which points at you or your wife, I'll be back."

Kaine held Laura's quivering body tighter. "You know where to find us."

The BIA agent started to walk away and then stopped. "She says your kid is lost out here. Want us to stay and help?"

Kaine shook his head. "We'll be fine."

For a moment, Laura was about to argue that they could use all the help they could get, and then she saw the hatred passing between Kaine and Oates and thought better of it. They had enough problems without having to contend with an internal war between the searchers.

"No thanks," she finally said.

Longtree cast one more look from her to Kaine, pocketed the cuffs and took the bowl of pottery from Oates.

The FBI agent looked suspiciously at Laura. "We'll need you to stop by the office and make out a report about these."

She nodded.

"Now, if you're done here, we have to find our son," Kaine said pointedly and stepped back to let them know he wanted them gone.

Neither of them was foolish enough to argue with him.

Kaine watched the two agents disappear into the brush and then turned to Laura. "Are you all right?"

She smiled. She couldn't stop looking at him, couldn't believe he was there, alive. "I should be asking you that. I thought you were—"

Even with the flesh-and-blood man standing before her, she couldn't say the words. Tears filled her eyes. One escaped and trickled down her cheek.

Gently, he brushed the moisture away with the pad of his thumb and then cupped her face. "I was lucky. The mud left behind by the flood broke my fall." He smiled and looked down at the wet soil caked on his clothes from his booted feet to his waist. "It took me better than a half an hour to pull myself out of it."

He kept talking, but she wasn't really listening. She was too busy looking at him and making sure this wasn't just a dream. Instead, she ran her hands over his face, neck and arms for reassurance that he was indeed there, alive and all in one piece.

"I'd kiss you, but I really stink." He glanced over his shoulder at the stream. "Maybe I should take a bath and then we can talk."

She nodded, her eyes still brimming with happy tears. "I'll make you something to eat. You must be starved." Still she wouldn't let go of him. She searched his face, touching the scratches and bruises, outlining his eyes with her fingertips. "Oh, to hell with the mud." She pulled his mouth down to hers and melted into his arms.

Kaine clutched her close. He'd thought of nothing but this from the time he fell over the cliff and heard her tell him she loved him. It had been the thing that had kept him going as he made his way through the canyon.

Laura.

Ever since he'd met her, she'd been the driving force in his life, even when she wasn't with him. And he wanted her now more than his next breath. But not until he'd removed half the Arizona desert from his skin. Gently, he pushed her away.

"Remember where we were." He turned her toward the fire. "You go cook. I'll go wash."

Laura laid out a cold supper for him, zipped the two sleeping bags together as she'd seen him do before, and shed her clothes. Then she slid into the sleeping bag and watched him bathe. He'd broken a stem of the yucca plant off, squeezed the sap into his hands, and used it to wash his torso and shampoo his hair. Beads of moisture trickled over his skin as he rinsed the yucca suds from his body. She held her breath. Without a doubt, he was the most beautiful specimen of manhood she had ever seen or ever hoped to see.

Muscles rippled beneath his coppery skin. His tight buttocks lay just above the water's surface, tempting her to go to him and touch them, to touch him all over, once more assuring herself that he really was there. But she contented herself with watching him.

Silently, she thanked her God and the Navajo gods for sparing him and giving them another chance.

Darkness closed in on the clearing, and the creatures of the night began their lullaby. Laura sighed and closed her burning eyes. She'd just rest them until Kaine was finished with his bath and his meal.

✛   ✛   ✛

Kaine unzipped the sleeping bag and then lay down beside his sleeping wife. He threw the top flap of the bag over them and then pulled Laura's warm body against his. As if understanding their need for privacy, Shadow crept away into the darkness.

Looking down at Laura, Kaine felt his heart swell with love for her. At the same time, he experienced a loneliness far beyond anything he'd ever felt before. He knew that, just because she loved him, there was no guarantee that she wouldn't leave. She'd done it before. Hadn't she? The chance that she'd soon be gone from his life was by no means an impossibility.

What then, my friend? How will you fill the lonely nights in your cold bed? With more dreams of what can never be?

He lifted a handful of her hair and rubbed the silky, night-black strands between his fingers and then lifted it to his face and inhaled the flowery fragrance.

These days with Laura left him weak just remembering them. No one, not even *Shimá*, his beloved mother, had touched him so completely, so deeply. Swooping down like a bird of prey, Laura had stolen off with his heart the first day he saw her. Even as he told himself to keep her at arm's distance, it had already been too late by the night he had opened the door and looked into her careworn face. He'd just been too stubborn to admit it.

When he hanged from that rope and saw death staring him in the face, he thought he'd lost her for good, that he'd never get the chance to hold her again. Yet here she was, all flesh and blood, and sexy as hell.

For a scant second, he gave in to the thought of following her into her world, but just as quickly, the idea vanished. He'd die anywhere away from the People and *Dinétah*, the land of his people. He may not believe in the Ways anymore, but the land still flowed through him as surely as his blood did.

Painful memories of his month in Washington lobbying for the Indian Artifacts Preservation Bill assailed him, memories of long sleepless nights punctuated by bleating automobile horns and the incessant rumble of a busy city outside his hotel room window. Only his ability to call the spirit of the *Dinétah* to him, just as he'd taught Laura to do, and vivid memories of Laura beside him in their bed had kept him alive, but how long could he live on memories?

How long indeed? his subconscious prodded, bringing the reminder of the days and nights to come without Laura back into sharp focus.

Suddenly he needed to preserve her in some way, soak up her essence as he'd taught her to absorb the sun, flowers, and colors of the earth and store it in his soul for the time when she'd no longer be beside him. Reverently, he laid his hand on the smooth skin of her hip, feeling the heat of her flesh warm his palm and spread to the cold corners of his heart. He bent over her and inhaled the fragrance of her hair, her skin, her breath.

He memorized her from head to toe with his senses, storing each curve and valley for the time when memories would be all he'd have, when he would use them to summon her spirit and touch her with his mind to drive away the darkness.

He felt himself swell with the explosive need to join his soul with hers, to add one more memory to his growing storehouse. Shifting toward her, he caressed the unmarred skin of her cheek. She stirred and rolled to her back, shoving aside the sleeping bag and offering him the sight of her naked body.

Sucking in his breath, he stifled a groan and stared down at her golden beauty. Her lips parted, inviting his kiss, but he held back. A wisp of black hair shrouded one breast, hiding the dark rose peak from his eager gaze. The delicate curve of her neck reminded him of a swan he'd seen on a lake in Washington, long and elegant.

Lord, how had he ever believed he could be near her and not love her completely? It would have been like sitting a starving man down before a sumptuous feast and telling him not to eat.

A shaft of moonlight fell across the "V" of her thighs. At the same moment, she raised her leg, bending it at the knee. The memory of other nights, of her wild abandonment in his arms, brought a smile to his lips and an arrow of heat straight to his groin.

His voice came from him thick and heavy with desire. "*Sidoh, tikan, yá' át' áéh.*"

"Has anyone ever told you there's a distinct strand of voyeurism in you?" Laura's sleepy whisper drifted up from the folds of bedding. "What did you just say?"

"Hot, sweet, beautiful."

Her eyes opened and at once became languid and dreamy. A smile grew on his lips. He wasn't a man easily given to smiles unless something really pleased him. And Laura's passionate nature definitely pleased him. In fact, his pleasure in her was rapidly approaching physical discomfort. His grin broadened when she tentatively tried to repeat the words he'd said in Navajo.

"You need lessons," he told her, brushing a strand of hair from her cheek, using the innocent gesture as an excuse to feel her skin.

Stretching lethargically, her back arching and throwing her breasts into prominence, Laura took delight in the darkening of Kaine's eyes. "I need lessons, but not in anything that requires speech," she purred, brazenly folding her arms around his neck and pulling his mouth down to hers.

Keeping their lips apart by a hair's breadth, he looked down at her with a devilish grin. "What are you up to now?"

"I'm trying my damnedest to thoroughly corrupt you, but you're not making it easy."

A throaty laugh came from him, washing her face in his warm breath. Just before he claimed her lips, he mumbled, "Then do your damnedest."

Laura pressed her full length against his bare torso. Her lips opened, eagerly sucking him inside.

Ever since she'd awakened and found him deep in a study of her anatomy, she'd wanted him. One of the hardest things she'd ever had to do was lay there passively while his velvety gaze burned a trail of desire over her exposed flesh. She'd grown used to the phantom touch of his eyes. What she hoped never to grow complacent about was the way they ignited her passions.

His hands sought and found her breasts, enveloping them in the rapture of his grasp. His touch burned as he gently kneaded their aching fullness and feasted on her eager mouth. The smell of his sun-washed skin brought a tingle of desire to her sensitive body. Was there nothing about him she didn't love?

His mouth left hers and nibbled a trail of hot, wet kisses over her chin, down her neck and chest, and into the valley between her breasts. As his lips closed over a turgid nipple, a vision of how he'd appeared moments ago, taking pleasure in just looking at her, enticed Laura to perpetuate the vision.

His hair had been ruffled and damp from his bath, his eyes hooded and heavy with passion; the stark beauty of him had been a powerful aphrodisiac to wake up to. Like a wild animal zeroing in on its mate, she'd extracted his special scent from the others being pushed around by the breeze wafting up the canyon. A need for him had flourished in her, becoming a throbbing demand.

Her hands feathered over his bare skin, reliving by touch what her eyes had consumed earlier; what until a little while ago, she had thought lost to her forever. Her foot skimmed the hard muscles in his well-defined calf. Her busy fingers molded and memorized the vibrating tendons in his back and buttocks. A low moan from him brought delight to her heart.

Kaine rolled to his back, taking her with him with an arm hooked around her waist. "Touch me more," he begged, the words mingling with his rasping breath. "Learn my body as I've learned yours."

His words magnified the sparks rushing to her nerve endings, encouraging her to fulfill his request.

Her fingers caressed his naked chest, twirling the tips of the brown buds capping his well-developed pecs. Wasting no time when she heard his throaty moan of pleasure, she moved on to explore his stomach. Bending her head, she laved at the dimpled indentation of his navel.

The rush of heat spearing through her made her clench her thighs to calm the pulse building in the musky cavern of her love.

Her head dipped lower, and the velvety tip of his arousal nudged her cheek. She knew his scent, knew the sound of his rich deep voice, knew the feel of his body lodged within her and knew the sight of his handsome face. What she longed for now was to memorize his taste.

Slowly, she turned her head and worshiped him with her lips. His body arched, and an earthy, almost primal groan tore from him. She intensified her efforts in a bid to give back to him a small measure of the pleasure he'd given her.

"No more," he rasped, pulling her up to cover him. He kissed her deeply, hungrily, tasting himself on her mouth.

Twisting, he flipped her to her back. Her legs parted, ready to receive him. One quick, deep thrust and he was where he most longed to be—buried in her heat.

Laura's body arched to meet him. Her high-pitched cry of pleasure pierced his ears. Her fingernails dragged pleasurable, painful paths across his back. He tried to withdraw, fearing his passions had driven him to be too rough, but she held him fast with her long legs wrapped securely around his hips.

Their mutual cries rent the night and then stillness settled over their entwined bodies.

Hunger gnawed at Kaine's stomach, waking him from his dreamless sleep. Easing himself away from Laura's sleeping form, he shivered when the cold desert air hit his bare skin. He threw another log on the dying fire and then fumbled around for the food she'd lain out for him earlier. It wasn't a steak dinner, but the dried beef and hardtack were enough to ease the hunger pangs brought on by over a day without food.

He didn't eat all of it. Just enough to fill some of the emptiness. They'd need the rest for the days ahead. If they had the other backpack, they'd have had more food. Now, two people had to survive on food for one. And he had no one to blame but himself.

He couldn't believe how stupid he'd been back on the trail. For Christ's sake, he was a seasoned guide. He knew these trails like he knew Laura's body. He should have been watching what he was doing when he took the backpacks off instead of watching Laura. Maybe then, he wouldn't have lost his footing.

However, being stuck in oozing mud up to his waist for what seemed like hours and then having to walk to the arch without food seemed just punishment for his inattention. It had also given him time to think, and for the first time in eight years honestly evaluate why Laura had left him and resolving that also helped him put aside his anger at her for keeping Peter's birth from him.

He'd dragged her, a city girl, into the wilds of the Arizona desert to a reservation filled with people who lived a life totally foreign to her and then left her to fend for herself while he ran off to Washington every other week. Was it any wonder she couldn't hack it?

Then, when she'd left, he'd dug in his feet and nursed his bruised ego, instead of going after her. Why would she ever think he cared about their child? Why would she seek him out to tell him?

Laura stirred in her sleep, drawing his attention to her. Love welled up in him so strongly that he had to bite his lip to keep from crying out.

Shadow sidled up to him and rubbed his face on Kaine's hand as if begging to be petted. Kaine obliged, absently.

"What do you think, Shadow? Is it too late for me to make amends for my stupidity back then? You think she'll forgive me and stay so the three of us can become a family again?"

And maybe it'll snow in the desert tomorrow, he thought. Shadow licked his hand.

"Laura's so sure you're Changing Woman. If you are, why can't you speak? Was that lick a *yes* or a *no?*"

Shadow's tail beat the night air furiously.

He sighed and patted the dog's head. "Yeah, I get the message. I have to figure this one out on my own."

Predawn darkness still cloaked the canyon when Laura awoke to nature's call. Slipping from the sleeping bag carefully so as to not wake Kaine, she stood over him for a moment, just looking at him. How peaceful he looked. Her heart beat faster just being near him. She was still having trouble believing that he was actually alive. Then she laughed quietly. If nothing else convinced her of his wellbeing, the ache in muscles she hadn't used that actively in eight years verified it for her.

Dragging her gaze from her sleeping husband, she put on her clothes and headed off toward a large rock at the base of the arch. Shadow trotted along behind her.

Ablutions completed, she straightened and looked up at the star-studded sky. Faint pink and purple rays of sunlight painted the heavens. Stars twinkled weakly as the onset of another day stole the stage from them. She stretched and headed back toward their camp. Shadow, who had been laying to the side waiting for her, stood and started to follow along.

Maybe today would be the day they'd find Peter, and then her life would be complete. Well, almost complete, she qualified. There was still the question of whether Kaine wanted to start a life with them. After all, sex had always been the one part of their marriage that had worked flawlessly. It was beyond the bedroom that they needed help. She still had no idea if he loved her or not and she would settle for no less.

Suddenly Shadow stopped; that warning ridge of standing hair appeared down his back, and then he bared his teeth. Before she could see what had caught his attention, he lunged at the darkness.

Recalling what had happened the last time he'd dove into the darkness, Laura called him back. He plunged on, disappearing into the murky morning light.

A chill of foreboding climbed up her spine. "Shadow, come back here. Shadow—"

An excruciating pain shot through her head and then her world went black.

The day had just barely begun when Kaine awoke to find the empty sleeping bag beside him. He dragged himself upright and looked around for Laura. Assuming she was off taking care of her morning ritual, he made coffee and sat down to wait for her return and the coffee to brew.

When several minutes passed and she didn't come back, he whistled for Shadow. The dog did not respond. Growing increasingly concerned, he headed in the direction Laura's footprints took him.

"Laura?"

He waited and listened. No answer.

"Laura?"

Still no answer.

Then he saw the footprints. Not just Laura's footprints, but also Shadow's, a man's and several animals. There had been a scuffle, then both Laura's and Shadow's footprints disappeared. But the footprints of the man and one of the animals deepened, as if they were carrying something . . . or someone.

Kaine's first impulse was to race after them, but he knew he had to take this slow and think it out. Instead, he returned to the campsite and packed up the sleeping bag, threw out the coffee he'd just made and doused the fire with sand. While he worked, he thought through what he knew.

He's almost certain the footprints will lead to the caves above Canyon de Muerto. The logical place for them to take Laura would be back to their lair, and all the Navajos knew that the skinwalkers inhabited the dank hollows gouged out of the canyon walls. Not ones to work at anything but evil, they were parasites who lived off the residue of others, in this case, the leavings of an extinct civilization. That it was a box canyon with no exits that

Kaine knew of made it that much more convenient for them to trap the Navajos who wandered into their domain looking for lost sheep.

He checked the gun to make sure it was loaded, tucked it into the back waistband of his jeans, and covered it with the tail of his shirt. Throwing the backpack over his shoulder, he trudged off toward the part of the canyon that had meant death for many an unsuspecting traveler.

Kaine had no trouble following the trail of Laura and her captors. The tracks followed the meandering stream through the canyon floor. Sunk in the soft mud at the edge of the stream, they were easy to follow . . . too easy.

Those cunning creatures knew exactly what they were doing. They knew if they took Laura, they'd ensure the chance that they'd eventually get him, too. What man wouldn't go after his wife and child if they were in danger?

Well, he could play their game—up to a point. He'd find out in which cave they were keeping Laura and Peter and then take a roundabout route—one that they had not been planning on him discovering—to get to them. Hopefully, he could sneak his little family out before they knew he was there. If not, he was prepared to fight, to the death if necessary, to get his loved ones to safety.

The sun was hung high in a blindingly blue, cloudless sky when he spotted the narrow entrance to the death canyon. Taking cover behind a thick stand of mesquite saplings, he watched for any movement that would give away their location.

The tree's thick fernlike foliage gave him complete cover; but even more, the ripened beans were a great way to supplement the dwindling food supply with something nutritious and filling. As he hurriedly pulled handfuls of the beans from the tree and stuffed them into the back-pack, he recalled the times during his childhood when he'd stolen away and filled himself full of the sweet treat and then caught the devil from his mother for ruining his appetite. He smiled. It had been a long time since Kaine had thought of his mother with a smile and not a deep stabbing pang of guilt.

A rustling in the bushes behind him brought him up sharp. His body tensed and ready to spring, he turned slowly toward it. The bushes parted, and Shadow ambled into the clearing. Kaine drew a deep relived breath.

"Shadow! How'd you get away?"

He reached toward the dog to welcome him back with a scratch behind his ears and a thorough petting, something he knew the dog loved. But, to Kaine's surprise, Shadow pulled back from his hand. The dog's normally bright, discerning gaze was dark and lackluster. The skinwalkers must have put him through hell before he got away. Even his coat was dull and unkempt.

"It's okay, fella. I'm not going to hurt you." He reached for the dog again, but again he backed away.

Obviously, Shadow needed time to recover from the trauma of having been taken by the skinwalkers, so Kaine backed off.

"Okay." He held up both hands. "No touching. Can you take me to Laura? Where's Laura?"

Shadow's ears perked and then he turned back to the direction from which he'd come. Kaine grabbed the backpack and quickly followed him into the bushes.

The trail led through more bushes and zigzagged around boulders and through a grove of mature mesquite trees. It finally ended at a small opening that Kaine figured he'd just fit through. Pushing the backpack through first, Kaine slid on his back and wiggled through the opening, finding himself in a narrow slot canyon.

Following the tracks that led along the precipitous wall, Kaine looked around him, awed by the grandeur wrought by wind and rain. In spots the high walls curved in, blocking the sun and resulting in the bottom being almost as dark as night. Where the top of the chamber opened to the sky, the walls were vibrant yellow, the tones deepening to orange as the sun worked its way toward the lower levels. At the floor, slashes of blues and purples cut across the rocks where the sun barely reached.

The walls, where the softer sediment had been eroded, were scalloped, and indentations marked the wind-smoothed surface. In some places, the cavities extended back for several feet, forming cave-like alcoves, but without the three-sided protection of the caves higher up the canyon walls.

From where he stood, he could see just a slice of the canyon, but, even though he'd only ever seen it from atop the canyon rim, he knew it from memory. The canyon itself formed a bowl, with one opening to enter and leave. The walls went almost straight up from the quarter-mile-wide floor, which was cut through with a stream that disappeared below the far wall, probably into some underground caverns. Scattered here and there were mesquite trees and some saguaro cacti, the dead blooms of the flowers hanging from the cacti's outstretched arms like white, deflated balloons.

It was understandable why the earlier settlers who inhabited this box canyon chose it. The walls were full of hundreds of caves, a natural, readymade, fortress.

Now, all he had to do is figure out which one the skinwalkers were keeping Laura and Peter in. He removed the backpack and tucked it back into one of the alcoves. When he found them, this would be the escape route he'd choose to get them out of here safely. He'd pick up the backpack on their way out.

Feeling for the lump nestled against his back to make sure the gun was still in place, Kaine followed Shadow as he wove his way through the curves of the slot canyon. The dog stopped a few feet from the mouth of the crevasse. Kaine eased up behind him and surveyed the caves for any sign of his wife and son.

The stench of death seemed to hang in the air, reminding him of the ritual of the skinwalkers and the many bodies they'd probably burned here to get the corpse dust they used to sicken their victims before they killed them and the ritual started all over again. From the strength of the odor, he decided they must have had a ritual burning not long ago. His stomach turned with dread and fear clutched at his heart.

Laura's head throbbed. Though her eyes were closed, she could feel the warmth of the sun on her face, yet her immediate surroundings felt dank and chilly. The rays falling across her eyes felt like tiny knife blades being pushed into her eyelids. Quickly, she squeezed them closed in an effort to block the pain.

Despite her efforts, a thundering ache pounded through her temples and radiated from a spot at the back of her head. Rubbing the tender lump she found under her hair, she tried to recall how she could have come by it. She and Kaine had been quite physical the night before, but she didn't remember hitting her head. Recalling the night before brought a smile to her heart.

Then it came to her. She hadn't hit her head. Some-one else had done it . . . someone who'd been hiding behind the rocks around their encampment.

Gingerly, she opened her eyes and blinked against the harsh beam of sunlight. Cautiously, she looked around at what appeared to be some sort of cave. The light that had pierced her eyes was coming from an opening about twenty feet away from her. The sun was shining brightly, sending meager shafts of warmth into the damp darkness. She shifted slightly so the sun was off her face.

Where in God's name was she? How did she get here? How long had she been out? Had Kaine noticed her absence? Was he looking for her or had he gone on to find Peter without her?

"Well, you finally woke up."

Laura spun toward the strangely familiar voice. Her aching head cried out in protest of the sudden movement. Squinting her eyes against the pain, Laura could barely make out a figure in the darkness at the back of the cave. Then the figure stepped forward into a ray of sunlight and Laura gasped.

"Anne? What are you—" The pain slicing through her head made it hard to think, to rationalize why her best friend would be *here*.

Laura bit off her questions. Now that Anne had come closer, Laura couldn't believe the change in the woman with whom she'd shared her most closely guarded secrets.

Anne's eyes, the same eyes Laura remembered as velvety brown, friendly and always laughing, were now cold and menacing. Instead of her warm brown pupils, they were an eerie red, and diamond-shaped like those of an animal. Her lovely copper-colored skin had paled to an ashen gray. And her mane of shiny, black hair was now shaggy, grayish and unkempt and lacked any luster at all.

It reminded Laura of the skinwalkers' coats. On the tail of that thought, another raced into her mind, one that chilled her to the bone. She backed away, unwilling to accept what her mind was telling her.

"Afraid of me, Laura?" Anne advanced, her lips curling into a smile or was it more a snarl?

"Where's my son?"

Anne threw back her head and laughed and this time, there was no mistaking it. The sound that emerged was a growl, an animalistic growl that sounded very much like the noises that had come from those beasts the night they'd attacked Kaine. Anne was one of them. She was a skinwalker.

"Don't you mean yours and *Kaine's* son?

Ignoring the taunt, Laura advanced on her. "Where . . . is . . . my . . . son?" Laura's tone sounded almost as feral as Anne's had. Each word was spoken through clenched teeth.

"He's fine, Laura." She threw a furtive glance toward the back of the cave.

"He's here?" Laura lunged forward. "Let me see him. I want to see him now!"

Anne caught her upper arms in a surprisingly strong grip and forced her back. "Not yet. You'll see him eventually, but not now."

Rubbing the spots where Anne's fingers had bruised her flesh, Laura stared at the woman she had thought of as a friend since she'd come to Tucson. How could she have misjudged her so completely?

"Why, Anne? Why did you do this?"

"Do what? Take Peter to the powwow? Befriend you?" She emitted a guttural, growl-like laugh. "Why else? To get to Kaine Cloudwalker, of course."

"Why Kaine? Why not some other shaman?"

"Because Kaine has what we need."

It didn't take Laura long to put two and two together and figure out what that was. "His ability to heal animals?"

Anne pointed an unusually long fingernail at her. "Exactly."

Then, as though looking for someone, Anne strolled to the cave opening and peered out—leaving Laura, who had been waiting for her chance, to edge her way to the back to find Peter. Suddenly, she came up against something big and hairy. She screamed and jumped back, swiveling to see what it was. Another skinwalker stood on its hind legs peering at her through the same red eyes Anne had.

"I told you that you could see Peter shortly, Laura." Anne motioned toward the other skinwalker. "You remember David, don't you?"

Laura's mouth fell open. "David? Your son?"

"Yes. Handsome boy, isn't he?" She laughed again, this time it took on all the aspects of a baying coyote.

Laura's legs gave out. She dropped down on a rock ledge protruding from the side of the cave. Why hadn't she noticed anything different about them? They'd lived next door to her in a little house, tucked into a respectable neighborhood. David had gone to school with Peter every day, and Laura and Anne had laughed over lunch dates and cheered wildly for their sons at Little League games. Everything about the single mother and her son had been so . . . normal.

As if reading her thoughts, Anne explained. "Don't blame yourself, Laura. We're very good at what we do. Skinwalkers can change into whatever form suits our purpose best. Because we needed to get to Kaine, becoming your friend and your son's friend filled that need. Then luring Kaine into the canyons to find his missing son took care of the rest."

"But you knew Kaine had no idea that Peter was his. How did you know that it would be Kaine who came looking for Peter?"

Anne frowned. "This plan has been in the works for a long time, Laura, and we've thought it out very carefully. As for making sure Kaine was the one who brought you to look for Peter, well, let's just say that, when they find the *real* Lieutenant Klah of the NTP, his health will be very poor."

Laura remembered the picture of the smiling children on the coffee mug, and her heart saddened for their loss.

Anne's expression hardened. "Be assured Laura, even

without putting one of ours into that NTP uniform to make certain you went to Kaine for help, we would have gotten him here one way or the other, have no doubt about it.

"As for getting Peter here . . . well, that was a bit more difficult. Of course, if you weren't such a doting, over-protective mother, it would have been much easier. You did make my job much more difficult and very compli-cated, always being around him, never letting him out of your sight, needing to know every move the poor child made. But after you told me about how interested Peter was in his heritage . . ." She snapped her fingers. "It was a breeze. The powwow was the perfect answer."

At the back of the cave, Anne's skinwalker *son* prowled on all fours, crossing the cave and then retracing his steps, like a sentry walking a picket line. She stared at him, try-ing to equate this wild looking beast with the sweet little boy she'd made peanut-butter-and-jelly sandwiches for and who had stayed overnight with her son. His eerie red gaze bored into Laura. As if he knew what she was think-ing, his teeth bared in a twisty kind of almost smile, and then a low growl rumbled from him.

"Of course, then I had to lure Peter away. He proves to have your stubborn streak, Laura, but a promise to visit the reservation where his father lives was too big a temptation for any little boy to pass up. Once we left the powwow, I made sure he didn't resist." Anne paused, as if waiting for Laura to reply.

"What did you do to him?"

Anne's answer was a twisted, noncommittal smile.

"You bitch!" Laura lunged for Anne's throat. But David interceded, raising on his hind legs and baring his teeth. Saliva dripped from his lower jaw. His front paws were raised even with his head, razor-sharp talons protruded from each toe. Remembering what those claws had done to Kaine, Laura backed away.

"Smart," Anne said, stroking David's mangy coat, "a bite from one of us has dire consequences." When Laura looked at her questioningly, Anne smiled. "Let's just say that I wasn't always a skinwalker."

An icy shiver stole down Laura's spine. So that was why Kaine had sacrificed his body to hold the beast's head away from him. He knew the consequences of being bitten by one of these monsters.

"You still haven't explained specifically why you want Kaine." Laura hoped if she kept her talking, she could distract her long enough to slip past the skinwalker guard and find Peter.

"My pack has contracted a sickness."

"*Your* pack?"

"Yes." Her red eyes narrowed menacingly on Laura. "Since you chose to kill my father the other night, as his oldest offspring, the pack is now mine." Laura detected the feral tone of an animal defending its turf. "And my pack is sick. Once they come down with whatever it is that's infected them, nothing we do can cure them. As a result, our numbers are shrinking." Anne snarled. "I can't have that. Our strength is in our numbers."

Laura couldn't summon any sympathy for their plight and had to tamp down the elation that came with Anne's pronouncement.

"Since Kaine's special brand of magic is curing animals," Anne went on, "we not only want him, it's vital that we get him. So you see, Laura, this is not just a frolic for us. The perpetuation of our species is at stake."

"And after you get Kaine, what about Peter and me? What will happen to us?"

"Well, you must be punished for murdering my father, so . . ."

Laura swallowed hard. Anne didn't need to elaborate. Laura could guess Peter's and her fate. The more Anne told her they more she'd have to go on to help her and Peter out of here—if she ever got to him.

Fighting to keep control, she spoke in an even tone. "But you could kill us now and Kaine would never know."

"Ah, but I'd want him here for the happy event." Her smile was one of the purest evil Laura had ever had the misfortune to witness. "Besides, I never said we'd kill you. Since our numbers are shrinking, we'd make sure you joined us." Her top lip curled back.

A cold dread passed over Laura. It took every ounce of her strength to keep from screaming at the complete horror of this situation, to not charge at Anne and hope for the best. But she'd be no good to her son dead. Instead, she continued to keep her voice under control. "But if you kill Kaine then how will he help you?"

"You're not listening, Laura. We won't kill any of you. You'd be of no use to us dead. Once you're bitten, you will become one of us to help replenish the pack. When Kaine is one of us, he'll use his skills to save *his* people, *our* people, *my* people."

"And if we refuse?" Laura wasn't sure she wanted to know the answer to her question, but the words tumbled out before she could stop them.

Anne walked to the side of the cave and picked up a large pottery bowl that had been resting on a ledge. She brought it to Laura and thrust it under her nose. Laura drew back from the putrid smell rising from the gray dust that filled the bowl.

"What is that?" Laura coughed and covered her nose.

"Corpse dust made from grinding the bones of our prey. Blown into a human's face, it can kill them in days, very slowly. Of course, if we chose to just sicken our victims as we did with Peter and that damned dog of yours, then you'll just sicken and eventually drift into a coma, unless we choose to reverse the process."

Laura's heart stopped. Terror clogged her throat. "Peter's sick?"

Anne smiled. "I'll let you see for yourself."

Laura jumped to her feet, eager to see her son. Anne motioned for the skinwalker guard to move aside and let them through. They walked down a long, dark tunnel leading to a small chamber at the back of the cave. The only illumination was a thin beam of sunlight coming from an opening in the chamber's roof.

When Laura stepped closer to what looked like a pile of dirty rags, she saw Peter immediately and rushed to his side. Beside him was Shadow, still and lifeless except for a slight movement of his chest. Evidently, they had no idea of Shadow's true identity or they would have killed him immediately. When she bent toward Peter, one of Shadow's eyes opened, stared at her and then closed. For a dog that was supposed to be in a coma, this startled Laura, as did the alertness of the dog's gaze.

Instantly, she understood. Shadow pretended sleep to be near Peter, to guard their son as the dog had guarded Kaine and her throughout their journey.

Laura knelt next to her son and pulled his head to her lap. She stroked back the black hair lying over his forehead and looked down into his sleeping face. His complexion was waxen. His lips pale. His skin cold and clammy. Looking at him from a strictly medical point of view, Laura would have said he was in the final stages of a coma and would lapse into death very soon.

Looking at him with a mother's heart, she refused to accept that. If she had to take on these animals with her bare hands, *Peter would not die*.

She leaned closer to his face. The same stench she'd smelled coming from the bowl Anne had shown her accosted Laura with each shallow breath Peter took.

"Peter, sweetheart. Mommy's here. I won't let them

hurt you, baby." Peter didn't respond. Though Laura hadn't expected him to, his lack of reaction twisted her already lacerated heart. Holding Peter close, she looked at Anne who was standing nearby, leering at the scene, revulsion in her expression. "He needs help. Let me take him away from here, please."

Anne shook her head, her wild mane of hair wobbling comically around her face. "No. He stays here until Kaine shows up." She turned to the skinwalker. "She's been in here long enough. Bring her back outside."

Though Laura clung to Peter, the beast's strength was beyond anything human and her own a feeble attempt to overcome or match him. He easily tore her away from her son and dragged her back to the front chamber of the cave. Small spots of blood erupted on her arms where his claws dug into her flesh.

Rubbing at the smarting punctures, she glared at Anne. "How can you do this to a little boy?" she spat. "He's done nothing to you or these . . . things. Let me take him to a doctor."

"A doctor won't help what ails him, Laura. I'm the only one who can cure your son. If you do as I ask, then maybe, just maybe, I'll allow him to live and join you and your husband in your fate." Anne strolled casually, as if out for a Sunday walk, to the front of the cave, stepping into a puddle of sunlight that ironically gave her a spiritual appearance. She twisted as if in physical pain and then quickly stepped back into the shadows.

Fighting to hold back her tears, Laura refused to let this bitch see any weakness in her. "And what is it you want me to do?" she asked much more calmly than she felt. Inside her heart was breaking and her mind was screaming her son's name at full volume.

"I want you to sit here," she pointed at the cave mouth, "and watch for your husband. When you see him, beckon for him to join you. Tell him you've found Peter. If you try to signal him in any other way, the boy dies." She bared her teeth in that half-snarl, half-smile. "Understand?"

Laura nodded. She could only hope that when Kaine saw her sitting here so casually without Peter that he'd figure out something wasn't right.

"Good. Willoughby," Anne called toward the back chamber. "Bring the blanket."

"Willoughby? From the trading post?"

"Yes, one and the same. It seems Mr. Willoughby has a greedy streak and doesn't wish to spend his retirement trading trinkets with Navajos and doling out supplies to tourists who want to gawk at the scenery. So, he enlisted our aid."

"Your aid?"

"If we showed him where to find the burial site of some Mimbres pottery, he'd help us get Kaine. Why do you think the woman at the trading post so willingly gave up the information about having seen a child drinking from the stream in this very canyon? Who do you think left the shirt for you to find?"

Laura was beginning to think that not one person she'd met in the last week was not a cohort of this evil bitch.

"And who do you think buried the pottery you found under the arch?" Anne clicked her tongue. "Unfortunately, neither you nor those damn government men were supposed to find it. Now, that the agents have taken it, poor Willoughby is out of luck." If it were possible, her smile tuned nastier. "Of course, Willoughby has enough pottery stowed in the back of the cave that he won't miss one bowl and a few worthless shards."

"Then why is he still here?"

"Because we aren't quite finished with Willoughby, are we David?" The skinwalker sentry growled, his lip curling into a vague semblance of a smile.

Just then a slender, balding man, hovering on the doorstep of seventy years and wearing bib overalls and a red plaid flannel shirt, came from the back carrying a colorful Navajo blanket. The trader avoided Laura's accusing gaze, spread the blanket in front of the cave's mouth and then quickly retreated into the small chamber.

Laura glared after his diminishing figure, then looked down at the blanket. It was the one the old woman had been weaving in front of the trading post. It reminded Laura of the pendant. She laid her hand against her chest to make sure it was still there. Warmth flowed into her cold palm.

"Sit," Anne commanded.

Laura obeyed; she clutched at the pendant and

concentrated with all her being, aiming her thoughts at Kaine. If this thing had the power Laura believed in her heart it had been imbued with by Changing Woman, then maybe she could communicate with Kaine. Her fingers had no sooner closed around it than she sensed Kaine as if he were sitting next to her.

❖   ❖   ❖

Kaine had been anxiously scanning the caves cut into the box canyon's walls for over two hours and had seen nothing. There was no sense trying to search them all; there were just too many, and it would take hours.

Shadow laid beside him, still unwilling for Kaine to touch him, his strange eyes centered on Kaine. He had no idea what the skinwalkers had done to him, but it seemed to have altered the dog's personality drastically. Aside from the personality changes, his appearance had changed. The fur that had been fluffy and clean was now dirty, matted, and disheveled. The sunburst on his chest was so grimy it was nearly obliterated.

Truth be known he gave Kaine the creeps, and he'd have been much happier if the dog went off on one of its frequent side trips. But it seemed content . . . no, not content . . . *intent* on staying close to Kaine.

He dragged his gaze away from the dog and scanned the caves for the hundredth time. Perhaps when night came, since skinwalkers were nocturnal by nature, they'd start moving and he could get some idea of where they were keeping Laura and Peter. He sighed and leaned back against the smooth wall of the slot canyon.

Closing his eyes, he thought of Laura and wondered absently if Peter looked like her. Kaine tried to picture a miniature version of her, but each time he saw a small girl with coal-black hair and large eyes looking up at him with such love and trust that it made his heart ache. Maybe it was an omen of things to come. Maybe someday, if Laura could find it in her heart to love him enough to stay with him, they would have a little girl like that.

Laura. Why couldn't he have loved her as she should have been loved, deserved to be loved, when he had the chance? Now, if he didn't find her, he may never get that chance.

The pain that shot through his heart nearly made him cry out. Then it was followed by a burning yet comforting warmth, right in the center of his chest; and that removed all of the pain. He laid his hand over it.

Kaine.

He bolted upright, but kept his eyes tightly closed, afraid of disturbing whatever was happening to him.

Kaine.

The dog growled, but Kaine ignored him.

I can feel you near me. I know you hear me. Look up.

He opened his eyes and did as Laura's voice instructed. For a moment, he searched in vain for any sign of her; then, on the ledge of a cave high above the canyon floor and almost directly in line with his vision, he saw her. She was sitting close to the edge, her hand at her chest, her head lifted toward the cloudless sky.

I'm here, he thought, propelling his voice back to her with everything in him. *I'm here, Laura. I hear you, and I can see you. I'm coming. Hang on.*

Chapter 18

A stormy night sky canopied the canyon as complete as if it had been enfolded beneath the wings of the angel of death. The darkness was infinite and absolute. Kaine couldn't see his hand in front of his face.

Despite being confident of his courage, apprehension laid in a tight ball in the pit of his stomach. What if he couldn't find them? What if he found them and the skinwalkers had already killed them?

Pushing the doom-and-gloom thoughts aside, he concentrated on the direction in which he'd been moving. Afraid to turn on the flashlight and alert the skinwalkers of his presence, Kaine stumbled along in the darkness purely by instinct toward the cave where he'd seen Laura.

Shadow walked beside him. Keeping a distance between himself and the human at his side. As if making sure Kaine was still with him, he'd occasionally turn those eerie, yellow eyes toward him. Oddly, they glowed as if with an inner light source.

Suddenly Shadow bolted forward and took the lead. He paused, looked back at Kaine and then proceeded on at a pace that accommodated Kaine's unsure movements. When they reached the bottom of the cliff in which the cave was located, Shadow paused again. Raising his head, he sniffed the air and then took a path leading up from the ground level.

Kaine followed. "I hope you know where you're going," he mumbled at the dog's back.

✤　✤　✤

Laura's back throbbed like a toothache from sitting still for so long, but she remained unmoving, clutching the pendant in numb fingers and speaking to Kaine in her mind. Since he'd answered her earlier, there had been only silence. But she didn't give up. She kept up the steady stream of mental chatter, hoping her voice would guide him to her and Peter.

When she still heard nothing, she had to give up. Instead, she concentrated on getting to Peter. If only David could be distracted. She stole a glance at him. All his attention was still on her.

The light had all but disappeared; only a flickering torch someone had lit and attached to the cave wall almost out of sight of Laura remained. Out of the corner of her eye, she could see Anne leaning against the wall . . . waiting. David prowled in the background just behind her. So far, she hadn't seen any of the other skinwalkers. Were they all sick? Were Anne and David all that was left?

Even if they were the only ones left, Kaine had no idea what awaited him. He'd be ambushed. She had to do something, but what? The one thing in her favor was that so far she'd only seen David and Anne and none of the others in the pack of skinwalkers. If she waited for Kaine to come, maybe she could catch Anne off guard, and then maybe she could get to Peter and leave Kaine to take care of David.

"You realize that you may not be able lure Kaine here," she said to the watching woman. "He hasn't cared enough about me in eight years to search for me. What makes you think he'd care enough now?"

Anne straightened abruptly and came to stand over Laura. "You mean you haven't told him about Peter?"

Laura dropped her gaze to her lap, but kept a close watch on where Anne was standing out of the corner of her eye. "No." Unfortunately, her anxiety flavored her voice.

"Liar!" Anne grabbed a handful of Laura's hair and snatched her head back so that she was looking directly into those evil, red eyes. "Don't lie to me." She stared at Laura for a long moment and then smiled. "You've told him. I can see it in your face. He knows about his son and even if he cares nothing for you, his blood is in that boy's veins, and he won't let him die. These Navajos are far too loyal like that. They'd lay down their lives for a relative."

She let go of Laura's hair abruptly and pushed her away. Lara tumbled backward.

Turning to David, Anne spoke as she walked toward the chamber where Peter lay. "Watch her. I'm going to find Willoughby to bring her food." Anne disappeared inside the depths of the cave.

Laura watched David as closely as he did her. Could she overpower him? She looked at his paws and saw the lethal claws that protruded from each toe. Again, she recalled what those claws had done to Kaine. David would tear her to shreds, and she'd never be able to help Peter. She *had* to find a way to get Peter and herself out of here.

Just then, Willoughby appeared carrying a bowl of something that smelled almost as foul as the corpse dust. He set it down in front of her and fussed with the edge of the blanket.

"She hates light," he murmured so low Laura could barely hear him. "I can distract her son, you kill her."

Laura nodded almost imperceptibly. "Why are you doing this?" she asked in a whisper.

"Shouldn't hurt a child," he mumbled.

"Willoughby! What are you doing? Give her the food and go!"

Anne shoved him away. He lost his balance for a moment, then righted himself and scurried off to the back chamber.

"Old fool," Anne snarled and then cast a look at Laura

that said: *Don't try anything.*

Laura turned away, her mind busy thinking about what Willoughby had said. She pretended to be interested in the food. It was something red and raw, something that turned her stomach just to look at. She set the bowl aside.

How could she overpower Anne? How could she kill her without a weapon? In desperation, Laura grasped the pendant.

My son will send you a weapon.

Having heard it so many times by now, Laura instantly recognized the voice in her head as Changing Woman. The son she spoke of must be Monster Slayer. Another gift from the child who had given her the corn pollen. Was she expected to kill Anne with corn pollen? She desperately hoped it would be something more substantial, something she could cut this witch's heart out with.

Sighing heavily, she glanced at the sky. She felt utterly helpless to do anything about the inevitable ambush that was awaiting Kaine; and worst of all, that she'd enticed him into the very mouth of the beast. Her shoulders slumped. Dark clouds blocked out the moon. Thunder growled in the distance. Lightning sliced through the heavens, illuminating the depths of the huge thunderheads above her. Then another flash came right above the canyon, slicing a beam of lightning down toward the cave.

Laura felt a sharp pain in her thigh and looked down to see a shiny dagger sticking into her flesh. She pulled it out. Amazingly, no blood stained her clothes and the pain disappeared instantly. She studied the dagger. Was this the promised weapon?

It was shaped like a small lightning bolt, and it lay cold against her palm. Then it began to vibrate from within, as it were filled with some unleashed power. Reflected in the shiny metal was the face of the *tewa*, the sun god she'd seen on the pendant worn by the woman at the hospital fair.

I gave this as a gift to my son, Monster Slayer. Because of the kindness you've shown him, he wants you to have it. Use it wisely.

The voice, this time a man's, echoed through her mind. Laura's fingers closed around the dagger. She glanced toward the back of the cave where Anne was standing beside David. David continued to skulk on all fours, his acid red eyes glowing brightly in the dim light. She prayed that Willoughby would do his part as he said he would. In any case, she would be ready.

✤   ✤   ✤

The climb to the cave became steeper and steeper, until Kaine and Shadow were ascending the canyon wall at what felt like a forty-five-degree angle. The muscles at the back of Kaine's legs began to ache. Sweat coated his body. His breath came hard. But he pushed on, knowing his wife and son's lives were in his hands.

Several hundred feet above him, he detected a very

faint light coming from the cave where he'd seen Laura. Knowing how much skinwalkers detested light, he knew nothing good lay beyond that light. They were using it as an enticement while they lay in waiting for him.

As they got closer to the light source, he could see Laura sitting just inside the cave's entrance. He wanted to rush to her, but he knew that would be the stupidest thing he could do. She was the bait. He was the quarry. The second he showed himself, she became expendable.

Shadow moved forward. Kaine followed. They began the climb upward again. Kaine split his attention between watching the path, his footing, and keeping an eye on Laura. After several more minutes, they'd stopped again, this time just beyond the entrance. He was no more than a few feet from Laura.

He picked up a small pebble and tossed it. It hit her on the cheek. She flinched but not enough to really notice. She swatted at her face as though an insect had bitten her. His heart dropped.

He started to toss another pebble, but Shadow lunged forward. Just as the dog passed through the entrance, it looked as though he'd been engulfed in a small, dusty tornado. Inside the churning dust Shadow seemed to swirl and twist as his body morphed and took on a new form.

When the dust settled, a skinwalker stood in his place. Its gaze fastened on Kaine. He growled deep in his throat and then launched his body at Kaine. Kaine quickly steeped aside, and the beast flew over the side. A shrill almost human scream came from the animal as he plunged to the canyon floor, hundreds of feet below.

Kaine knew his presence was known to whoever was in the cave. He bounded forward and grabbed Laura's arm to pull her out of the way.

"Look out," she cried.

The word had barely left her lips when Kaine was knocked down by another skinwalker. They rolled in the dirt. The beast's claws ripped at his shirt. Kaine managed to elude the thrashing claws and got to his feet before the beast grabbed him again. He fastened his hands around its throat and tried to push it away. It raised its claws above Kaine's head and started the downward thrash that would once more rip Kaine's flash to ribbons. But Kaine caught the back of the animal's hind legs, behind the knees with his foot, and it buckled to the ground.

Making a fist of both hands linked together, Kaine brought them down on the back of its neck. It fell forward and lay still. With the toe of his boot, Kaine rolled the body off the cliff.

He looked up to find Laura being held around the throat by a woman. "Who the hell are you?"

"She's Anne Yatzee, the woman who took Peter to the powwow," Laura said, her voice choked by the pressure the woman was applying to her neck. "Peter's in the back of the cave."

"Alive?" Kaine held his breath, and then she nodded.

"Barely. He's very sick."

"And he'll stay that way and worse, if you don't do what I ask." Anne glared at him through the same unearthly eyes the dog he'd thought was Shadow had. The only difference was the dog's eyes had been yellow and Anne's were blood red.

"And what is it you want from me?"

"You have to heal my pack of their sickness."

"Do I look stupid?"

Anne tightened her hold. "Then she dies, and so does the kid."

If he wanted to save his family, he had but one choice, agree. Laura's and Peter's life was worth too much to try to bargain with the other woman. However, that didn't mean he had to keep his word. "Agreed. Now, let her go."

Anne pushed Laura at Kaine. He caught her in his arms. "You okay?"

Laura clung to him. "Yes, but we need to get to Peter. He's very, very sick."

Anne circled them like a wolf ready to pounce. She got herself between them and the cave entrance. "Don't try anything. I'm the only one who can stop the sickness infecting the boy. Kill me and he dies, too."

Kaine felt Laura shiver against him. "We won't try anything," he said, holding Laura tighter.

Laura looked past Kaine at the woman she'd called her friend. She had a choice to make, let her live and risk them all being infected and turned into skinwalkers. Kill her and possibly take her son's life along with Anne's.

Laura decided that either way Peter would die, but she preferred it be in his normal form and not that of a blood-thirsty beast that lived off the corpses of others.

She fingered the lightning dagger she'd hidden in her jeans pocket.

"Move away from her," Anne commanded.

He set Laura aside, but moved slightly to put his body between them. "Where are the ones you want healed?"

Before Anne could answer, Laura stepped around Kaine and threw the dagger at Anne. It glittered brightly and seemed to give off its own light as it traveled toward its intended target. With a muffled *thud*, it stabbed deep into her chest. She screamed, and her agonizing cry echoed around the canyon like a thousand cries of death. She clutched her throat and crumpled to the ground. Smoke started seeping from her body and soon obliterated her. Moments later, the smoke cleared and all that was left was a puddle of black fluid. The evil that had flowed through her veins. In the center of the puddle, the dagger glowed brightly and then vanished.

Kaine turned and grabbed Laura to him. "Where's Peter?"

Taking his hand, Laura led him to the small chamber. She wasn't certain that what she'd done was using the lightning bolt *wisely* as she'd been instructed to do, but she could not let Kaine heal those monsters so they could terrorize more Navajos. Hopefully, they could find a way to save Peter without Anne. They better find a way. She'd gambled her son's life on it.

Together, they sprinted down the tunnel leading to the small chamber. They found Willoughby bending over Peter, swabbing his forehead with a wet cloth. Beside the boy lay the limp body of Shadow.

As soon as Willoughby saw Kaine, he straightened. For a moment Kaine and Willoughby locked gazes. Laura held her breath. The look on Kaine's face was one of such anger that she thought he'd grab Willoughby and shake him until he didn't have a breath left in his body. Evidently sensing the same thing, the old man backed away from the boy.

Willoughby looked at Laura. "Anne?"

"Dead. David, too."

She dismissed the old man quickly. Her concern was entirely for the boy. But as she stepped forward, she stopped and allowed Kaine to precede her. He knelt beside Peter and touched his face as if he were a porcelain doll that would break if handled too roughly. His expression, which had been so thunderous moments before, was now gentle and held an awe she had never seen before.

"My son," he said softly. "My son." The torch light illuminated a single tear as it rolled down Kaine's cheek.

Laura felt as if a hand had reached inside her chest and squeezed her heart. How could she have been so cruel as to keep Peter's identity from him? It never occurred to her that Kaine would need his son as much as Peter needed his father. Her selfishness had robbed them both of eight years of knowing each other. At that moment, though she had no idea how she'd manage it, she made a decision. If they got out of here, she would see to it that Kaine and Peter had as much time together as she could arrange.

Roughly, Kaine wiped the tear away, but he couldn't seem to tear his gaze from the child. This was his son, made up of the best parts of himself and Laura. A product of their love.

He looked at Peter's gray complexion and how still he lay. Had he found him only to lose him? He refused to believe that. Once they got him away from here, he'd find a way to save Peter if he had to carry him on his back all the way to the nearest hospital himself. But he also knew that no hospital would be able to cure Peter.

"We need to get him to a hospital," Laura whispered, laying her hand on Kaine's shoulder.

Kaine's shoulders slumped the merest fraction. He shook his head slowly, keeping his gaze on Peter. "*Bilagáanaa* medicine is not going to help him."

"You're wrong," Laura cried, clutching at his sleeve. "You have to be wrong. If we just get him to the—"

Kaine sprang to his feet and grabbed her by the shoulders. "This is not a white man's sickness, Laura. It's caused by corpse dust. The white man has no medicine to fight this."

Slowly, the meaning of Kaine's words sank in. Despair flowed through her, sapping her strength. "Then . . .

Anne was right." Laura paled. If it hadn't been for Kaine's hands holding her up, she would have crumbled at his feet. "Oh, my God. What have I done?" She put her hand over her mouth. Tears filled her eyes and then cascaded slowly down her cheeks. "I killed Anne and now there's no one left to heal Peter."

Just then Shadow, who had been lying as still as death beside Peter, sprang to his feet and bounded past them to the tunnel entrance. He stopped and turned back and then barked. Everyone stared at the dog. Shadow ran a few feet down the tunnel and then came back and barked again.

"I think he wants us to follow him." Kaine bent over and picked up Peter's limp body.

When they would have gone down the tunnel to the front of the cave, Willoughby stopped them. "Some of the sick skinwalkers are deeper in the cave. The rest are out hunting, but the sun will soon be up, and they'll be coming back very quickly after that. If we go that way," he pointed to where Shadow stood poised to run, "we'll run right into them."

Kaine paused, unable to decide if following Willoughby would be a good idea. While he was making up his mind, Willoughby reached into a notch in the cave wall and pulled out several pottery bowls.

Eyes widening, Kaine stared at the bowls. "What the hell are you doing with them?"

Laura nudged Kaine. "He's the one that buried the bowls I found back at the Rainbow Arch. He made a deal with the skinwalkers to get you here, if they helped him find more pottery."

It was good thing Kaine was holding his son, or he would have done what he first wanted to do when he realized Willoughby was a part of the scheme. Instead, he just glared at him. "You son of a bitch."

Willoughby shrugged helplessly. "I thought it would be a good way to get money so I didn't have to die penniless in that damned trading post. You'd have done the same thing, Warrior."

Kaine made a sound deep in his throat that sounded like a feral growl. "I would never sell my heritage to *anyone* for *any* reason. But above that, I would never sell out a man I called friend."

Laura tugged on his sleeve. "We don't have time for this. There's a storm coming, and it'll soon be dawn. The skinwalkers will be back. We don't have a choice. Unless you know another way, we have to follow him out of here."

Kaine continued to glare at Willoughby. He knew this canyon, but not the maze of caves and slot canyons surrounding it. He looked down at Peter and knew he'd follow the devil into Hell if it would save his son. That fact alone gave them no choice but to follow Willoughby and hope that he led them to safety, and not their ultimate deaths.

"Let's go," Kaine grumbled. "But if you even *look* like you're going to cross us, I swear on this child's life, I *will* kill you."

Thunder rumbled in the distance. Kaine figured it was a couple of miles to the west. He glanced at the sliver of sky he could see through the small opening at the top of the slot canyon. The churning thunderclouds blocked the sunlight and were growing in size and ferocity. If those clouds dumped their rain while they were on the bottom of the slot canyons, the chances of them surviving the resulting flashflood were nonexistent.

He'd grown up wandering through slot canyons and arroyos. He knew the dangers that lurked within their facial beauty. He'd experienced the subtle changes brought about by the forces of nature and some of the tragic results. He knew some were blind alleys and some gouged hundreds of feet into the earth. He knew that the dead ends could seal a man's fate as surely as a cornered rabbit.

Kaine sprinted forward, dread in his heart and a

prayer on his lips, Peter's body held close against his chest. Following Willoughby into another crevasse in the precipitous wall, he looked around him, his dread growing with each passing moment. Behind him, Laura, the backpack hanging from her shoulders, stumbled along as quickly as she could, trying valiantly to keep up with them.

While some of the walls were smooth as silk, others had a series of pockmarks dotting them that were just large enough to provide foot- and handholds for climbing. He'd never be able to climb to safety using them and carrying Peter, if that was the only option. What they needed was a clear path to one of the alcoves high above them.

Often the canyons had been widened by repeated floodwaters, causing expansive indentations; they were frequently large enough to build entire villages, as the Anasazi had at Canyon de Chelly. However, never having explored this part of this particular canyon, Kaine didn't know if there were any such alcoves here.

When the rains came and the slots flooded, there were few places high and dry enough to provide safe shelter from the churning waters that would wash down the crevasse at a moment's notice.

The ominous rumbling in the distance grew closer. Aware that the storm didn't have to be overhead for the flashfloods to come, he felt the raw edge of fear reminding him they were running out of time and needed to exit this place as soon as possible. He glanced back at Laura and saw the fear clearly written on her face.

Laura clutched the backpack straps tighter, fighting with every bit of her strength not to show Kaine how frightened she was. She'd followed in his footsteps as he'd guided her through the maze of sandstone corridors.

"Turn left," Willoughby called back to them, and then seemingly disappeared into a solid sandstone wall.

When they reached the spot where he'd vanished, they found another crevasse opening. Peeking around Kaine, she could see Willoughby trudging on, the pottery clutched tight to his chest. Her legs were aching from trying to keep her balance on the sand-slicked downhill slope, but she pushed on, wondering if they'd ever see civilization again, if they'd ever get Peter the help he needed before—suddenly her back stiffened.

That's a defeatist attitude, Laura.

This wasn't the first time she'd been faced with a hopeless situation. She'd never given up before, and she'd be damned if she'd do so now. Hell, she just buried a knife in the chest of another being. Wimps didn't do things like that.

In front of her, she saw Kaine's footsteps falter. He'd been carrying Peter nonstop for over an hour without resting. Sooner or later, even a man of his strength had to weaken. But he'd never stop.

"I have to rest," she called out and then swung the backpack to the ground and flopped down.

"We can't stop now." Kaine's shifted Peter so that his head rested against Kaine's shoulder.

She looked up at him. "I have to."

Kaine glanced at the sky and then nodded. "But just for a minute, then we have to go on." He sat beside her with Peter on his lap. Laura pushed the wave of hair so like his father's coal-black tresses off Peter's ashen forehead. Willoughby stood nearby, wisely keeping a distance between him and Kaine.

"If only I hadn't—"

Kaine grasped Laura's hand and cut her off, seeming to know what she was going to say without hearing the words. "You did what you had to do back there."

She nodded, afraid to speak. When she did, tears choked her voice. "But if I hadn't killed Anne, she could have saved Peter."

"And we'd all be part of her pack by now." Kaine lifted her chin with his finger. "You made the wisest choice you could have under the circumstances." His brow furrowed. "What was that you threw at her anyway?"

Laura hesitated. *She'd made the wisest choice.* She felt better. She'd really need confirmation of that. But she still hesitated to answer Kaine's question about what she'd thrown. Kaine already felt she'd given all the inexplicable things that had been happening to them too much credence. Would he believe her? She took a chance. "A small lightning bolt."

Silence that could have been sliced with a dull knife followed.

"Where did you get it?" he finally asked.

She glanced at Willoughby and then leaned closer to Kaine so only he could hear her. "The little boy, Monster Slayer, sent it to me to thank me for helping him."

She leaned back and waited for Kaine's rant to begin about her belief that the Navajo gods had a hand in almost all that happened to them in the past few days. But it never came. Instead, he glanced at Peter's placid face.

"I wish they'd send us something to cure him."

"They don't have to," Willoughby put in. "You already have it."

Both she and Kaine looked at the old man clutching the pottery bowls and keeping his distance. What did he mean they already have it? Anne said she was the only one who could reverse the effects of the corpse dust.

"I don't understand," she said.

"Him." He pointed at Kaine. "He's a shaman, and he can sing a Way over the boy to do what Anne would have done."

Laura's head jerked toward Kaine. All color drained from his face. "Is he right? Can you do a *sing* to cure Peter?"

Kaine's insides tied in instant knots. Bile rose in his throat. There was no way he'd even try to heal Peter. He'd done that once with someone he loved and lost the battle. He would not take the chance with his only son.

He stood abruptly. "We need to move on."

Laura grabbed his sleeve. "My medicine can't help him. If yours can, you *have* to try. *You have to.*"

Kaine almost gave in to the plea in her voice that seemed to emanate from her very soul. But then a vision of his mother flashed before him, and he shook his head. He would not risk Peter's life by doing something he hadn't believed in for years. "No. We'll take him to Window Rock to a doctor."

"He'll be dead by then," Willoughby said.

A gasp escaped Laura, and she turned to Kaine with large pleading eyes. She placed her forefinger on Peter's wrist. "He's right, Kaine. His pulse is already growing weak and threadlike. We can't wait much longer."

Kaine shook his head. "Let's go." He shifted Peter's body to a more comfortable position then strode away from her. He stopped not far from them in front of what appeared to be a solid wall of sandstone. Laura had learned quickly nothing in these canyons was as it appeared. Too many times, she'd thought they'd reached a dead end and found another corridor waiting around a bend in the wall.

Laying her head back against the hard rock wall, she tried to think what she could do to persuade him. Her own panic scared her senseless. The cold seeping into her took charge of her thoughts. She shivered uncontrollably, but wasn't sure if it was entirely from the cold temperatures or the sound of distant thunder.

She suddenly understood Kaine's need to get moving. She jumped to her feet. "Let's go. We've wasted enough time." Kaine was waiting just past Willoughby. When she met his gaze, he quickly looked away and turned to stride down the trail.

✣ ✣ ✣

Kaine eased himself and Peter from behind an outcropping of sandstone. A few more feet and they'd be on the floor of the slot canyon and then they could find a path up to a safe spot above the flood. Thunder rumbled ominously. It was closer, a lot closer.

Balancing his son in his arms, Kaine scrambled the remaining distance to the floor, his blood running cold at the close proximity of the thunder.

"We need to go back up, higher, off the canyon floor."

Willoughby and Laura glanced in the direction from where they'd just come.

"There's nothing back that way. We'd be trapped on the ledge before we could get high enough." From where he stood, Kaine cast a glance over Laura's head and saw a narrow path leading to a deep alcove in the wall just above her. "There. There's a cave where we can get away from the water." Willoughby looked at him as if he'd lost his mind.

A bright flash of lightning sent light zigzagging over the walls. The following crash of thunder vibrated the ground beneath their feet as it reverberated down the labyrinth of sandstone corridors. A drop of water fell on Peter's forearm. Looking up, Kaine saw the beginning of what would quickly become a miniature waterfall running from a crack in the canyon wall.

Seconds later, every groove and crack sprouted a slender waterfall. For a moment the scene was lovely, but all too quickly, its beauty turned deadly as the water's flow increased at a rapid rate and emptied onto the floor.

"If we don't move now, when this canyon floods, we'll all drown." Kaine's voice rose above the din of the water falling from above.

Sprinting to Laura's side, Kaine hoisted Peter over his shoulder in a fireman's carry and then grabbed her and shoved her toward the path.

"Climb," he ordered, pushing her toward the alcove.

"Hey! Wait for me." Willoughby started to follow, but dropped one of the bowls.

Laura turned to see what happened. The bowl had shattered into a dozen pieces. The old man fell to his knees, muttering about his own carelessness, and began gathering the pieces, placing them inside the intact bowl he still held.

Kaine placed his palm under Laura's buttocks and gave her a hard boost up the path. "Keep going. Don't stop."

"What about Willoughby?" she cried, her feet fumbling for solid footing close to the left side of the ledge, and trying not to look over the drop on the right side. She turned sideways and plastered herself against the cold sandstone wall.

"Keep going," Kaine called up to her.

Laura didn't ask for any more of an explanation. She'd seen this before, not more than days ago. She reached as far as she could, and clawed at the walls until she found protruding rocks to help boost her along up the steep incline. She could feel Kaine right behind her as he called out directions and encouragement.

The strength in her arms had nearly given out, but she managed to struggle over the edge of a wide opening in the wall. Kaine scrambled into the small cave behind her.

She turned back to the edge. "Willoughby."

The sound of thousands of waterfalls gushing from the walls onto the hard-packed earthen floor and the rumble of rushing water drowned out her voice.

She clutched at Kaine's shirt front. "Help him," she screamed to be heard above the din.

Kaine shook his head and mouthed, "It's too late."

Laura looked back at the man crouched over the broken fragments of bowl. Just then, a wall of red-brown churning water charged toward him. Full of collected silt and debris, it appeared too thick to move so fast. It tumbled in raging, turbulent torrents with standing waves of three feet carrying with it trees and large boulders as if they were sticks and small pebbles. Laura heard her scream echo above the roar of the encroaching flood.

From their perch high above, Kaine held her and Peter close. Laura watched in frozen horror while the water closed over Willoughby and sucked him along on its wild rampaging journey. A couple of times she noticed a leg or an arm protrude from the mucky water; but then he disappeared completely, and she saw no more of him. Turning, she buried her face in Kaine's shoulder.

Long minutes later, the many waterfalls slowed and stopped abruptly, as though some unseen hand had turned off a faucet. The rampant waters continued to rush through the canyon for almost an hour before they too gradually subsided.

Kaine levered Laura away from him and looked into her ashen face. He shook her gently, but she didn't respond, only continued to stare at the place where Willoughby had disappeared beneath the water for the last time. The place that was now empty of any trace of the man or his treasures.

"We can go now," Kaine said, hoisting Peter into his arms again.

Laura spoke not a word in reply, but placidly allowed him to guide her down the steep path to the floor below.

When her feet touched the solid, slippery ground, she shook off his hands and stood back, waiting for him to lead the way out. Kaine moved ahead of her, glancing back from time to time to make sure she was still there. Her stoic face told him she was in shock and speech would accomplish nothing.

As they stepped from the crevasse into the open canyon, Laura pushed past him and walked without saying a word in the direction of the Rainbow Arch. He shifted Peter back into the cradle of his arms and followed.

✤   ✤   ✤

They walked silently for what seemed like hours. Soon, up ahead, Laura could see the stone arch spanning the canyon. Shadow slipped out of the bushes and trotted along beside her. She hadn't even noticed that he hadn't been with them in the slot canyons.

Long ago, she'd come to terms with Willoughby's demise. What she could not come to terms with was Kaine's stubborn refusal to sing the Way for Peter. When they reached the site of her old encampment beneath the arch, she dropped the backpack and sank down on a rock. She untied the sleeping bag from the backpack brace and spread it out on the ground.

Kaine gently laid Peter on it and then collapsed beside him.

"Do you want your son to die?" Laura asked quietly.

"What?" Kaine's head snapped toward her. "Of course not!"

"What do I have to do to convince you that it was not your fault that your mother died, that this situation is totally different, that if you don't do something our son will most certainly die?"

Kaine stared down at Peter. He could barely see his chest rising and falling. Laura was right. Peter was dying.

Then he felt her arm circle his shoulders. "I'll help you. I'll do anything I must to help you do the *sing*."

He took a deep breath. Was Laura right? Would his mother have died anyway? Was her cancer too far advanced for his healing powers to help her? Was her sickness something that went beyond the powers of any medicine to heal?

Either way, he didn't have a choice. If he did nothing, Peter would die. If he did the *sing* unsuccessfully, Peter would die.

But what if you do it successfully? Step into the eye of the dream, Kaine.

The familiar voice of his grandfather rang inside his head.

Suddenly, knowing what he had to do, Kaine stood and then walked away into the brush, leaving Laura to cradle her son's head in her lap and let her tears wash his face.

Moments later, she could hear the plaintive sounds of a flute filling the air. Kaine. She raised her head and absorbed the music. It seeped into her body and her mind and through it she experienced Kaine's emotions.

She could hear the sadness in Kaine's soul; hear his indecisions, his battle with himself about the dilemma he faced. The sharp staccato notes told her of the pain of losing his mother and the separation from his heritage and teachings. After that, the notes became soulful and lonely, as if that self-imposed separation had torn a piece of his soul away, leaving him raw and isolated. The music stayed that way for a long time.

Suddenly, it changed and became alive, vibrant, and active, washed free of all tension. It told of hope and a new beginning. Then it went silent.

Chapter 20

Kaine emerged from the stand of mature mesquite trees and then walked back to where Laura sat on the sleeping bags with Peter cradled to her body. When she saw the resolution in his expression, her heart filled with hope.

"You're going to do it."

He nodded and then sat beside her. "You said you'd help me with the *sing*."

She nodded, and a smile transformed her sad face. "Just tell me what you want me to do."

"First of all, once I start, you can't interrupt me." She nodded. "This is not a fast process. It will last for a couple of days. I'll grow tired, but you still can't interrupt, for any reason at all." Again, she agreed with a nod. "There are things we have to gather."

She eased Peter from her lap and made him comfortable on the sleeping bag. "What?"

He pulled the pendant from beneath her shirt. His fingers grazing her skin sent a shiver through her despite her efforts not to react. "I'll need this."

She grabbed it away from him. "Why?" The pendant had been her stabilizer, her source of comfort for a very long time, and she was reluctant to part with it.

"I have to do several sandpaintings during the ceremony, and I'll need the colored stones from the pendant."

Still she hesitated to give it up. "What will you do with them?"

It was his turn to hesitate. "You have to understand that the colors in your pendant are sacred to this ritual. If the paintings are not done exactly as they should be, the healing will not take place." He paused, and then took her hand. "I'll have to pry them from their setting and then crush them into dust."

She gasped. "Dust?"

He nodded. "I'll also need the bag of corn pollen that the boy gave you."

Reminding herself that this was for Peter, Laura made no further argument. She removed the necklace and placed it in his hand. As she dug into the backpack for the leather pouch of pollen, something occurred to her. "Do you think we'll be able to find everything you need?" Then she felt the pouch and gasped. Despite having used a great deal of it to heal Kaine's wounds from the skin-walkers, the pouch was full again.

Kaine smiled and took it from her. "Considering who's been very instrumental in this whole adventure, I have no doubt that everything will be provided."

Just then, Shadow proved him right by appearing with some sagebrush sticks in his mouth. Kaine removed them, patted the dog on the head and then added them to the growing pile of items he'd need to do the *sing* over their son.

"Prayer sticks," he explained in response to Laura's frown.

Laura watched Kaine painstakingly arrange everything he had collected. She stilled his hands with her own and then looked deep into his eyes. "Are you okay?"

A long moment passed and then he nodded. "I'm fine. Doing the *sing*, even though it will last for so long, is the easy part. Waiting to see if it works is the rough part."

Laura encircled his shoulders with her arms, and then laid her cheek against his. "It'll work. We have to have faith. Surely they wouldn't have put us through all this only to take Peter from us."

Kaine kissed her cheek lightly, and then pulled away. He twisted and leaned over his son. Gently, he brushed Peter's dark hair from his ashen face, and then caressed his cheek. Pushing himself to his feet, he looked over the items spread out on the ground.

Choosing a spot, he leveled the sand and then using his penknife, began the task of prying the stones from her pendant and grinding them with a rock on a flat stone until nothing remained but colored dust. He kept each color separated from the others, and added other ground stones he chipped from the canyon walls—oranges, bluish blacks, and deep browns.

"I think everything is ready," he finally said. He stepped back and stared down at Peter.

This time Laura had no trouble reading her husband's thoughts. He was worried, frightened and filled with apprehension. She followed him to the bushes surrounding the campsite and watched silently as he cut chunks of yucca from a tall plant.

"I need something to put the juice in," he explained.

Quickly, she retrieved one of their cooking pots.

Kaine squeezed the juice from the yucca into the pot and then set it near the stream. He looked at her, and she smiled her encouragement. As though that were sufficient to imbue him with the confidence he needed to proceed, Kaine smiled back at Laura, and she saw he had lost all the anxiety and fear. At that moment, she knew he'd be fine.

Slowly, he began removing his clothes until he was totally naked. He stepped into the stream and, using the juice from the yucca, began bathing.

Without him telling her, Laura knew the ritual had begun. She returned to where the bedroll was laid, stretched out, and then pulled her son's body close to her side to wait.

When Kaine emerged from the stream, he dressed

then came to where he'd leveled the sand. He sat facing the east and then taking small portions of the crushed stones, he began to draw a picture by allowing the colored dust to seep through his fingers, controlling how much was allowed to slip through with his thumb.

Laura watched in fascination as the sandpainting very slowly took form. She understood none of symbolism in the figures Kaine placed in the drawing, but she was in awe of his talent for the artistry with which he did it. As he worked, he began telling a story out loud that she was sure had something to do with the sandpainting.

Once the main figures were completed, Kaine outlined three sides of the painting, leaving the side across from him, the eastern side of the painting, open. The outline very much resembled that of a rainbow. This Laura understood from listening to Ada tell Peter tales of his Navajo ancestors. The rainbow protected the figures in the painting as well as leaving the east side open for the dawn to enter.

Hours later, when the painting was completed, Kaine began to chant. While the singsong cadence *should* have kept Laura awake, it didn't. She found herself laying back beside Peter and closing her eyes, soothed by the sound of Kaine's voice and finally at peace, knowing something was being done to cure Peter.

When she awoke again, the sun had already started to warm the ground. She checked Peter for any signs that the ceremony was working and found him the same as he'd been since they found him in the cave, pale, with a weak pulse and shallow breathing. She did detect an absence of the putrid odor that had come with each breath he took. Hope rose in her.

Nevertheless, she glanced at Kaine, hoping he hadn't realized that Peter's condition had not significantly improved. To her relief, he didn't seem to be aware of her or Peter and had centered his total concentration on performing the *sing*.

Laura made herself coffee and while it cooked, slipped away to wash her face in the stream and perform her usual morning rituals. By the time she returned to where Kaine had been sitting cross-legged before the artwork, he had removed the sandpainting he'd so painstakingly drawn the day before and was throwing it to the eastern wind.

Once done, he smoothed the soil again and began a new one. She watched the same process take place; this time the sandpainting was different. Again, he drew figures she didn't recognize.

Unable to stand the tedium of the ceremony, Laura poured herself a cup of coffee and walked to the edge of the stream. She sat on a rock and sipped at the steaming brew. As she did so, she reminisced about Peter's birth, his first tooth, his first steps, his first day of school, all events that she'd cheated Kaine out of by holding onto her secret like a spoiled, willful child.

By the time her coffee had cooled, she was aware that the chanting had stopped. Rising, she hurried back to find Kaine lifting Peter's limp form from the sleeping bag and gently depositing him inside the circle of the sand-painting. He drew some corn pollen from the pouch, and while chanting, sprinkled it over their son. The yellow dust blended with his ashen complexion making him look even sicker than he was.

Impatience had begun gnawing at her, and she longed to ask Kaine how much longer this would take. When would Peter be well again? But she had promised not to interrupt him and truth be known, she was terrified that doing so would be a bad omen for the outcome. She bit her lip and remained silent.

Kaine returned Peter to the sleeping bag, and she saw no change in his condition. Laura went back to the stream. Tears streaked her face. She could not let Kaine see any doubt. She contented herself with intermittently chewing on a mesquite bean and praying to her God that her son would live.

The day wore on, more chants were sung, more stories repeated, still Peter lay motionless. Then, just before sun-set, Laura returned to the sleeping bag to check on Peter. Kaine was sweeping the sandpainting from the ground and onto the rug in which they'd wrapped Peter and carried him out of the cave. Once he'd removed all trace of the painting, he cast the gathered colored grains away, scattering them into oblivion.

He turned to Laura. "It's done." Fatigue lined his eyes, and his shoulders slumped. She wanted to hold him until he slept.

"You should rest," she told him.

"No, not until I know."

Without the strains of the chant filling the air around them, it seemed eerily still. Laura could tell that Kaine was afraid to even look at Peter. Afraid he'd failed yet again to save a loved one.

"Mom?"

Both of them hurried to Peter's side. He was sitting up looking from one of them to the other.

Laura brushed his hair form his forehead. His coloring was a healthy pink and his lips cherry red. His eyes, dark and velvety like his father's, were alive with questions. She felt his skin. It had lost the clammy feel of a dying person and was now warm and dry.

Laura looked at Kaine. "You did it," she said, her eyes filling with tears. She wanted to hug him, to kiss him, to tell him how grateful she was for giving her back her son, but she held back. Now that Peter was healthy again and they'd soon be leaving, the hopelessness of their situation reasserted itself. "You did it, Kaine."

"Yes, I guess I did." Kaine let out a long sigh. "Thank God," he muttered, relief written all over his features.

"No," Laura corrected. "Thanks the *gods*."

"What's going on? Where's Mrs. Yatzee and David?"

He eyed Kaine suspiciously. "Who's he, Mom?"

Along with his health, it seemed Peter's inquisitive nature had returned. Now, she had to tell him who this man was who had just saved his life. On other occasions, Peter had always been very good about taking the unexpected in stride. But this was different. She had no idea how he would take it. She'd always told him his dad lived somewhere far away from them, so at least she hadn't been stupid enough to corner herself with a lie about him being dead and now having to explain his resurrection.

"Peter, remember I told you your dad lived on the Navajo Reservation?"

The boy nodded, still glancing at Kaine who sat very still as though expecting the worst.

"Well, you were a little lost, and I needed help finding you so I asked this man to help me. Peter, this is Kaine Cloudwalker, your dad."

"Hi, Peter," Kaine said tentatively.

Peter eyed Kaine for a moment; then a curved-up grin and a look of total comprehension spread from ear to ear across his face. "Oh, yeah. Now I remember."

Laura and Kaine exchanged looks of confusion. "You remember what?" she asked.

"When I got lost, a nice lady kept showing up in my dreams. She said not to worry 'cause my dad was coming to get me."

At that precise moment, Shadow appeared seemingly from nowhere and gave a sharp bark.

Chapter 21

Laura stood in the front hall of Kaine's house watching the interchange between father and son. In the past few days since Peter had recovered from the corpsedust effects and they had traveled back to Kaine's, he and Kaine had forged a bond so quickly that it surprised her. It was as if they'd known each other forever.

In fact, it was so complete that she sometimes felt like a stranger standing on the outside fringes of their lives. At those times, she reminded herself that they had eight years of catching up to do. Still, sometimes it hurt not to be included.

The two of them had spent hours walking in the wilderness surrounding Kaine's home. When they'd returned, Peter had some new tale to tell her about Spider Woman learning to weave or one of the Monster Twins slaying an enemy. She'd never seen her son so animated before. And she'd never seen Kaine so absorbed in another person.

That only fueled her envy of Peter's relationship with his father. How she wished they could have mended their shattered relationship as easily.

Despite Kaine and Peter finding the father/son relationship easy to slip into, she and Kaine had been cordial, but stiff, carefully walking on eggshells around each other, careful not to touch and neither of them ready to reveal what lay in their hearts. Finally, when she could stand no more of being close to Kaine, but so far away at the same time, she announced that they had to return to Tucson so Peter could get ready to start the new school year.

"Mom, do we have to go?" Peter pleaded. "I want to stay here forever." His sad eyes brightened. "I don't have to go back to Tucson to go to school. I could go to school here, couldn't I, Dad?"

Kaine glanced at her, and then quickly looked away. She wondered if he was wishing for the same thing Peter was, for them to stay and become a real family. But they let the moment slip away without saying anything.

Besides, chances were it was probably just her wishful thinking and all Kaine's look had meant was he wanted his son with him as much as Peter wanted to be there and not any wish for them to patch up their tattered lives together.

"I'm afraid you have to go home with your mom, son."

Peter's face wilted. He kicked at the floor with the toe of the sneakers Kaine had bought him the day before in town and thrust out his lower lip. "Aw, Dad, why can't I stay?"

The word *Dad* brought an instant grin to Kaine's face that tugged at Laura's heart and for the hundredth time stabbed her with a pang of guilt at having deprived them of a life together.

"Well, for one thing, I don't have a bedroom for you. Sleeping on the sofa for a couple of nights is okay for now, but you can't do that forever." Kaine stepped back and smiled. "Tell you what. I'll clean up the storeroom and paint it up a bit. Next time you come, you'll have your own room. How's that?"

Peter nodded, and then hugged Kaine around his legs. "You're the greatest."

Laura turned away. She didn't want this picture stuck in her memory to remind her of what could never be between her and Kaine and how much Peter would be missing out on. How much *she'd* be missing out on.

"Will you come to see us?" Peter asked as Laura guided him toward the front door.

Holding her breath, Laura waited for Kaine's answer. He shifted his gaze and met hers above the boy's dark head.

"Well, I guess that depends on what your mom thinks about that."

In truth, Laura wasn't sure. On the one hand, seeing Kaine and not being able to walk into his arms or feel his lips on hers would tear her heart to ribbons. However, on the other, enduring the exile of not seeing him at all would hurt beyond reason. She decided that the latter would be the worst of the choices for both her and Peter. Peter deserved to have his father in his life as much as possible, and Kaine deserved to know his son.

"You're welcome in our home anytime," she finally said, avoiding eye contact with Kaine and fighting to check her tears.

"All right!" Peter, who had been staring at her expectantly, punched the air and did a little victory dance.

Laura had to laugh. For being so ill only a few days ago, he'd made a remarkable recovery. It was as if he'd never been infected by the skinwalkers. He was the exuberant little boy she'd watched leave to go to the powwow not all that long ago. What was even better, he seemed to have no memory of his ordeal and was convinced he'd been lost for the entire time and sleeping in a cave. In his mind, he'd had a great adventure. Laura wasn't at all sure that Changing Woman hadn't had something to do with that, but however it had happened, she was extremely grateful.

"Wait until David finds out my dad's a real Navajo." Peter's face glowed with excitement and pride. He straightened his back and looked for all the world like a miniature cock rooster.

"Don't forget, that makes you half Navajo as well," Laura told him, never wanting Kaine to doubt that she would encourage Peter to be proud of who he was and what that meant.

"Yeah. David is gonna be sooo jealous."

Kaine and Laura's eyes met over the boy's head. So far, they had managed to avoid any details about David or his mother. But, obviously, that was no longer an option.

"Ah, Peter," Laura said, moving to touch her son's shoulder. "David had to go away. He won't be living in Tucson anymore."

Peter's happy smile disappeared. "Why?"

"Well . . ." Laura searched for the right words to explain the inexplicable. She looked to Kaine for help.

"His mom had family business she had to take care of," Kaine put in quickly. Laura sent him a silent *thank you*. "They'll be living somewhere else now."

"Bummer. I'm gonna really miss him." Though obviously not happy about losing his best friend, Peter seemed to accept that he and his mother had moved to a new location.

Kaine put his hand on Peter's shoulder. "I know you will, but you'll make new friends, right?"

Peter nodded. "So, when can you come see us?" he asked, bouncing back to the original subject with all the resilience of a child.

Kaine laughed. "I don't know."

"Next week?" Peter begged with a pleading note in his voice. "And can you show me how to make one of those?" He pointed at a reproduction of a sandpainting of Father Sky and Mother Earth hanging above the mantel. Laura now recognized it as one of the sandpaintings Kaine had used in the *sing*, and Peter had taken a great interest in the painting ever since they'd arrived at Kaine's house.

"All right, next week, but I'm not sure you're ready for sandpainting yet, but we'll see." Kaine looked at Laura. "Will you be okay driving back alone?"

How she wanted to say *No, come with us. Be with us. Stay with us.* Instead, she just nodded. "I'll be fine. After all, I have this young man's chatter to keep me awake, and I'm sure he won't let me go more then ten miles at a time without a pit stop for food or a drink or a bathro—"

"Mom!"

Laura and Kaine laughed.

"I guess modesty knows no age limit," Kaine said, laughing and ruffling his son's hair.

An awkward silence fell over them. The kind of silence that comes before making a reluctant exit. Laura wanted to beg him to let them stay, to be a part of his life, but she had to hear the words, and he showed no indication that he wanted things that way.

"We better get going, buddy. We have a long drive ahead of us." Laura avoided looking at Kaine.

"Okay." Peter grabbed his mother's backpack and the overnight case that held the new clothes they'd gotten for him from the floor, heading out the door to the car. "See you next week, Dad."

"See ya," Kaine called, his eyes feasting on Peter. "Son," he added softly.

Another stiff silence hung between them. "Well, I'd better go." Laura hesitated. "Thanks for all you did for Peter and for me, Kaine. I don't know how I can say that enough. I'll send you a check for what I owe you as soon as I get back to Tucson."

"No."

She stopped her progress toward the door to stare up at him. "What?"

"I can't put a price tag on my son's life." He took a deep breath. "Laura, I—"

She held her breath. What had he been about to say? Did he want them to stay? If he did, he'd have to ask them himself. She refused to help him say it. She had to know that she and Peter were wanted because he needed them with him, not because they had forced themselves on him. She did not want him regretting it down the line.

He shook his head. "Never mind. Have a good trip." He reached for her and hugged her close for a long moment before releasing her and stepping back.

She swallowed her tears and quickly walked past him out the door. "See you," she called.

With pain-filled eyes, Kaine watched her go, knowing in his gut she was walking out of his life, but unable to find the words to stop her.

❖   ❖   ❖

A month had passed since Laura and Peter had gotten

back to Tucson and fallen easily back into their daily routine just as if the time in the Canyon Country had never happened. As though Kaine had not again been part of their lives, he dropped from sight once more.

His promised to visit Peter had fallen through when he'd had to take a tourist into the canyons. But he'd promised their son that as soon as he could, he'd come to see him. Several of her coworkers had warned her that such was a glaring sign that Kaine was becoming a deadbeat dad. Having seen him with Peter, she couldn't believe that of Kaine.

Kaine loved his son almost from the moment he knew he had one. He would never hurt Peter that way. Still, the phone didn't ring for him to make a new date to visit, and Peter was becoming antsy.

"Carl Taylor's dad lives with him. Why can't Dad live here?" Peter asked over and over. "Then I could see him all the time."

Laura danced around an answer, trying in vain to find a way to explain to her young son why adults split up, why marriages didn't work, why she loved a man who didn't love her. When she finally told him it was because his father had to be close to the canyons and his job, Peter accepted it for a few days, and then they were back to square one—why couldn't Kaine live with them?

But today he'd added a new twist. "Why can't we go live by Dad? He can't move the canyons here, but you can be a nurse any old place."

That statement for a small boy had set Laura to thinking about how close Peter had come to death because there were no medical facilities close by and of the little boy with the injured thumb who could well have been some Navajo child and not the son of Changing Woman. The fact that Peter hadn't been suffering from a malady that *bilagáanaa* medicine couldn't cure—and that the child had been the son of a god—didn't negate the fact that the area was in dire need of more accessible medical facilities. Besides, there was nothing that said they couldn't combine the best of the Navajo rituals and Anglo medicine. All they needed was somewhere to do it. And she thought she knew the perfect location.

As time wore on and she went about her nursing duties, the thought prayed on her mind and used up her entire train of thought when she wasn't at her job. Eventually, on her break, she found herself sketching plans for a clinic that would serve many of the outlying areas. By the time she got home, she made Peter a quick dinner and then made a dash for her computer and did some extensive research on government grants and real estate for sale in the Big Rez area.

A week later, on her day off, she met with an attorney and a real estate agent and listed her house for sale.

✦   ✦   ✦

Kaine felt like shit. It had been over a month since Peter

and Laura had gone back to Tucson, and he still hadn't done anything about going to visit Peter.

He'd promised Peter again and again that he'd come see him, and then made excuse after excuse as to why he couldn't. Deep inside, he knew it was because he just couldn't bring himself to go see Laura and his son and not want to bring them home with him and be a family. He wasn't sure he could stand the pain of her saying no.

Although he was now at peace with his mother's death and had started getting that part of his life back on track, his nights were littered with dreams of the time he and Laura had spent in the canyon, the night they'd made love and the joy of holding his son for the first time. His days were much the same. He missed them as much as he would have missed the sunrise over the buttes. Yet he couldn't bring himself to do anything about it. Nor did he make any attempt to finish the old house and put it up for sale. It seemed as if his life had come to a standstill waiting for someone to show him the next step.

Instead, he sat here alone in his living room night after night feeling sorry for himself. He took a long drink of the beer that had grown warm in his hand. It reminded him of the night that his grandfather and Changing Woman had come to him in the dream.

The wise man welcomes sleep and risks all by stepping into the eye of the dream. When he emerges, he brings with him wisdom, strength and a full heart. Step into the eye of your dream, Kaine Cloudwalker, before it is too late.

His grandfather's words from the dream played through Kaine's mind like a mantra. Back then, he'd laughed at them as foolishness, but now . . . now, he finally saw the wisdom in them. Laura would not make the first move. He would have to go to her. He would have to step into the eye of the dream and prove to her that he could make a life for them.

A knock roused him from his thoughts. He trudged to the door, pissed because he didn't have time for visitors. He had plans to make, plans that might well include leaving the Big Rez for good.

Flinging the door open, he took a step backward when he saw who stood on his doorstep.

"Can we come in?" asked Jim Longtree. Behind him, FBI agent Henry Oates peered over the BIA agent's shoulder.

Kaine stepped back and made a sweeping motion with his arm that indicated they should come in. "What brings you two out here?" he asked, leading them into the living room.

"That Mimbres pottery we found with your wife," Oates said, looking around the room with an assessing eye.

Kaine didn't resume his seat and didn't offer them one. He wanted them gone and making themselves at home would only prolong their visit. "What about it?" He was primed to come to Laura's defense if necessary.

Muted streaks of late sunlight slashed across the rug, as if even nature knew about their different points of view and had lain down a demarcation line between them.

"She's been cleared." Longtree eyed the sofa as if waiting for Kaine to offer him a seat. When he didn't, Longtree continued. "We found out who's been stealing the pottery."

Kaine waited for him to continue. When he remained silent, Kaine spoke. "Let me guess . . . Willoughby."

Oates mouth gaped open. "How did you know?"

A chuckle escaped Kaine. "Let's just say a little blue-bird told me."

He sipped his beer, realizing how inhospitable he was being by not offering either of the two men any of the usual warmth a host would normally make available to visitors, but he didn't care. He needed to get on with his plan to go to Laura and Peter.

"Anyway," Longtree went on, "we searched Willough-by's after we got reports that he was seen sneaking into his trading post a few weeks back with an armload of what looked like pottery. It didn't seem right that a man would be sneaking into his own place of business or that Willoughby had suddenly started dealing in trading Indian artifacts."

"How did you know about Willoughby?" Oates persisted, eyeing Kaine.

Kaine related what had happened in the canyons, leaving out the parts that might make Oates pass out cold on the floor. Not that he hadn't been tempted to tell him about the skinwalkers and the corpse dust and all the rest just to watch the color drain out of the man's florid, fat cheeks. But though the entertainment value would have been high, Kaine had other things to do.

"So Willoughby's dead?" Longtree said.

Kaine nodded. "Yup."

"And you found your son and he was okay?"

Kaine nodded again.

Both men looked at each other, then back to Kaine. "Well, I guess that settles this case," Oates said, sounding thrilled that it was over.

Kaine walked to the door and opened it wide and without saying so, told them they could leave anytime now. Longtree got the hint before Oates and led the other man to the door. When they were standing in the open doorway, Longtree turned back to Kaine.

"I never guessed you ran into Willoughby out there. I figured you knew about Willoughby because your wife bought his trading post and had it torn down for her clinic."

Clinic? Laura? Here?

Kaine fought to keep his face from showing any reaction. Inside, his stomach was doing flip flops, his heart raced in time to his mind, and his breathing threatened to stop entirely. Not trusting his voice, he nodded at Longtree and Oates, then closed the door behind them and stifled the yelp of triumph that hovered on his lips.

Chapter 22

Laura stepped back to admire the rug she'd hung on the wall in the newly painted reception area of her clinic. The deep reds and golds reminded her of the one the weaver had been working on outside when this had been Willoughby's trading post. It had been the sole reason she'd bought the rug from the shop in Tucson.

She looked around the small clinic she'd built after they'd torn down the store and brought in the doublewide mobile home. It wasn't elaborate and most of the equipment was secondhand, but it would provide a place for her and the doctor she gotten to agree to come here once a week to treat the neighboring Navajos. It was a good start to what she hoped one day would be a larger facility.

The other doublewide that had been placed behind this one would provide a comfortable home for her and Peter, who had been ecstatic about moving closer to his father and who had declared her the *bestess mom ever.*

"What do you think, Shadow?" she asked the black dog that had shown up on her doorstep the day she'd moved in. Shadow was looking a little ragged around the edges, as if age was catching up with him. His muzzle was peppered with white hairs, and his gait had slowed noticeably.

Nevertheless, he barked and wagged his tail enthusiastically.

What would Kaine think?

Refusing to think about that, she walked closer to the rug. Unbidden images of the old woman, her gnarled fingers guiding the shuttle between the threads, came to mind. Laura leaned forward and inspected the edge closely.

If Ada had been right about the reason they didn't complete the border, this weaver's spirit had not been imprisoned in the design. But Laura knew there were more ways than one to lose your spirit, ways that weren't visible to the naked eye, ways that reached down inside you and locked it in a dark shell of hopelessness.

She leaned her forehead against the rough wool weave. Would the pain ever go away? Would she ever be able to make it through a day without reminders? She'd hoped working on the clinic would keep thoughts of Kaine at bay, but it seemed everything and everyone brought him to mind.

Pushing herself away, she turned and froze in place. Her gaze locked with a pair of velvet, dark eyes peering at her from a chiseled face half-hidden in the shadow of a wide-brimmed black Stetson. Gripping her fingers together tightly to still her suddenly trembling hands, she took a step back.

"Laura."

"Hello, Kaine."

"Your door was open."

She glanced past him as if to confirm his words. "I was trying to cool the place off." However, since Kaine had arrived, the temperature in the room seemed to have risen several degrees.

Laura stared at him as if she'd never seen him before. She devoured him with her eyes and soaked up his essence with her skin. She'd missed him, of that there was no doubt, but until this very moment, she hadn't realized just how much.

Kaine looked around nervously. Now that he was face-to-face with her, he felt like a school kid going before the principal, fumbling for something to say that would excuse his bad behavior. "I heard you were opening a clinic here."

Laura smiled, satisfaction written all over her expression. "I'm not surprised. Word has spread very fast. I've had to turn people away and ask them to come back next week, so I can get set up."

"It's a good thing. The People needed it." He took a step toward her and then stopped, fighting the need to touch her and knowing that he didn't have that right.

Nodding her head, she tore her gaze from his. "I know. I just didn't want you to think . . ." She shook her head as if to clear her thoughts. "It doesn't matter." Taking a wide route around him, she went into the area that served as a kitchenette. "Want some coffee?"

He couldn't help the grin that blossomed on his lips. "Sure." Her answering smile coaxed the chill from his bones.

"It's been here for a while. Might be a bit strong."

"I'll have some anyway." He'd drink roofing tar just to stay with her a little longer.

Standing back, he feasted his fill on the sight of her, feeding his starving heart. She was wearing a tight red T-shirt and brief cutoffs. Her feet were bare, and her hair was braided in one long pigtail that swung against the delicious curve of her buttocks like the tail of a playful cat.

Kaine shifted his feet and looked for somewhere to sit to hide his growing discomfort. He didn't want her to think he'd come with the notion of dragging her off to the nearest bed. Not that it hadn't occurred to him when he first set eyes on her. But he wanted to talk first, to settle things if they could, to heal the wounds and try to rebuild what they'd once had.

"Thank you."

Her voice grabbed his attention. "For what?"

"You saving Peter's life," she told the coffee mug as she poured coffee into it.

"No need. You've already thanked me. Besides, he's

my son. I could have done no less." He looked through the open door. "I should be the one thanking you."

She swung to face him. "Why?"

He hitched his thumb toward the open door. "I saw the sign out front. She would have been proud you called this place the Wanda Cloudwalker Clinic." Emotion choked his voice.

Laura blinked, and then looked away, immersing herself in wiping up a few drops of spilled coffee. "You're welcome." She paused in her task. "Why did you come here today?"

Evidently, the small talk had ended. He swallowed hard. He'd rather be facing a herd of charging buffalo than be doing this, but he gritted his teeth and forged ahead. "I need to talk to you . . . about Peter."

A surge of disappointment flooded her.

What did you expect him to say? That he loves you, and he'd come to talk about getting back together?

Despite the taunts her niggling conscience threw at her, Laura couldn't let go of the possibility entirely. Something about his voice, his attitude wouldn't let the hope die completely. Hoping she wouldn't regret it, she pushed him farther.

"What about him?"

For a time he stared at the stiff line of her back, then he opened his mouth to explain, but fear kept the words locked in his throat. Others pushed ahead of them and tumbled over his lips before he could stop them. "Why did you decide to open this clinic? Why here?"

Laura almost dropped the coffeepot as she slid it back onto the coffeemaker. Although she should have been expecting it, the question had come out of leftfield, catching her totally off guard. She been waiting for him to ask it since he'd come in. It was just that she hadn't expected it so soon. She hadn't even begun to formulate an answer, one that wouldn't give away how big a part he played in her decision to open this place for his people. She took a deep breath.

"A few weeks ago, someone told me I could be a nurse anywhere." She heard his sharp intake of air. She turned slowly to face him, the coffee forgotten. "He said his dad couldn't move the canyons, but I could be a nurse in any old place. He was right."

"Peter." He flopped down in one of the molded plastic chairs.

"That's right. He can be a very wise little boy when he sets his mind to it. It seemed only reasonable I use my knowledge here, where it would do some good helping the Navajo people."

Laura stared at him in expectant silence. She wasn't going to make this easy for him. "Why did you *really* come here today?"

Glancing up at her, he leaned forward, resting his elbows on his denim clad knees. The material of his blue chambray work shirt stretched across his muscled back. Laura's mouth went dry. She looked quickly away.

His hat shaded his face, obscuring his expression. "There haven't been many times in my life when I was sorry for anything. There haven't been many times I've had to say the words either." He raised his head, his gaze searching her face. "Laura, I don't ever remember a time when I was more wrong about anyone than I was about you. I never should have asked you to live out here when we got married. I'm sorry."

"Why? Did you think I was that fragile?"

He nodded and looked at the floor, unable to meet the accusing look he knew must be on her face. "You were a city girl and I dragged you into the desert into a foreign place to live with people who had an entirely different way of life than you were used to—"

"Kaine, for the record, living out here was no hardship. I loved it. I loved the people, the land, the legends. I didn't leave because I was unhappy with where you'd brought me." She choked back her tears and whispered, "I left because I couldn't stand you not loving me enough to want to be with me."

Kaine stared at her for a long time, as if processing what she'd just revealed. Then suddenly, he rose and walked from the clinic. Laura's heart sank. Had she been too blunt? Was he walking out on her? She was still trying to decide when he stepped back into the clinic carrying a large, rectangular package wrapped in brown paper. He extended it to her.

"Consider it a Grand Opening gift."

Wordlessly, she took the package and laid it on the table. Glancing toward Kaine, who stood with his back to the window, she tried to see his expression, but it was hidden beneath the brim of the hat. Untying the string, she folded back the paper. She had to blink several times before she could believe her eyes.

"My God, Kaine. It's the Rainbow Arch."

"I found it in a shop in Window Rock, and I wanted you to have this to remember that night."

Her gaze shot to him. Words lay trapped in her throat, held in place by the lump of emotion. His whole body seemed poised, ready to spring at the slightest provocation. Frantically she tried to gather her scattered thoughts.

"I never want to forget it, and now, I want to make sure you remember, too, always."

She smiled. "Like I could forget."

"Well, sometimes it's good to have reminders of the importance of things we take for granted."

"Like what?"

"Like I had something very precious that few men find. I had it right here in my arms, and I let it slip away once and was about to let it happen the second time. Like I'd be a fool not to tell you I love you and want you to forgive me."

Laura's eyes filled. Kaine's face blurred.

"I've answered all your questions, now how about you start answering mine? Why are you here?"

Sobs bubbled up in her throat making speech almost

impossible. "Because. . . ." She swallowed. "Because I wanted Peter here, near you, so he can learn his heritage from his people and his elders and not just on weekend visits."

Kaine took a step toward her. "There are seventeen-and-a-half-million acres of reservation from which you could have picked. Why here, Laura?"

She shook her head. He was close enough for her to see his eyes, to smell his special scent, to feel the warmth radiating from his flesh. "I wanted to be near you. Where else would I go?"

Taking her hands in his, he drew her close. Looking down into her sea-green eyes, seeing himself in their endless depths, he shook his head. "Not good enough." He framed her face with his hands. "Say it, Laura. I promise you'll never be sorry. I'll never hurt you again. Please, baby, say it."

With gentle fingers, Kaine tilted her chin up and covered her lips with his. The fire was there, but so was an infinite tenderness, a promise for tomorrow and all the tomorrows to come. But even more, there was trust. He'd lain his heart open for her to do with whatever she saw fit. Only love will allow that kind of gamble.

Laura felt as if a dam suddenly burst inside her, freeing the words he wanted to hear. "I love you, Kaine. I love you so much. I couldn't stand living with half the state between us."

His dark eyes glowed with happiness and a faint hint of moisture as he looked down at her. His big hand cupped her cheek. His head descended for a gentle kiss. "When I first saw you, I knew I loved you. When we first kissed, I knew it was forever. I love you, Laura Cloudwalker. You've brought me more happiness than any man could ever hope for. The Cherokee have a saying for what you make me feel. *You walk in my soul.*"

Turning her face, too choked up to reply in words, she kissed his hand and covered it with hers.

"I'm sorry for not saying 'I love you' often enough, for letting you think I didn't care when I cared more than you will ever know. It damn near killed me when you walked away."

"I'm sorry," she whispered. "There was just so much . . . so much hurt in me. I couldn't talk to you then, but later I should have. I should have told you about Peter—"

His hand over her mouth gently stopped her apology.

"There are no words to excuse not showing someone how much you love them. It should be a part of that love. I had to learn that the hard way, but I have. I never want to lose you again."

He sealed his pledge with a kiss and then leaned back to flash one of his killer smiles at her. "There's something else for you outside. I couldn't bring it in here."

"Why not?"

"You'll see." He chuckled at his private joke and led her through the clinic. Keeping an arm around her, hugging her securely to his side, he opened the door and placed her squarely in front of him.

"What on Earth?" Her gaze fastened incomprehensively on three pinto horses tied to the tailgate of a pickup truck.

His broad chest vibrated against her back as a deep, satisfied laugh rumbled from him. "They're part of the proposal."

"Proposal?" She swung around to face him.

While she waited for him to answer, he pulled her outside, closed the door, and guided her to the mobile home she and Peter shared in the back. They stepped inside, and he closed and locked the door.

"Where's Peter?"

"He's on a field trip to Washington, D.C. with his school class. He won't be home for a couple of days." She stared at him. "Tell me about this proposal. What kind of proposal is it?"

"A marriage proposal."

Her mouth fell open even as a broad grin curved her lips. "But we're already married."

"In the Anglo way. A Navajo shaman should be married in the Navajo way. Besides, we need to restore the harmony of the People." Kaine grinned slightly at his own humor, but his face quickly became serious. "Well?"

Kaine was going to become a shaman, verification that he was at last at peace with his mother's death and that he played no part in it. Elation filled Laura.

She drew back and adopted a playful haughty look. "Mr. Cloudwalker, if you're waiting for an answer to a marriage proposal, I think you'd better make it properly."

Maneuvering her into the bedroom, Kaine pushed her down on the edge of the bed and knelt on one knee in front of her. Clasping her hand, he looked at her with serious eyes. "Miss Kincaid, will you do me the honor of spending the rest of our lives together as man and wife?"

When he looked her directly in the eyes and purposefully removed his hat and threw it on the bed, her blood pressure jumped several notches. He was home for good.

"Yes!" she cried, springing off the bed and launching herself into his arms, sending them both sprawling across the floor. "Yes! Yes!" she repeated, raining kisses all over his face.

Squirming from beneath her, Kaine stood and drew her up into his arms. "I love you, you crazy woman, and I plan on telling you every day for the rest of our lives, so you'll never doubt it again."

Taking slow steps backward, he sat on the edge of the bed and pulled her down on his lap. Covering her mouth with his, he put all the pent up emotions of weeks without her into the kiss, slowly easing her back onto the mattress.

Laura wrapped her arms around him and gave herself up to the ecstasy growing by leaps and bounds as it swamped her. Gasping for air, she pulled a breath away. "Is this one of the Navajo Ways of sealing a marriage proposal?"

A sly grin painted his lips. His fingers began inching their way up under the hem of her T-shirt. "No. It's *my* Way."

Laura lay back and let the shadow of her husband spread over her, protecting and warming her with his love.

Epilogue

Laura surveyed herself in her bedroom mirror. Had she forgotten anything? She wanted her wedding day to be as perfect as any Navajo's bride's.

Smoothing the folds of her white ankle-length skirt, she picked up the flat basket she was to carry to the *binahagha' hoogan*, the ceremonial hogan Kaine had had erected in the nearby peach orchard. Setting the basket aside, she fussed with a last-minute adjustment to her lavishly embellished silver-and-turquoise squash-blossom necklace, tucking the clasp beneath the collar of her blue velvet blouse.

Never being one for much jewelry, she felt overdone, but Kaine's cousin Diana had been adamant about what she was to wear. In addition to the heavy necklace, each wrist was encircled with matching silver-and-turquoise *keetohs*, ones that would also match the bow guards Kaine would wear. A silver *concho* belt of four-inch oval disks connected by silver-set turquoise nuggets cinched in the waist of her wedding blouse. She wondered that she could even walk under the weight of so much metal.

Looking again in the mirror, a thrill rippled over her with the idea that she was about to take part in a ceremony that looked deep into the Navajo past for its origins, a ceremony rich with meaning.

It would have been so much more meaningful if Kaine's mother could have been there and his grandfather, Brother to the Owl, could have conducted the rituals as the clan shaman.

Automatically, her hand went to her throat to search for the rainbow pendant. She missed it, but refrained from mentioning it to Kaine. Using it to help cure Peter had been worth the loss.

Shaking away her unhappy thoughts, she concentrated instead on the man waiting for her in the hogan. Today she would become Mrs. Kaine Cloudwalker for the second and last time. She draped the wedding shawl around her shoulders and picked up the basket. Thinking about the special wedding present she had planned for Kaine, she cast one quick look in the mirror and left the room.

The walk from the house to the hogan was a solitary one, one during which she thought of Kaine and how much she loved him.

By the time she walked through the hogan door and looked at the man who had filled her thoughts, her face radiated her love. An answering love welled up in Kaine when he looked into her eyes. Loving Laura was like stepping into another world where the sun always shone and the birds always sang. He still had to pinch himself to believe his good fortune.

Rising from his seat on the west side of the room, he walked toward her, his hand extended to take hers. He felt a slight tremble in her fingers when they curled around his, and gave hers a reassuring squeeze.

Laura couldn't believe this handsome man clothed in the same colors and wearing like jewelry was the man who'd barged into the clinic and taken her breath away less than two weeks ago. As they walked beneath the smoke hole in the roof, the sun danced over his hair in shimmering blue highlights. Could she love him any more than she did right now?

Guiding her to her place on the blanket, Kaine waited while she sat, then assumed his place beside her. She placed the basket in front of Kaine, just as his cousin had instructed.

To their left, Peter made up her family members. To Kaine's right sat his cousin and several other distant relatives. The rest of the room was filled with friends, most of whom had come from the far reaches of the reservation and whom Laura had never seen before today.

The clan shaman stepped forward carrying a double-necked earthen jar and rawhide bag. He knelt before them and poured water from first one side of the jar then the other, Laura and Kaine washing their hands in turn beneath the stream.

"This is for purity," Kaine told her quietly.

Upending the bag into the flat basket, the shaman spread a mixture of ground, raw, blue corn and ashes evenly over the bottom of the basket. Reaching beneath his shirt, he extracted a small bag of yellow corn pollen.

"This is a blessing," Kaine explained.

Carefully, the Holy Man sprinkled a line of pollen over the mixture from east to west.

"The beginning and end of the day."

Crossing that line with another from south to north, he sat back and raised the basket to the couple.

"This signifies the beginning of life and the end of life. Now, we must taste some from each section." Kaine demonstrated by dipping his fingertips into the first section and then placing it in his mouth. He repeated the procedure until he'd sampled some of the mixture from each segment. Laura followed his lead and was rewarded by his approving smile and his cousin's affirming head nod.

The basket was then passed to Peter. He did as he'd been instructed, but made a face and swallowed hard. After Kaine's cousin had sampled her share, the basket made the rounds of the gathered guests.

When the shaman handed it to Laura, along with the double-necked jar, she set them carefully aside, knowing they would become treasured possessions, symbols of their joined love.

"Well, Mrs. Cloudwalker, how does it feel to be an

old married lady?"

Kaine's warm breath on her ear sent shivers over Laura. "That's it? We're married?"

He nodded and touched her lips lightly with his. "That's it."

It was all over so quickly; she could hardly believe it was true.

At that moment, Laura knew what she truly felt for this strong, handsome man by her side—her husband. No matter where he made his home, it would be hers also. No matter where life took him, she would be at his side. No matter what hardships he faced, she would face them with him.

Before she could tell him, the guests began to file outside to the arbor which had been constructed to shelter them while they devoured the food Kaine's friends and family had spent days preparing.

But even all the beef, lamb stew, watermelon, fried bread, salad, and cake he stuffed into him didn't seem to erase the hunger from Kaine's eyes every time he looked at her. With her eyes, she told him the same hunger gnawed at her.

Dutifully, after the meal was done, they opened gifts. Kaine's cousin had given them matching *keetohs*, each bracelet formed in rich silver and adorned with two pieces of turquoise. A tiny piece of silver wire connected the two pieces.

"So you'll never be separated in heart or spirit," she said softly so as not to wake the sleeping baby on her lap.

Taking Laura's hand, Kaine looked deep into her shimmering eyes. "We don't need *keetohs* to make sure of that."

The remaining gifts went quickly and soon the guests were filing past them on their way out. Each person stopped to impart wise advice about what to expect from marriage and how they should treat each other. Kaine respectfully thanked each in turn, not once relinquishing his tight hold on his wife's hand.

An ancient woman dressed totally in black was the last to leave. Taking their joined hands in hers, she spoke to them in her native tongue. Her speech was so rapid and so glottal, Laura couldn't understand it, but she recognized the voice from her dreams. When it was apparent the old woman had concluded, Laura turned to Kaine for a translation.

"She said, live your lives lightly and walk in beauty."

Kissing the old woman's wizen cheek, Laura felt her slip something soft between her palm and Kaine's. She looked down and found a doeskin pouch closed with drawstrings.

"It's from the Old One," she explained. Then twitching her lips, she tilted her white-capped head toward the owl perched in a tree on the ridge behind them. "He said you should have it the day your hearts truly became one."

Laura's eyes opened wide. She stared at Kaine. He grinned. Turning back to the woman, Laura found they were alone.

Still amazed at this new revelation, she pivoted back to Kaine for some explanation. He was absorbed in examining four tiny doeskin-wrapped bundles he'd dumped from the larger pouch into his palm.

"What is it?"

"It's the Old Man's medicine bundles from the Four Sacred Mountains."

"What's it mean?" Laura knew of the four mountains marking the land given the *Diné* by the Holy People, but she'd never heard of these medicine bundles.

"It's the most powerful blessing he could give us. We have to put it above the doorway of our home so it blesses everyone who comes into our house and the house itself."

Picking up one of the bundles, Laura sniffed at the end. The pleasing odor of pine needles, wood, earth, and wild herbs mixed together to tickle her nose.

"To assemble these bundles, the Old Man had to go to each of the mountains to gather the required items." Kaine took the bundle from her and tucked it back into the larger one. "It's a long, tedious trip even for a young man. Some of it he'd have to travel on horseback, but the majority he'd have had to cover on foot." He shook his head in wonder. "I can't believe he did this for me . . . for us."

"I can," Laura said, remembering all the things he and Changing Woman had done over the past months to see to it that the harmony of their People and of this little family was restored. Her hand went automatically to her chest in search of the pendant.

"I have a wedding gift for you." Kaine dug into the pocket of his pants. A moment later, he handed Laura a folded square of white cloth.

She took it and immediately felt the weight of whatever was concealed inside. But more than that, she felt a familiar calm steal over her. Slowly, she folded back the cloth. In her palm lay the rainbow pendant, intact and restored to its original beauty.

Kaine took it from her trembling fingers and fastened it around her neck. "It will always remind us of the journey we took to find each other again."

Laura kissed his mouth lightly in thanks. "Do you remember the lingerie I wore the first night of our honeymoon nine years ago?"

Carefully, Kaine placed the bag in the basket at their feet and reached for his bride. Cradling her against him, he kissed her temple. "Do I remember? I never forgot. From the first night I saw you in that indecent little scrap of red lace, I knew there was something incredible about you."

Laura arched a brow. "Indecent? Then I guess I'd better throw it away."

"Not on your life, woman. Some day I'm gonna see you in that thing again." A full grin spread over his face. "That's the damnedest, most disturbing piece of clothing I've ever seen on a woman in my life." His arms tightened. "I wanted to make love to you all night."

Snaking her arms behind his neck, Laura smiled coyly.

"All night, huh?" She distinctly recalled the heated look he'd leveled on her that night and how her body had responded.

That was all she could take of this seductive byplay. Pulling from of his embrace, she closed the hogan door and walked to the circle of sunlight coming through the chimney hole in the roof. When Kaine took a step in her direction, she held up her hand to stop him.

Reaching behind her head, she loosened the elongated bun into which her hair had been fashioned earlier by Kaine's cousin. As the weight of it cascade down her back, she shook her head to loosen the strands.

Kaine inhaled sharply. Was there ever a woman anywhere as beautiful as Laura? He exhaled slowly, his gaze glued to the woman in nature's spotlight.

Very deliberately, she removed her jewelry and tossed it to him to add to the basket. The metal still carried the heat from her body. He fingered the last piece while she toyed with the buttons on her blouse and looked at him through lowered lashes.

"You sure you're up to this?" Her voice had dropped to a sultry growl.

Thinking of what was going to happen when she was free of those clothes, Kaine couldn't get his voice to work. There was only room in his mind for that glimpse of red lace he caught when she'd opened the last button.

Her hands paused on the next button. Then she released the catch on the *concho* belt and let it drop from her fingers.

Kaine's entire concentration centered on the blouse slipping from her shoulders and the enticing bits of red lace coming into view. His knees grew watery. His hands opened and closed spasmodically with the need to touch her. He had the feeling this entire show held importance for her in some way, so he forced himself to remain rooted to the spot.

Instead he devoured her with his gaze, feasted his eyes on her upper body cloaked in that same lace teddy that had driven him crazy on their last wedding night.

Dropping her hands to her waist, Laura made a few quick movements and the skirt puddled at her feet like an early snow fall. Fire raged through Kaine as he watched the light bathe her body in an unearthly glow. The sun on the red lace seemed to set her flesh ablaze, engulfing her in flames that beckoned to him.

"No one wears the sun like you do," he whispered, finally finding his voice and answering the need in him that pushed him from his frozen state just as Laura extended her arms and wiggled her fingertips in invitation. Like a man in a trance, he walked toward her.

Raising his hand, he touched her tentatively, expecting her to vanish into thin air. The initial contact with her warm flesh made him suck in his breath while his blood pounded in his temples. He pulled her pliant body to him, nestling his arousal against the sun-warmed lace covering her stomach.

"How's your harmony now?" Laura whispered into his descending mouth.

"Destroyed, totally destroyed," he answered, pulling her down to the rug-covered floor.

"Good."

Though night was falling, outside the hogan a rainbow sprang across the sky and next to the entrance, an old black dog vanished in a puff of smoke. The soft hoot of an owl pierced the growing twilight.

Inside, Kaine and Laura stepped into the eye of the dream.

For purposes of my plot and reader clarity, I took liberties with some of the Navajo myths and beliefs.

The term "shaman" is not used by Native Americans for someone who has healing or spiritual powers. This is an anthropological word and originally referred to far eastern cultures. "Hataalii" is the actual Navajo word, meaning chanter or singer. However, because most people are more familiar with "shaman," I used to it to prevent confusion.

Navajos believe that all ghosts are evil and therefore go out of their way not to encounter them. As a result, they never refer to the dead by name, but rather as "The Old One" or the "Little Mother." Using generic names prevents the ghost of that person coming to them and infecting them with a sickness. For reasons of clear character identification I did not do this in this book.

I extend my apologies to the Navajo Nation for any misconceptions I may have inadvertently caused.

A Special Preview Chapter From The
Award-Winning Author, Elizabeth Sinclair

Miracle
in the Mist

Elizabeth Sinclair

PRESS®

ISBN#1932815651
ISBN#9781932815658
Jewel Imprint: Amethyst
US $6.99 / CDN $9.99
www.elizabethsinclair.com

PROLOGUE

December—Tarrytown, NY

As Anna Hobbs maneuvered her walker to the front of the Tarrytown Library's main room, then lowered herself into the brown leather chair, Durward Hobbs' gaze followed the sure-footed movements of his wife. No longer did she baby herself and spend her days closed up in their small apartment because of her increasingly acute rheumatism. Since they'd come back from the village, she'd reverted to that emotionally strong, gregarious woman he'd fallen in love with over a half a century ago.

Nowadays, Anna Hobbs had a special glow about her that drew people to her. With her snow-white hair encircling her head like a halo, her blue eyes shining, her cheeks rosy with anticipation, and her smile so friendly, she reminded him of one of the angels in the stained glass windows at church. Her always cheery voice warmed him inside, just like a rainbow after a surprise summer shower.

He studied the children gathered around his wife's feet, waiting expectantly for the weekly story hour to begin. With a smile, he settled into the hard wooden chair at the back of the room and waited for Miss Anna, as the children called her, to start her tale. For a while, she thumbed through the worn volume in her lap, trying to decide where to start. As she studied the table of contents, she spoke to prevent the children from becoming restless while they waited.

"In the early 1800's, a boy named Washington Irving lived here in the Hudson Highlands. When he became a man, he wrote stories about his birthplace, which were published in a book called *The Sketch Book of Geoffrey Crayon, Gentleman.*" She held the book aloft. The cover showed loving wear, but endured, as did the tales it held. "Some of them make us laugh. Some make us shudder." She shook, as though frightened. The children followed suit and giggled. "It's nearly Christmas and Mr. Irving's stories are more for Halloween. But I'm afraid there are so many wonderful Christmas stories that it'll be hard for me to choose. Do any of you have a favorite?"

"Miss Anna, please tell us the story of Emanuel." The request came from Elethia Stanton, a young girl with a quiet voice and the face of an angel. She cradled a worn teddy bear in her thin arms.

Though her smile seemed genuine to an observer, Durward knew her cheerful mask hid a deep and profound sorrow.

Anna glanced at the child, then looked at Durward and nodded almost imperceptibly, confirming what he already knew. This was the child they'd been waiting for.

Anna turned back to the gathering of young expectant faces. As always, when requested to tell the tale of Michiah Biddle and the mist, Anna's face broke into a beautiful smile. But Durward paid little attention to his wife at that point. He sat up straighter, stretching to see the girl better.

"That's the best tale of all," Anna said, laying the book aside, then leaning forward, warming to her subject.

Durward knew his wife loved telling this tale above all the rest.

She scanned the faces in the room. "Do any of you know who Michiah Biddle was?"

A unified "no" came from the children. The young girl listened intently to Anna's every word. Her grandparents stood beside her, her grandfather's hand resting protectively on the girl's slim shoulder. A bright red bandana concealed her hairless head, but nothing could hide the sadness that filled the old man's eyes.

Durward took comfort in the fact that the sadness would soon be a thing of the past. He and Anna would see to that just as soon as the story hour ended.

"Michiah came to the New World a long time ago, when the United States still belonged to England, before New York became a state. He brought with him his wife Rachel, whom he loved more than anything else in the whole world. Together, they built a cabin out near the river."

Half listening to his wife's soothing voice, Durward concentrated all his attention on the girl and her grandparents. The girl smiled, but her grandmother and grandfather exchanged apprehensive looks above the girl's head. Clearly they doubted. Durward smiled to himself. He and Anna had doubted, too, but no more.

Anna continued with her story.

"Michiah and Rachel lived very happily in their little house. After a few years, Rachel had a baby. They named him Emanuel for Michiah's great grandfather. From the very first, Michiah adored his small, inquisitive son. Emanuel had a serious nature and asked questions Michiah, a man of little book learning, found difficult to answer. Where did the robins go when the snow came? Why did the river flow down and not up? Where did the clouds come from?

"When Emanuel reached the age of twelve, Rachel became very sick. Michiah was beside himself with worry that his beloved wife would die. What would he do without her? How would he go on? Searching for solitude to pray, Michiah went into the woods to the top of a hill, a hill where he often sat to think while he watched the Hudson River flow lazily to the sea.

"On this day, a mist had gathered in the glen, blocking Michiah's view. An odd mist, thick and white, it glowed softly from the inside. He stared at it for a long time until his curiosity got the better of him, then, descending the hill, he walked into the fog.

"Later, when Michiah came out of the heavy mist, then climbed back up the hill, the mist had disappeared, but something wondrous had happened to him inside that white cloud. He knew in his heart things would be better. When he arrived home to tell his

3

wife and son of his strange adventure, he found Rachel fixing dinner for the first time in weeks. In his joy of Rachel's recovery, he forgot to tell his little family what had happened in the glen.

"Michiah went back to the hill many times after that, but the mist never reappeared. One day he took Emanuel with him, and while they sat side by side on the top of the hill, Michiah told his teenaged son the story of the mist.

"The young boy questioned his father about what he'd seen in the mist. Michiah said he'd seen nothing, but he'd felt such overwhelming peace and love that, if it hadn't been for Emanuel and his mother, he would have been content to remain there forever.

"Emanuel, captivated by the story, returned time after time to the hilltop, waiting for the mist to reappear, but it never did."

The group began to stir, as if ready to leave. Anna put up a hand. "Wait. That's just the beginning of the story. The best is yet to be told."

Durward turned his attention from the child back to Anna. His heartbeat quickened in his chest. He slid a little farther forward on the chair. She smiled. Not outwardly. Her face didn't change, but Durward could feel Anna's smile inside him, as if he'd just walked into an open meadow filled with sunshine.

"Two days after his fourteenth birthday, Emanuel's parents died of a fever that swept the valley. Emanuel was very sad, and no matter what anyone said or did, they couldn't cheer him up. He buried his parents together on the hilltop overlooking the glen where his father had seen the mist.

"That same day, some said, the mist reappeared, and Emanuel walked into it. Others said he just ran away into the woods, unable to bear the sorrow of losing both parents, and the Indians got him. Whatever happened, no one ever saw Emanuel again." She paused. "Except for—"

"Except for who?" a young boy called out.

"Shh," his mother admonished. She sent Anna an apologetic smile.

4

Anna went on, undisturbed by the interruption. "Except for Josiah Reeve."

"Who's he?" asked a little girl in the front row.

"Josiah Reeve ran the local livery stable. A stingy man, he'd hoarded all his money and kept it stashed in a secret hiding place, refusing to give anything to the poor. 'If they can't earn an honest dollar, then let them die an honest death instead,' he'd say.

"Two years after Emanuel disappeared, one of Josiah's horses ran off, and he chased it into the woods. Josiah saw a glowing mist in the glen." The children gasped. "Yes, it was the same mist Michiah had seen. He went into the mist, thinking his horse might have wandered into it and couldn't find its way out.

"When he came out, finding that he'd only been gone for a few minutes astonished him. He thought it had been days. When the town's people didn't believe him, he tried to convince them by telling stories of what he'd seen in the mist. Wondrous tales of an entire village. He told of local people who had disappeared from their little settlement and who now lived inside the white cloud and had strange powers. *And* he had seen Emanuel, not as the boy who had vanished, but as a full-grown man." Anna's voice took on a wispy quality Durward knew well. "But, what he remembered most was the love he'd found there, a love so powerful that no man could resist its pull."

Durward smiled and glanced at the young girl. He knew about love. Love happened when Anna touched him, and he felt a peace beyond description. Love happened every time he looked into her face. Love happened in the heart of every child who listened to her stories.

"When asked to give the name of this village he claimed to have seen," Anna went on, "he said the people called it Renaissance, which means rebirth."